Dark Soul Series

Vassago

Randi Cooley
WILSON

Published by SECRET GARDEN PRODUCTIONS, INC.
Edited by Victoria Rae Schmitz | Crimson Tide Editorial
Copy edited by Liz Ferry | Per Se Editing
Cover Design by Regina Wamba | MaeIDesign.com
Book Formatting by Vellum

VASSAGO (A Dark Soul Novel, Book #2)/Randi Cooley Wilson
Printed in the United States of America
Second Edition January 2019
ISBN-13: 9781793264152

Dark Soul

SERIES

abandon all hope.

CONTEMPORARY ROMANCE

IF | A NOVEL

THE MONSTER BALL ANTHOLOGY

ISLE OF DARKNESS

HAVENWOOD FALLS NOVELLAS

COVETOUSNESS

INAMORATA

GYPSY HEART

PRISON OF ASRIA

Vassago

*For those who have let love slip through their fingers,
but in the end, fight for it.*

Do not be afraid; our fate cannot be taken from us;
it is a gift.

Dante Alighieri, *Inferno*

PROLOGUE

VASSAGO

I stand emotionless, exposed to the Devil. Two soulless eyes look me up and down in a threatening manner. I knew my day would come. Even so, when the Devil stands before you, ready to take your soul, nothing in existence has prepared you for the moment.

Lucifer smirks at me, mocking my fear, which I try not to outwardly show. Doing so would feed his vengeance and wrath. As if he needs any more reasons to punish me. I've broken two of his golden rules: never let your adversaries see, or sense, your trepidation; and never fall in love—there's no place for weak mortal emotions in the Circles.

My gaze shifts slightly from Lucifer's cruel glare to the vacant brown eyes behind him. Like a good legionnaire,

Lore appears calm. Unaffected. Her façade is firmly in place. Yet, through our bond, I sense the turmoil the goddess endures at the scene playing out in front of her. As she tries to mask her unease, her bottom lip twitches. The movement is so slight that most beings wouldn't notice it. But I do. Because I notice everything about her. The twitch is her way of letting me know she is prepared to fight.

With a small shake of my head, I tell her not to interfere. The goddess's gaze narrows, displeased at my warning. It's not her place to protect me. Stolas stands to her left, and Leviathan to her right, both on alert in the event the she needs to be restrained.

I've existed far longer than I thought I would in the Circles. I have killed. Tortured. Destroyed souls. And loved—a mistake that is now costing me my existence.

"I warned you, Vassago." My father's voice is cold and detached. "Dark souls must shed all mortal emotions. When you were branded with the red serpent, I thought you understood that." His eyes flick to Lore, then back to me. "And yet, you've been tempted."

"Even the Devil was once tempted by love's warmth," I bait him.

At the remark, Lucifer's chin lifts and his minions behind me whip me with the long, heated switch my father favors. The dark magic running through it burns the demon skin on my back, leaving nasty, open marks where my black tar-like blood oozes out.

"Shut the fuck up." The Devil snarls at me.

"My Lord," Lilith's voice cries out. "I beg of you. He is our son."

"No son of mine is fooled by love's false pretenses!" Lucifer's voice booms.

The crop hits my back again and I grunt in pain but remain upright, spreading my arms out and sticking out my chest. I don't flinch. Doing so will show feebleness, which will only add more slashes to my punishment. My father hates weakness—helplessness.

Seeing that I won't be defeated by his torture, Lucifer holds my gaze and steps away from me, toward Lore. With each step he gets closer to her, my heart pounds in my chest. When he reaches her, my heart is beating so rapidly, it's fucking difficult to breathe.

Stolas swallows, but doesn't interfere. My half-brother keeps his focus on me. Prince Stolas is the heir to the Circles' throne; as such, he knows better than to challenge our father unless absolutely necessary.

Lucifer's cruel gaze snaps in my direction as I take in the image that will forever haunt me. Without blinking, his hand wraps around Lore's throat. The goddess doesn't wince—she is, after all, a dark-souled warrior. Her lips press together as her eyes hold mine.

With little effort, Lucifer cuts off her air supply and yanks her forward, slamming her into the wall. Bile rises in my throat as I watch his fingers tighten and squeeze until she looks as if she's ready to pass out. Distressed, her runes begin to glow.

"What the fuck is this?" Lucifer barks out, studying the marks.

The gold running through her hieroglyphs matches my own, indicating we've bonded. Anger coils within me that his hand is touching what's mine. The woman I love. My nostrils flare in anger and it's all I can do not to attack him. Stolas's and Lev's eyes remain steadily on me, but my gaze stays entangled with Lore's.

She watches me, as if she's pretending she's somewhere else, when the back of Lucifer's hand cracks over her face, bruising it instantly. With my mouth closed, I grind my teeth.

I can't stop him.

If I do, he will take that as disloyalty.

That I've chosen Lore over the Circles.

If I make one step in her direction to try to protect her, my father will end her existence as my punishment. In this moment, I have to trust that if he goes too far, Stolas and Leviathan will stop him. Or at least try to. I stare at her beautiful face, now swollen and purple. A nasty bruise is already forming. The ugliness is embedded in my memory.

"Are you ready to apologize for your insubordination, Vassago?" Lucifer growls.

"I agreed to your punishment." I use a bored tone, attempting to appear unaffected.

My father tilts his head, considering me with an odd expression. One that confirms he doesn't have a conscience. There is not one goddamn ounce of remorse in his body. He laughs darkly and turns back to face Lore. With both his hands, he rips the front of her clothing, exposing her bare body.

"I've changed my mind," he taunts. "Perhaps Lore should be punished instead."

She spits in his face and I watch as he backhands her again, on the other cheek this time. He hits her so hard the cracking of her bones vibrates around the room. Then, with a loud snarl, Lucifer picks her up and tosses her against the wall as if she's nothing more than a ragdoll. An angry groan falls out of Lev as she hits the stone and slides down it in agony.

And yet, through the entire thing, Lore is silent, watching me.

In this moment, rage replaces every feeling, every emotion, and every thought in my body. All I see is vengeance—red murderous rage. One day, I'll destroy everything my father has built—everything he loves.

"You've made a mistake, Vassago," Lucifer's voice is quiet. "One that should cost you everything." He approaches me, staring into my hard gaze. "Including your existence."

The sick feeling in my stomach intensifies with every menacing breath he takes.

"Then I guess you finally have an excuse to get rid of your half-human son."

"It would seem so," he agrees.

"Then do it already!" I provoke him.

"Tell me she means nothing," he demands viciously.

"She means nothing to me," I lie.

"And if I fuck her?" his tone crass.

"Be my guest," I spit out.

"Kill her?"

"Do it." I don't hesitate when answering him.

If I do, he will actually kill her.

After he tortures her in front of me some more.

Neither of which I will survive.

"Let this be your final warning. In the Circles, you fuck anyone you want. But if you fall in love with another being, I will end their existence. You are not human. You are a dark soul. The son of Lucifer. Brother to Stolas. And in your world, only darkness exists."

I don't blink.

It's time I accept my fate, so Lore won't suffer.

"Are we clear, my son?" he asks.

My jaw clenches at the reminder that Lucifer is my father. "I serve the Circles. My loyalty is to you, my Lord."

His bloody hand lifts and he takes my cheek in his palm, staining my skin with Lore's blood. "Lilith may be a whore, but you are my blood. Created in my likeness.

I'd rather cut my own heart out than have one of my own cease to exist, because of love," he says.

I dip my chin, acting as though I agree and accept his forgiveness. Lucifer gifts me a proud look and pats my cheek before stepping away from me and standing straighter.

"Strike him until he's lying in a pool of his own blood. Keep doing it until I have decided he has learned his lesson. Or he dies," he orders, and storms out.

After a few hard blows, my vision blurs and I fall to my knees. Stolas picks up Lore's limp form and disappears with Lev and my mother following closely behind.

For the first time tonight, I exhale.

She's safe.

For now.

Never again will I allow her to be in this situation.

She won't have to endure my father's threats.

Or his hands on her.

From this moment on, Lore means nothing to me.

PART II

HOPE LIES IN ETERNAL DARKNESS

1

FADING ECHOES

VASSAGO

I watch his silhouette. It moves with grace through the darkness toward the girl's restless form. He lifts his charcoal-stained fingers and with the gentlest of touches, caresses the top of her head. She sighs in her sleep, his touch soothing her, ending the nightmares that haunted her slumber. A visible shudder runs through the demon at the sound of her soft, content exhale. Come morning light, he'll be nothing to her.

Not even a memory.

With each passing moment, the prince's mood becomes more and more disconsolate as the two lovers become fading echoes of what they were. The memories they shared are now shadows, passing one another in the night, without recognition.

Tonight, he turns his back to the sun. The light she

breathed into his soul has been extinguished. Now there will only be darkness in both their worlds.

Fitting for a dark soul—the prince of the Nine Circles.

Incongruous for a divine soul—the oracle of lost souls.

"You're better off here, Hope," he whispers.

The clock on her bedside table ticks. As the seconds fall away, the sound echoes around the room. It cuts through the silence that surrounds us. The moon refuses to shine on the earth realm this evening. The night sky has darkened into a black abyss.

Bending over her sleeping form, Stolas closes his eyes, his breath caressing the back of her neck. For a moment, I think he's going to press his lips to her snow-white skin. At the last second, he stops himself.

With a sharp exhale, he jerks away. I remain silent.

As his half-brother, it seems the least I can do—give the demon prince a proper moment to say his final good-byes to the woman who stole his heart. An odd sentiment coming from me—his enemy and ally.

Though Stolas is unaware that I'm either, yet.

After all, I am a Seeker.

I make my way through the world being silent.

I'm the darkness you never see coming, until it's too late.

I exhale slowly, becoming annoyed at his wavering. Stolas needs to be strong enough to do this—to walk away from Hope. I know he never meant to fall for her. Regardless, he must let her go. He's chosen. Chosen to sacrifice. Chosen to give her up to prevent a war and save her divine soul. Chosen to accept his birthright within the Circles, by our father's side, without his newfound reason for being.

His sacrifice is necessary—he and I both know the dangers in letting our father think she's alive. We're all too familiar with the price of being princes in the Nine Circles.

And love? I know better than most dark souls that there is no place for the human emotion in our world of suffering, pain, and torture. A love like theirs, it won't—can't—last forever.

"Is everything in place?" Stolas asks me in a detached voice.

As I stare at Hope, I become lost in my own thoughts. A long time ago, I made the exact same decision—to walk away from the woman I loved in order to protect her.

"Vassago?" He prompts, using a hard tone.

I blink away the painful memories.

"Everything has been accounted for, my Lord."

Stolas stands taller, turns, and meets my gaze.

"Father can never know she's alive."

I hold his steely gaze. "He will not," I vow.

And I mean it.

No one can know the way he loves her. It would be

seen as a weakness and used as a weapon against what we've been trying to accomplish for years. If Lucifer found out the divine oracle was still breathing, he would tear her apart—for sport. My brother and I are cursed to roam the earth and otherworldly dimensions alone.

"Her memory?" he inquires, distressed. "Of me? Of the Circles?"

The Circles. The dark empire our father built is changing, morphing into something I no longer recognize. With each passing moment, Lucifer becomes more and more lost in his own thirst for revenge. It both fuels and blinds him. Soon, it will be his demise.

Stolas is next in line to the throne. The firstborn, pure-blooded son of Lucifer and Tazia, an archangel with whom Lucifer fell in love. The divine are born of fire, and because of this, the Council of Archangels was mystified to learn Tazia was pregnant with Lucifer's child—an unfeasible achievement between angels and an intolerable offense against the divine, as are most free-willed choices made behind the gates, even if they're made in the name of love.

Instead of considering Stolas a miracle, the council concluded that both he and Tazia must cease to exist. To protect her son from death, and at the council's orders, she begrudgingly agreed to allow Stolas to fall with Lucifer—to be his pure-blooded heir—hoping that someday her son's divine blood would rise to the surface. That he would one day turn on the Circles and Lucifer, aligning with the divine and peacefully uniting Heaven and Hell.

The agreement was conditioned on two provisions: Tazia was to fall, and the divine would create a human oracle. Tazia's soul was to be reborn human, the very thing Lucifer despises. Over the centuries, with each of her rebirths, she has been permitted to recall Stolas as part of her punishment. And the human oracle, Hope, can read dark souls, a gift bestowed upon her to tempt Lucifer into capturing and using the soothsayer for his own selfish desires. They knew Lucifer wouldn't be able to resist the power, or the oracle's beauty. At the time of the council's choosing, the oracle's purpose would be to safeguard Stolas and enlighten him about his true reason for existing, which Hope did.

She was created for my brother's protection—the divine's loophole. Tragically, he fell in love with her. And she with him. Now Stolas must chose: love or birthright.

Our father sent me to find the oracle. I am his second-born son, a Seeker whose gift is to find any soul, divine or dark. When I'd found Hope's soul, it was broken. She was in Switzerland, being treated for self-harm tendencies and schizophrenia at a mental healing facility called Shadowbrook. After I'd located her, Stolas was directed to bring her to the Circles—a test—confirmation the future heir was loyal. We agreed, thinking Father wanted to use Hope as a weapon against the divine. To read dark souls as an advantage.

We were wrong.

After finding himself provoked by the archangel Gabriel into a vow of protection, Stolas learned of Lucifer's intent to end Hope's life. Needing to safeguard her, he reached out to Lucifer's brother and made a deal with the archangel. In exchange for the divine's protection of Hope, my brother promised to keep a tight rein on our father and offer the divine the appreciation of the Circles—a gift the Council of Archangels would never refuse, because in the end they want unification. With Stolas at Father's side, they now have an ally—one that ensures a chance for peace between the two realms, as prophesized.

Worried and untrusting of Gabriel, for the first time in my existence, my brother asked me to seek out his mother. The assumption is that if we place her near Hope, Gabriel will have no choice but to keep his word and protect both of them—because of his unrequited love for Tazia, even though she chose to love his brother.

It's because of Tazia that Stolas has a pure bloodline. Hence his divine given name, Stone, which Hope calls him. The dark souls call him by his demonic name, Stolas. Stolas may be the pureblood, and the heir to Father's legacy, but I am Lucifer's favorite son, held back from my rightful place by his side because my bloodline is tainted by my human mother, Lilith. My impure, mortal blood is a reminder of how weak I am.

"Vassago. Her memories?" Stolas snarls, gaining my attention.

"Lore wiped them," I state, bored.

He swallows. "Then there is nothing left for me here."

I dip my chin and ignore the way his face pales as he moves away from her. "It's time for us to return to the Circles and finish what we started," I remind him.

He nods. "I know."

I pretend I don't see the way his jaw clenches with each step away from her he takes. "She means nothing," I point out.

"Nothing." He repeats the word in a whisper, as if it's dirty.

"Hope is a danger to you, Stolas. Feelings are illusions. You need to empty your heart and free your mind of her. Any desire she created within you, you have to exile," I coax.

"You ask the impossible of me."

"You are a stranger to her now. In this moment, you've ceased to exist in her mind."

"And yet, I've memorized and will recall every part of her."

I step closer. "We are used to suffering, my Lord. With time, it will ease."

"And if it doesn't?" he poses, pinning me with a look.

"Then she dies. At Lucifer's hands. Tortured in front of you."

He needs to be reminded of the cruelty of our world. Hope doesn't belong in it. By the way he's hesitating, I give it a week before he loses his mind and breaks his oath, returning to her. The mortal's form becomes agitated in her sleep. As if she knows he's leaving her.

On a sharp inhale, Stolas looks over his shoulder one last time.

With a final resolve, the prince abandon's hope.

And we fade into the darkness.

2

PLAIN OF FIRE

LORE

I remain in the shadows as he moves with elegant strides through the black forest. Sleep eludes him, as it does all of us who make our home here in the Circles. The air is fiery, filled with the cries of suffering. They echo at night when the realm is swallowed by the darkness. Tonight, I sense the reason for his restlessness has nothing to do with the anguish surrounding us. The Seeker is plagued by the rise to power that awaits the prince.

I curl my fingers around my arms, pressing my fingers into the softness of my skin because they shake with the need to comfort him. To ease his troubled mind and carry his burdens. My lashes blink against my cheeks as I clear out the images haunting my mind. Images of what was once between us, but is no longer.

I crave his affection. And yet, all Vassago desires is

power. His loyalty to the Circles, and his father, are his only concern.

Bloodthirst claws at the back of my throat, but I push away the yearning for it. As a flesh-eating goddess, blood is like a drug to my system. Unnecessary for survival, but soothing to my heightened emotions—like attraction. Want.

The thirst is deepest when I'm around Vassago, because no matter how strong I am, when it comes to him, I am weak. My desire for him makes me weak. My love for him makes me weak. For those two reasons alone, I should not be here tonight guarding him.

I run my gaze over the Plain of Fire, taking in the bare, thorny, black-barked trees and boiling blood-red streams. In the distance, the desert sand is collecting the fire raining down on the blazing powder. In another realm, the beautiful amber flares might be considered a magnificent sight against the onyx sky. But this is the Seventh Circle. And here, the flames are a reminder of the blood on our hands, and that our souls are shadowed.

Centuries ago, my father, Tlaltecuhtli, an earth god, aligned with Lucifer and the Circles. He assumed it was for the greater good. The deity fought side by side with the fallen so that all beings might be granted the freedom to take control of their own destinies. My father sacrificed in the name of free will. As we all did.

In the end, the result of our war was nothing like we

had expected. Lucifer's thirst for revenge became the cause. Darkness overtook his mind and snuffed out the divine light. Cast aside, he became obsessed with pride and power. With blood. With death. With war. With vengeance.

He created the Circles out of pain, anguish and despair—lost love. A reminder that regardless of whether we are divine or dark-souled, love has no place in our world. It will only make you vulnerable, as it did him.

The harpies circle the sky, guarding the realm. Their gazes narrow while they search the forest and desert. Hunting, they seek out those who are violating the Circle's laws. Ironic—we live in a realm governed by laws and guidelines established by a being who revolted against them. It's a cruel paradox that Lucifer weaves.

Vassago stops walking. His gaze lifts and studies the female half-human, half-bird sentinels. I watch as he slides his long fingers into the front pockets of his tailored black dress pants. A classic crisp white button-down shirt lays across his broad shoulders and chest, slightly open at the top, revealing his smooth tan skin.

My eyes roam over him. As always, he has his sleeves rolled up to show off the fullness of his muscular arms. I take in the multiple scars and tattoos that run along the skin. Trophies of his torment. Each one is worn and shown off with a deep sense of pride—that he suffered.

That he survived.

A moment later, his gaze falls from the sky and slides over to where I am standing. He plasters a cocky expression on his face when our eyes meet. I should have known he'd sense me. I hold his intense gaze and inhale sharply. Vassago is beautiful in a raw and terrifying way —a heady combination that steals my breath whenever I am in his presence.

He lifts a hand and rubs it over his buzzed hair and then over the red serpent tattoo I know is crawling up the back of his neck, a noble branding given to him by Lucifer.

In the Circles, the serpent symbolizes rebirth. The tattoo is meant to remind Vassago that he must always shed any human qualities his mortal mother, Lilith, Lucifer's mistress, may have passed on to him. Like love. The honored mark is a reminder that he is bound to the Circles for eternity—the price for his royal immortality.

The subtle action is his way of reminding me that I must keep my distance this evening. It's our makeshift game. I chase. He pushes me away. Until we can no longer control how much to give and how much to take from one another. It's exhausting.

We were born immoral. I love him regardless. Even if it makes me weak. The only heaven I will be sent to is the one where I'm free to be with him. Where we find our own peace. I inhale again. If I lose myself in him, I lose it all. I can't fall under his spell tonight. Stolas sent me to guard him. My only priority and focus this evening is his safety.

His eyes drink me in as he stalks toward me. He always stares at me like this. Like a demon who can't ever get his fill. I used to love it. Now it just makes me feel pissed off.

Vassago's dark gaze is hard, demanding, possessive as he approaches me. I don't flinch. Even when he stops within a breath of me. Instead, I act like his presence is of no interest. His wicked smirk is unapologetic, because Vassago doesn't do gentle. He's all alpha.

"Goddess." His voice is deep.

I force myself not to shiver at the sound.

"Vassago."

I look directly into his eyes. They harden even further as a muscle twitches in his jaw. I try not to become addicted to his gaze again, because the one thing I can't get enough of is the way he looks at me— like I'm not evil. Like I'm not an immoral goddess.

Instead, he looks at me with the expression of a being who is totally undone in my presence.

Feeling my resolve cracking, I lift my chin and step back. Even though I know it's painful for both of us for me to put space between us.

He steps back as well and exhales.

"What are you doing here, Lore?" His tone is annoyed.

The emotion is thick in my throat as I try to find my voice. "I'm on detail."

I don't expand. I tend to be a woman of few words. I've never understood the human need for flowery pleasantries and fake verbal exchanges. It's a waste of breath and emotionally exhausting to pretend to listen to and care about others' words and rantings.

With narrowed eyes, he maneuvers his large frame around me and walks toward the large skyscraper he resides in. Silently, and a bit hurt, I follow him. There was a time when I was everything to Vassago. Now, it seems my entire existence infuriates him. The Circles have a way of altering beings, but Vassago's changes have been quick and recent.

Once we approach the sliding entrance to the building, covered in black-tinted glass, he storms in with me shadowing behind him. We step toward the elevators and as we do, I stare at my reflection in the doors in order to avoid making him the sole focus of my attention.

Instead of meeting his eyes, I concentrate on smoothing my silky straight dark hair, which is parted in the middle and falls to my lower back. My deep brown eyes remain fixated on the way the lights are shining off it. Mortals are always intrigued by my heritage. My Aztec bloodline has gifted me my exotic looks, along with tanned skin and high cheekbones.

The hidden runes on my skin glow gold as they

always do in Vassago's presence, reaching out to him. His matching runes respond to mine as they swirl across his skin.

It's another dark-souled trait that mortals cannot see. All except one mortal, the oracle who turned all our worlds upside down. She's the reason Vassago is in a foul mood.

The elevator doors open and without a word, we step in. He presses the button to the one hundred seventh floor. We don't make eye contact as we climb toward his penthouse. Within seconds, the doors slide open and we both move into the entryway.

I look around.Vassago's home is modern to the point of being uncomfortable. He goes to the kitchen and my eyes glide over to his large windows, taking in the breath-taking views of the Plain of Fire. Each of the nine Circles has a skyscraper in it where the dark souls live. The ruler of that particular Circle lives in the penthouse.

Here in the Seventh Circle, Vassago's building is designed in the shape of a bare-branched tree. The glass on the outside is tinted black, which causes the inside of the building to always be shadowed in a dull, muted, inky color. From up here, though, the fire raining on the desert is even more beautiful, even if dimmed by the tinted glass.

I sigh and step into the luxury penthouse. It has an open floor plan, with several freestanding polished stain-less steel gas fireplaces positioned throughout. The fire rises from glass stones, which Vassago collects from the desert. When the fire hits the blazing sand, it hardens into these beautiful pieces of gemstone. He likes to collect them on his walks.

The light hardwood floors and the white leather furniture are the only pops of color or brightness in his home. Even still, the white furniture is framed in ebony wood. Large circular onyx marble columns hold up the ceiling and the walls around us. Every wall is painted black. Occasionally, a piece of silver décor is positioned on the modern furniture.

I walk toward the kitchen, passing the black, white, and gray artwork on the walls. Taking a seat on a stool at the island, I watch as he places a glass of water on the marble counter. Everything in his kitchen is stainless steel, opaque, and masculine.

"You aren't needed tonight," he states coldly.

I don't miss the double meaning.

"My lord feels otherwise," I argue.

Vassago bends forward and leans his elbows on the counter, looking me directly in the eyes. "My lord isn't thinking clearly at the moment," he replies.

"I am here. At his directive."

He stands tall and begins to unbutton his shirt. When he yanks it off his toned upper body, I can't help but appreciate him. Tree branches shaded in black crawl up the insides of his arms, tattoos he wears proudly, a symbol of the Circle he oversees.

Once his shirt is off, he balls it up and steps around the counter. Pressing against my back, he grabs my long hair, wrapping it around his right hand as he pulls my ear to his mouth. "If you refuse to leave, at least make yourself useful and come fuck me, goddess."

3

FEARLESS AND YOUNG

STOLAS

Lost in anguish, I stare at the cobalt eyes staring back at me from the hearth. They fucking haunt me. With a quick flick of my wrist, I toss back the shot of tequila and throw the crystal tumbler into the fire. Her stare dissolves as the flames part and the glass shatters, like my heart. Falling into and becoming consumed by the fire. The burn of alcohol is the only thing that eases the guilt and ache of what I did —leave Hope in eternal darkness.

The light had officially drained from her eyes as I tightened the restraints. In that moment, I couldn't remember ever being fearless and young. I just knew that for the first time in my existence, I was terrified. Scared of something happening to her. I would do anything to protect her. Even if it means damning us both in the process.

Quickly, I stand and look around my penthouse. Her ghost is everywhere. Suffocating me into madness. I make my way over to the floor-to-ceiling windows, staring down onto the City of Lost Souls. The irony that I oversee the Eighth Circle, known for mental anguish, isn't lost on me. I watch the crimson drops of rain fall across the city. Reminders to those sentenced here of their sins.

Unfortunately, in the City of Lost Souls, there are no pardons, nor forgiveness that comes with repentance. Your mind is your own punishment here. Dark souls appointed in this Circle go through eternity trapped in their own heads. Mentally suffering at their own hands. It's called the Black Mercy. And it chastens me.

Before Hope, I'd never allowed another being to step foot in my home. It was my personal space, my sanctuary away from the agony and infinite suffering within the Eighth Circle.

Now, she shadows every corner. Her scent hangs in the air and her voice echoes in my memories. What was once my sanctuary is full of pain and suffering, my own.

Even though I'm doing the right thing, I know in my heart I'll never be free from the constant torture I suffer having let her go, protecting her. A mortal who owned me.

I growl and lean my arm on the window, looking down onto the concrete jungle below my penthouse in the skyscraper. The Circles used to own me, but now my soul and heart belong to Hope Annandale. My breath catches in my throat. It's like my lungs aren't working. In this moment, I wish for nonexistence.

Anything is better than suffering.

A knock thuds at my door. The sound is foreign, since no one is welcome here. My eyes scan the room before I watch my father and his minions burst through without an invitation, stalking toward me. In an instant, my guards—my best friend, Leviathan, and another one of my trusted companions, Avi—materialize, appearing at my sides protectively. Each can sense when I am in danger and appear at my location. And in my father's presence, I am always in danger.

Everyone is.

Leviathan's steel-gray eyes meet mine as his runes take on a deep blue color that matches the ocean in the Second Circle, which he oversees. He's dressed in his usual laid-back frayed jeans and white T-shirt, the black-lined wave tattoos crawl on his arms and neck.

Nervously, Lev brushes his caramel-highlighted hair back as he slides his focus to the African American girl staring at my father with nothing but gross disdain.

The petite curvy daughter of Medusa tilts her head as her runes take on a violet hue across her caramel skin. Avi's wild, untamed curls stand at attention as her honey-colored eyes slide to me, softening before hardening and turning back to my father.

This is the first time I've seen Avi since returning

Hope to Shadowbrook. The two had become friendly, and I know she is hurting just as much as I am. Hope's absence has left a deep scar in both of us. Friendships. Love. Caring. They're all vulnerabilities.

At the moment, Avi's and my desolation are examples of why.

"STOLAS!" My father's voice booms as he approaches.

"My Lord," I respond, dipping my chin.

"Where the fuck is she?" Lucifer roars. A cold gaze meets mine and a not-so-patient glare dominates my father's expression.

"Where is who, my Lord?" I keep my tone even.

"Don't play games with me," he snaps, his voice even, his eyes blazing with fury. His own two guards step closer behind him, watching Avi and Leviathan. "Where is the oracle?"

"Gone."

"Gone?"

I nod and remain silent.

Lucifer runs his long fingers through his thick raven hair as we stare at each other, assessing. A power struggle at its fucking finest. I have proven myself to my piece of shit father on more than one occasion, and to be honest, I'm tired of his trials and demands.

Anger surges through me from every angle as we play this game. Lucifer can never know that Hope is alive. And yet, if I lie to him, he will sense my deceit.

He narrows his eyes at me, cocking his head to the side. Waiting. I know what he is trying to do. He taught Vassago and me at an early age how to read beings. How to tell through body language who was full of shit. Who was lying. Who was pretending. Who was bluffing.

Leviathan and Avi stand stiff as boards on either side of me. Neither speaks or flinches, because even the slightest movement will be taken by him as an admission of betrayal. And no one betrays Lucifer. Our allegiance and devotion to the king of the Nine Circles is instinctual. Ingrained at an early age. Tortured into memory. A constant reminder of who and what we are.

"Explain," he orders.

"Leviathan, Vassago, and I learned that the oracle was created by the divine as a weapon. A key to be used against us. She was sent to test me. To see if I would turn on you, my Lord, and the Circles," I keep my voice quiet. "Tazia and the Angelic Council created her to tempt you, so that you would acquire her, wanting to leverage her gift of dark soul sight. Once in the Circles, she was supposed to turn my affections and end your reign."

Lucifer's face is expressionless as he listens to me recount the truth he already knew.

"I handled it. Her." I smile, casually, pretending not to care about Hope.

After a tense moment, Lucifer crosses his arms over

his chest and an amused expression appears on his face. "You've impressed me, Stolas."

"My intent wasn't to impress you, my Lord," I counter. "My reasons were purely selfish. I like ruling. And I plan to take my rightful place." I grit my teeth. "By your side."

He watches my every move with nothing but a guarded stare. The vein on his forehead pulses. For a long time now, I've distanced myself from him, spending very little time in his presence. Sharing the same air he breathes makes me fucking sick. It's time, though.

In order to keep Hope safe, I must accept my birthright. The designation Prince of the Nine Circles is no longer simply a title; it will now become a way of life. Something I will embrace and breathe every day of my excruciating existence down here.

"I am aware of what the oracle was created for," he admits. "Tazia and Gabriel are envious creatures who hide behind their pretend morals. The council is resentful of the power we now have. As I've said before, they are hypocrites, holding us to ancient rules and peace treaties that they themselves cheat around. You've proven your worth and loyalty. Exalting your place within the Circles. The oracle was never meant to exist. An insignificant human with divine gifts meant to threaten our existence. You did well, son."

"My Lord." One of his minions interrupts. "He didn't confirm she ceases to exist."

My father turns his attention toward his guard and in one swift motion removes a knife from his sleeve, slitting the guard's throat.

"If I wanted your opinion, I'd give it to you," he snarls at the demon's lifeless body, as tar-black blood pools around him. Turning his attention to his other guard, he spits out, "Clean this shit up."

"Yes, my Lord." The demon rushes to remove the body.

Lucifer's hard expression meets mine. "If I discover you have deceived me, and the oracle continues to be a threat to the Circles, Vassago will find her. And when he does, I will drag her into my Circle in front of you and squeeze her throat so hard that she will fight for every fucking breath. I will punish her in ways that you can't imagine. She will suffer. In pain. In agony. And then, when I'm done, I will do it all again. Over and over while she begs for mercy." His mouth contorts wickedly as he struggles to breathe at the thought of my betrayal. His eyes darken to soulless black orbs. His tan face turns a reddish-purple hue as his chest heaves with anger. "In the last seconds of her weak, human life, all she will see is me. All she will feel are my hands. My lips. My heat. It will be as if you didn't exist in her world. Ever. Then, when the life drains from her tortured, broken body, I will bring her back and repeat the torment all over again before I turn my anger onto you," he savagely spews.

I know he means every word.

I saw him do the same to Lore and Vassago.

"The oracle is no longer a threat, my Lord. To you or the Circles," I don't falter.

"You have been lost for far too long. Running wild and running free. It ends. In the morning, you'll appear in the Ninth Circle. At my side." He takes my face between his hands. "I have been waiting for this since your birth, Prince Stolas. Do not fail me."

"I will not, my Lord." I force myself to hold his gaze.

Leviathan and Avi remain silent, even as Lucifer leaves, waiting for my prompt. Numbly, I turn to my friends. Jealousy surges through me at the way they look at one another. It's familiar. Like when you want something you know you can't touch. All you can do is stare at it. Memorize the lines of the object. Love it from afar. Obsess over it. But never possess it. It's the way I look at Hope.

The reminder hurts like hell.

"Speak freely," I growl out.

"You do know he doesn't believe Hope is no longer a threat," Lev points out.

"I know he doesn't." My voice trails off as I confirm his point.

Avi sucks in a breath. "And yet he's allowing you to take your place?"

"He's using her as a focal point. So I don't lose sight of what he wants. Hence the threat to hurt her, just in case I still have any lingering feelings for her," I explain.

"Another test?" Leviathan scoffs.

My gaze snaps to his. "My entire existence is a test."

He nods, pulling out a cigarette. "No shit."

I drop my voice lower. "I want Vassago and Lore checking in on Hope once a week."

"You don't trust Gabriel and Tazia to keep her safe?" Avi asks.

"When it comes to Hope, besides the three beings in this room, I don't trust anyone with her safety."

"Then why Vassago and Lore? Why not send me and Leviathan?"

I meet Avi's hurt expression. "They don't have an emotional attachment to her."

She nods, understanding she's too attached to protect Hope.

"Besides, now that I'll be spending more time in the Ninth Circle, I'm going to need both you and Lev with me for protection. And strength," I add. "It was all I could do not to flinch when he ticked off all the ways he plans to torture her."

"Consider it done." Lev responds around his lit cigarette.

"Whatever you need." Avi offers me a sad smile.

The room falls into a tense silence.

"What I need, I can't have."

4

LOST SOUL

HOPE

I breathe in deeply. With my fingertip, I trace the outline of the snowcapped mountain on the windowpane. There are days, like today, that I don't recognize myself. The blue eyes reflecting back in the glass are vacant. The pale skin underneath them is marred by dark circles. They've permanently settled deep under my eyes, making me look exhausted all the time.

The medication I'm forced to take decreases my appetite, and I've become skin and bones. A shadow of what I once was. I'm a stranger to myself. My mind is confused. I can feel it in my soul—I'm lost.

"Nurse Gwen mentioned that you became agitated when she asked you to remove the charcoal drawing on your arm," a lulling voice says. "Would you like to discuss why?"

In the glass, I see Dr. Cornelius Foster's reflection watching me. The Idris Elba look-alike is sitting at his desk, quietly scrutinizing my disposition with his long, dark fingers tented under his chin. I don't turn around to answer him. It's too much effort.

Instead, I try to turn my mind off and remain silent.

"Is that why you left the retreat, Miss Annandale?" he pushes.

Lifting my left wrist, I pull it toward my chest, holding it close.

"It wasn't something you had when you first arrived," Dr. Foster points out.

After waking up from an apparent suicide attempt, I noticed the charcoal heart. The doctors and nurses kept telling me I drew it, but I don't draw. Let alone in charcoal.

A few days later, Nurse Gwen suggested I remove it from my arm, as I had been showering around it. When I refused, she threatened to sedate me and remove it. The idea sent me into an irrational panic. Since Shadowbrook isn't a lockdown facility, one night I slipped out and had it permanently tattooed onto my skin. I was afraid they would take it away. I need to keep it with me, always.

I just don't know why it means so much to me.

"Hope?" he prompts.

I clear my throat. Since waking up, I haven't spoken much. My voice sounds foreign and my throat is dry and scratched from lack of use. "It's important to me," I whisper.

"Why?"

My eyes dart around the Swiss landscape, landing on a tree outside of the doctor's office. Whenever I'm in here for my private sessions, the tree calls my attention to it.

"I don't know," I answer honestly.

With a heavy sigh, Dr. Foster falls silent. I turn to face him. His eyes soften. When they do, anger surges within me. The last thing I need is for him to feel sorry for me.

"Don't do that," I rasp out.

"Do what, Miss Annandale?"

"Look at me like I'm broken."

He cocks his head to the side. "Do you feel broken?"

I look down, frustrated.

"I feel . . . empty. Like a piece of me is missing."

"Depression is a mood disorder, Hope. It causes a persistent feeling of sadness. Of emptiness. A loss of interest. It affects how you feel, think, and behave. It can lead to a variety of emotional and physical blocks. It can make it feel as if life isn't worth living."

"Stop!" I exhale.

"Excuse me?"

I take two purposeful steps toward him.

"Your psychotherapy won't work on me."

His brows rise in surprise at my response. "Meaning?"

"I am not depressed. I am not suicidal. I am not . . . broken."

His voice is gentle. "A month ago, you tried to commit suicide in the library. Over a poem that wasn't on the shelf. Hendrix found you lying in a pool of your own blood."

I lift my chin. "I didn't do that to myself."

"Then who did, Miss Annandale?" he pauses. "The demons?"

Demons. As soon as the word leaves his lips, I freeze and my mind turns hazy.

Dr. Foster stands and walks around his desk. Standing in front of me, he crosses his arms and looks down into my eyes. "Help me to understand what you are feeling."

"I-I can't," I force out, quietly. "Everything in my mind is black . . . an empty void." I meet his concerned stare. "My thoughts are lost. Like I'm in a state of eternal darkness."

"Feelings of sadness, emptiness, and hopelessness are normal. Angry outbursts, irritability, frustration over small matters are all indicators. You're tired. You have a lack of energy. You suffer from insomnia. You have a reduced appetite and weight loss. Even now, I see signs of anxiety, agitation, and restlessness. These are all effects of depression. Normal effects. Symptoms that together, we can work through and overcome. I promise."

I stare at his lips as he speaks, but the words don't penetrate. In the deepest part of my soul and psyche, I know I'm not depressed.

"Are we done?" I ask, tired.

After a silent beat, Dr. Foster dips his chin. "For today. I'll see you tomorrow."

Once excused, I make my way out of his office. Closing the door behind me, I begin to walk down the hallway, but the sound of camera movement stops me. Looking up, I tilt my head and stare at one of the small lenses before turning my focus to the flashing red light. A strong sense of déjà vu hits me hard as I glare at the blinking red dot.

"Cameras?" I confirm.

"They're everywhere," a bored voice says flatly.

Startled, my gaze jumps around, looking for the other female voice. When I don't see anything, I chastise myself. Keeping still, I tell myself to calm down. I don't want it to appear like I'm talking to myself, or hearing the voices again.

Once I've evened my heart rate, I walk past the large, open lounge area. Patients are sprinkled around sitting on the velvet chaises and chairs. I ignore the hotel vibe of the facility. I've become used to the odd normalcy of it. It's designed to feel like a fancy retreat, a spa with guests.

My gaze shifts from the full wall of windows, which frames the grounds and snow-covered mountains, and lands on the baby grand piano in the corner. I shudder as I feel my throat tighten at the sight of the beautiful instrument. For some reason, it saddens me.

It's as if it hurts my heart to look at it.

Using my relaxation techniques, I close my eyes and imagine the piano in a field. At night. Engulfed in flames while I walk away.

The image calms me enough to open my eyes and keep moving until I reach the elevators and head up to my private suite. After closing the door, I exhale and stalk over to the large windows in my bedroom. My neurotic fascination with the Zen garden below is something else I can't explain. I'm obsessed with it. As if I'm waiting for something to appear in it. What? I have no idea. I've rearranged the furniture in my room so that I can sit in the chair and stare out at it for hours.

Curled up, I wrap myself in a blanket and focus on the spot near the pond—like I do every day. Pulling down the sleeves on my thermal, I twist my fingers around the edges and wait. And watch. Just as I'm about to doze off, a cool breeze brushes over me.

Unfazed at his presence, I keep my eyes on the pond instead of looking at him. I exhale slowly and then part my lips to speak. "I know you're there."

Silence.

"I sense you." My voice is hollow.

"Tonight? Or over the past month?" The deep voice asks.

"Does it matter?"

A dark rumble falls from his chest. "You do not fear me, then?"

"Am I supposed to?"

"Yes."

My gaze slides, meeting his cold eyes. "I don't."

The demon takes the empty seat next to me, watching me with a shady, soulless gaze. Logically, I know I should feel sheer terror in his presence. I don't. I just feel numb at his appearance.

And annoyed.

For the past month, he's shown up at least once a week, invading my space. Studying me, like I'm some sort of fascinating creature. He never speaks or approaches me. He just watches from the shadows. It's unnerving, and yet, I feel weirdly calm and protected when he's there.

He runs his palm over his cropped hair and down the back of his neck. The white button-down shirt he's wearing is crisp, the sleeves rolled to his elbows showing off tattoos and scars. So many scars. Maybe it's because the darkness is buried so deep inside of me that I can't breathe past it, but I know he's been tortured. Cruelly.

"Why do you stare out at nothing?" he asks.

"I'm lost."

"You won't be lost forever, mortal."

At the nickname, I stare at him as some sort of vision crosses my mind.

"Don't call me anything other than Vassago, mortal," he growls.

"Mortal?" I whisper under my breath.

The odd nickname takes me aback.

The memory turns to dust as my lips part.

I whisper, "Vassago?"

5

BACK TO THE SUN

VASSAGO

Nothing could have prepared me for what I see. On the outside, Hope appears fragile. Her fingers shake, but not out of fear—out of weakness. She's brittle and frail. It's fucking annoying. What are they doing to her in this place? And where the fuck is Gabriel? Tazia?

The prince's chosen looks like she hasn't eaten in months. Not that I fucking care, but Stolas will be displeased. If he saw her like this, looking sickly and weak, he'd burn the entire facility down.

The woman sitting next to me is no longer full of life, laughter, or love. She is no longer full of anything. An empty shell, she is hollow inside. A feeling I know all too well. It's easier this way. When you turn off your humanity. No longer wanting to feel anything. The moment when there is nothing left.

"Vassago?" she whispers, and my breath catches.

She isn't supposed to remember.

"You know who I am?" My voice is calm.

"Is that your name?" she asks, sounding confused.

"Yes."

"Do I know you?" Her steely gaze holds mine.

"No," I lie.

A wry smile appears on her chapped lips. "Liar."

"Why ask, if you already know?" I challenge.

"Why are you here?"

I make sure my eyes turn to ice. "I was asked to hunt you down and kill you."

Slowly she shakes her head. "Your threats don't frighten me."

"You don't fear monsters that lurk in the dark?"

Her eyes narrow. "Who said you're a monster?"

If I weren't so annoyed, I would fall into hysterics right here. I watch as her eyes slide back to the spot where she first noticed Stolas. She can't remember why she is drawn to the spot, but it's because it's where she first connected with him. And he with her.

"You should leave," she orders curtly.

"I can't." I grind out in an angry tone.

I'm pissed off that Stolas forced me to watch over her. Patience and kindness aren't part of my nature, especially toward frail humans. Seeing her like this, wispy, a foreign emotion wraps around me. One that I didn't think I was capable of feeling—pity. I think she senses that I feel benevolence for her, because her mood has suddenly changed.

Hope's mind is disintegrating from all the medicine they have her on. Unfortunately for her, like Stolas, she's turned her back to the sun and allowed the darkness to creep in.

Out of the corner of my eye, I watch her figure shift slightly.

"Can't? Or won't?" she asks.

"Either. So get comfortable having a devil on your shoulder."

Hope scoffs. "Devil."

She looks at me one last time, shaking her head.

Silence settles around us. After a while, her eyelids become heavy and flutter closed. I watch her sleep, admiring her unassuming beauty. I can see why my brother is attracted to her. Her long brown hair and matching thick lashes darken in the moon's light. When her eyes were open, the purple circles etched deeply under them on her porcelain skin made the blue hue even more prominent. For a human, she's attractive. Even more so, since she can sense dark souls.

She isn't afraid of us anymore. There was a time, when I first met Hope, when her eyes would widen with alarm, and she would shy away from me, or any of us. After all these years of wanting to be feared, it still annoys the shit out of me when beings are actually afraid. And now, she's not, which pisses me off even more. She's relaxed in my presence. Peacefully slumbering next to me. Other than Lore, no other woman is relaxed in my presence.

I don't like it.

It's easier for them to see me as a monster.

I don't deserve anything else.

I study the woman who turned the prince of the Nine Circles of Hell into the shell of a demon he used to be. Stolas lives every day with the constant reminder of his mistakes and regrets when it comes to her. The relentless torture he suffers from both loving and hating her control his every thought and action. Something else we share.

My mind wanders to thoughts of Lore and me. My heart pounds against my chest whenever I think about the goddess. I can't help but love and want her, even though I know I shouldn't, which makes me have to hate her.

I'm forced to push her away, because there is no way in hell that I would provoke fate. If Lucifer knew I cared for her, he would end her existence as a lesson and warning. Ironic that it's the same reason Stolas assigned me to look in on his human pet.

"I can't find peace without him." She whispers so low, I can barely hear her.

I look back over at her. Hope's eyes are still closed, and her breathing is relaxed. I can't tell if she is talking in her sleep, or if she's awake. She's mumbling incoherently, agitated.

Knowing I have an entire night of babysitting detail ahead of me, I disappear, materializing in the small kitchen outside of her bedroom. Her suite here at Shadowbrook is nice—small, but it has a tiny living area and kitchenette. Opening the fridge, I grab a bowl of grapes.

"You'd think after I walked away from her, pushed her away, I would have built up enough resistance to our bond. If anything, the urge to protect her has become stronger."

I turn and face Stolas, surprised that I didn't sense him.

He's standing, leaning his forehead against her bedroom door. A bottle of tequila is firmly clutched in his grasp. The liquid in it is half gone. One of his hands is gripping the doorknob. He's fighting everything inside of himself not to turn it.

"That is what happens when you give your word to an archangel and seal your fate to another's through a protection bond, Stolas. No one said it would be easy," I reply.

He turns around, sliding down her door, and sits with his back pressed up against it, his elbows resting on his knees. The anguish on his face says it all; he's feeling every last ounce of her pain and distress, wishing he could take it all away. He can't. He takes another swig from the bottle, leaning his head back against the door and listening to her whimper in her sleep.

"She suffers," he sighs.

"That is her burden," I remind him.

"It's because of me," he slurs.

"That is your burden." I watch him take a long pull.

"So it is," he mumbles.

"How often have you visited her?"

His eyes meet mine, full of sadness. "Every day since I left her."

I place the bowl on the counter. "For fuck's sake."

"Only on the days you and Lore aren't here. It's my way of being here for her. Not a night has passed where she has slept through the night, undisturbed by the nightmares that haunt both of us. Some nights, I slip into her room, and sit in the armchair by her bed, watching her sleep in the darkness, before I vanish like I was never there to begin with. Letting her think she was alone, when in reality, I am always here, protecting her."

I crouch down in front of him.

"You can't," I state.

"I can't not."

"You've placed her in Gabriel's protection," I point out.

"And look what has become of her," he snaps.

"Do you hear yourself? She is human," I snarl.

"She looks sickly."

"They have her heavily medicated."

"My point," he argues. "They can't take care of her."

"Hope looks weak and frail on the outside, but she is strong and determined on the inside. I mean, for fuck's sake, we wiped her memories and she still knew who I was tonight. She sensed my presence. She stares into the abyss, at the spot she first saw you."

His eyes widen. "What are you saying? That she remembers?"

"I am saying," I exhale slowly, choosing my words carefully. "You have a bad habit of underestimating her. Give the mortal a chance to prove herself worthy of you, my Lord."

"And if she dies in the process?"

"Then she dies. At this point she is better off dead. The second that you forget that, you will be faced with your demise. And hers," I throw back.

I can't give him peace of mind. There is a fine line between his life and hers. His love for Hope condemns her to death, either way. At some point, he will have to decide.

Placing the tequila bottle down, he rubs his hands down his face. "There days I can't even look at myself in the mirror anymore. I'm so fucking tired. How do you do it?"

"Do what?"

"Do this with Lore? Keep her at a distance. And don't lie and say you don't. I see the way you two eye-screw each other whenever you are in the same room," he accuses.

The truth of his pointed question causes me to jerk my head back, stunned. No one has ever asked me point-blank about Lore and me before. I swallow hard before answering.

"I won't allow her to know or see what I feel for her. I'll give her the world. She'll want for nothing. But I can't give her my love. I can't let her into the hollowness of my life. The darkness has settled in. I own it and it owns me. It will destroy her."

Stolas snorts and lifts his gaze to the ceiling. "You say it as if it's a choice."

"It is. One that I make every morning when I open my eyes. Because the alternative is that Lucifer finds out and uses her against me. Torturing us both in the process," I say.

After a few seconds, his eyes fall, and he looks directly at me. "My vow of protection, it haunts me. Hope is in danger here, Vassago. I don't trust Gabriel, or Tazia."

"You are going to have to control your emotions when it comes to the bond, until it wears off."

"And if it doesn't?"

"You are the prince of the Nine Circles. Do not allow a mortal to be your downfall."

6

ANCIENT CURSE

LORE

Vassago throws punch after punch at the bag. Like a hunter with his eyes on the target, he keeps his intense gaze focused in front of him, ignoring my presence. His hits come faster and faster as he boxes away whatever has angered and pained him after watching Hope today, to the point of physical exhaustion, which for a demon, is almost impossible.

Keeping my distance, I cross my arms and watch the beads of sweat drip from his forehead. I'm curious as to what is fueling his rage. The other night, I denied his impolite request to fuck him. I'm used to Vassago's crassness and rough edges, so his harsh invitation was no surprise. What was unexpected was how his expression fell at my rejection, as if I'd hurt him. Profoundly. Then he disappeared for the rest of the night.

He relaxes his arms and throws quick, snapping

punches, but I can tell his arms are becoming tired. Every so often he releases a push punch and the bag jolts in place with a hard smacking sound. After the third time, I step closer to him. His cold eyes snap to me and then look away, as if he's too disgusted with my presence to hold my eye contact.

"What's wrong?" I whisper, gripping his arm.

He snarls and narrows his eyes on my hand. "Do not touch me."

Regardless of how menacing he can be, I know he won't hurt me. Yet, I'm still terrified as I watch the muscles in his arm jump when he tries to control himself. Confused at his response, I freeze, and he curses, prying my hand away from the swirling runes that crawl along his skin. They come to life at my closeness and touch, recognizing his mate.

"Do me a favor; leave me be." His voice is hoarse.

I frown at his words.

"Whenever I close my eyes, you're all I see," he whispers.

Understanding the meaning of his words, I swallow.

"Vassago—"

"I can't fucking do it anymore. Don't get me wrong," he huffs out. "I'm a sucker for punishment. I mean, for fuck's sake, I'm the son of Lucifer. Mistreatment and self-torture are things I thrive on. But whatever this is between us—" He presses his lips together. "We're done.

We have to be. I don't have the courage to fall any more."

A heaviness settles in my chest, on my lungs, making it impossible to breathe. It's as if he's reached into my chest, grabbed my heart, and squeezed it until it no longer beats.

I step closer to him. "Do you not trust that I will catch you when you fall?"

He growls at me and steps back. "I don't want you to," he bites out. "I don't want you."

"Go to hell," I spit out, and turn to leave.

"I spend every waking minute there," he mutters under his breath.

His response infuriates me, and I can no longer control the demon inside. With a quick spin, I stalk back to him, kick out his ankles, and as he's starting to collapse, push at his chest so he falls on his back and looks up at me from the floor. Then, for good measure, I push my foot across his throat and stare down into his eyes as I press hard. He doesn't fight it.

"I don't know what has gotten into you recently, but I am done dicking around with you. You have issues? We all do. We all live in the Circles. You're pissed that you have to be your brother's shadow? Welcome to the world we live in. We all live in Stolas's shadow. And that pathetic little human that we're running around protecting, she has us all pissed off. Still, you don't get to take it out on me. You want out? To be done? Then be done.

Stop punishing me with your erratic emotions and actions."

A patronizing smile forms on his lips. "Going to kill me, goddess?"

I push my foot into Vassago's throat harder as lies underneath it, immobile, looking up at me. "We. Are. Finished," I spit out, accentuating the double meaning in my words.

With my chin held high, I storm out of his training room. A few moments later, I enter the elevators and head down two floors to my apartment. Infuriated with the Seeker, I storm into my home here in the Circles and slam the door closed, hoping the rattle is heard by him two floors above me, and kick it several times for good measure.

"Asshole!" I shout with a final kick.

"Bad day?" a Spanish-accented voice asks from behind me.

At the sound, I turn and take in the Aztec god sitting on my couch inch by inch. Like most dark beings, my father intimidates easily. Especially because Tlaltecuhtli is known as a monstrous, violent earth god. He tilts his head and studies me.

"Daughter," he greets, formally.

Coming to my senses, I approach him and dip my chin out of respect. "Tlaltecuhtli."

"Sit," he demands.

Without question, I take the seat next to him. Questioning him is not allowed; neither is calling him Father. Tlaltecuhtli makes me nervous, but not because I'm scared of him—because he is unpredictable and hard to read.

When retelling the Aztec myth of the earth god, mortals assume Tlaltecuhtli is a female deity. And while my father has both feminine and masculine attributes, he is certainly a male entity. His name means the one who gives and devours life. The deity represents both the earth and the sky. He is also known as the god in the Aztec pantheon most hungry for human sacrifice, demanding their hearts and blood as sacrifice.

He looks around my Aztec-inspired home, focusing his attention on the replica of a monolith that was excavated at the Templo Mayor in Mexico City. The sculpture was carved from a block of pink andesite and depicts my father's female form in a squatting position. Tlaltecuhtli finds the statue both amusing and a nuisance.

Since my décor is Aztec-themed, as a gift, he brought his only daughter a smaller version he compelled a human to create for him while in Mexico, before ripping out his heart and feeding off his flesh.

"Vassago causes you pain?" he asks.

We lock eyes, and for a split second, I see something familiar in his stare. Something I have always seen in mine, only now, it is being reflected back at me. A deep sense of sadness and loneliness. Averting my eyes, I focus on the crossed bones and skulls tattooed on his forearm. The great star sign borders the symbol. A reminder of his sacrifices.

"Not pain. Anger," I reply.

"He is complex. The weight of darkness falls upon him."

"He is a fool."

A deep chuckle falls from his lips. "Immortal or mortal, men in love often are."

I throw him an annoyed look. "Babysitting the human isn't helping."

"You speak of the oracle?"

"Yes."

"She is why I have come." He states. "I have met with Huitzilopochtli."

"The god of war and sacrifice?" I confirm.

My father dips his chin, validating my answer. "A war within the Circles will soon arise. A battle of revenge and redemption. It is a war of hearts met with great sacrifices."

"A war with the divine always shadows the Circles," I remind him.

"This time, the threat is not divine," he replies.

My brows pinch together. "Then who?"

"The pantheon."

My lips part in surprise at what he's revealed. "The pantheon?" I repeat.

"Tezcatlipoca has stepped in. Lucifer has become

vengeful and lost sight of his cause. The fallen forgets who legitimized his right to rule the land of the dead," he continues.

Tezcatlipoca is one of the most important gods in the Aztec pantheon. As the god of light and shadows, he is omnipresent both on earth and in the land of the dead. He was the deity who convinced the pantheon to pledge its allegiance to Lucifer and the Circles.

"The oracle's existence proves that Lucifer has become single-minded," he says.

"While I would agree, I'm curious, why share this with me?" I ask, with caution lining my voice. Something about my father's visit today doesn't sit well with me.

He shifts and hands me a black obsidian box. "A gift, from Tezcatlipoca."

I take it, slowly opening the top, revealing an obsidian knife cradled among black volcanic rock. Awed, my fingertips brush over the stunning weapon.

"Is this—" I whisper.

"The Weapon of the Smoking Mirror," he finishes. "It is."

The name is a reference to obsidian mirrors, which are shiny objects made of volcanic glass, a revered symbol to the pantheon, representing both the smoke of battle and the sacrifices made. To Aztec gods, black obsidian is created from the heart of the earth. The highly reflective stone is a vital part of human blood sacrifices.

In our world, whoever guards it protects the ancient curse.

After a moment, my eyes lift to his. "Why has Tezcatlipoca gifted it to me?"

"It is time to learn your purpose, Lore."

"My purpose?" I repeat.

"The weapon—the ancient curse—is your birthright to protect."

"Why was I chosen to protect the ancient curse?"

"The pantheon has chosen you because you have proven yourself worthy."

"Worthy of what?" I challenge.

"The oracle's creation causes upheaval in the land of the dead. The Aztec gods have declared that her divinity must be extinguished so that balance can be restored."

Looking around my home, I let his words sink in. "You want me to darken the mortal's divine soul in order to trigger a war between the pantheon and Circles?"

"The deities are displeased with Lucifer's reign."

"How does the pantheon feel about the divine and their quest for peace?"

"Peace between the two dimensions is of no concern to the Aztec gods," he replies.

"I see." I'm not surprised, but hearing him confirm their wishes saddens me.

"The divine are naïve. Unification will not happen. The Circles must continue to exist in order to keep balance in the mortal world and allow for free will. The oracle's divine destruction prevents unrest in the land of the dead. When we sided with the fallen, we agreed to protect the Circles. The end to her divinity protects the Circles." His voice is cold, detached.

"What about Stolas?" I manage.

"What about the dark prince?" he asks coldly.

"Stolas would never reign side by side with the pantheon, if he knew they were the reason for the oracle's lost divinity," I point out.

He pauses, watching my reaction closely. "Do not feel compassion for others, especially the dark prince. That moral attitude is beneath you. It's insulting to your honored calling."

"I do not." My reply is quick and firm as I'm reminded of my role.

He raises his chin. "The curse must be protected by the chosen goddess until it is time to wield the weapon. When it is, the goddess will reveal the weapon to the great red serpent, who will drain the life from the oracle's veins, releasing her divinity."

My lips part, shocked. "Vassago is to take away her divinity?"

My father stands, sliding his hands into his front pockets. "Why do you think you were placed in the Seeker's path? You and he have been allowed to share golden liquid in your runes. Your fates have been connected, since creation, for this very purpose. There are no coincidences where deities are concerned."

"Does Vassago know this?"

"Do not allow love for him to blind your calling."

My gaze lifts to my father's cold one.

"I shall not," I manage.

He places his hand on my head.

"You make me proud on this day, daughter."

I dip my chin and recite our creed.

"We do not serve darkness; darkness serves us."

7

RISE TO THE OCCASION

STOLAS

I stand outside the conference room and look through the glass panes at my father. It's hard to miss him. His tall intimidating build is muscular and solid. Regardless of whom he stands next to, Lucifer always seems to appear a foot taller than everyone else. The room is full of demons in a heated conversation. One I know I don't want to be a part of.

Through it all, I can't stop staring at Lucifer, who exudes dominance. He's dressed in an expensive suit, with his black hair slicked back away from his masculine face. The females in the Circles have always joked about how devilishly handsome he is, referencing his tanned skin, narrow cheekbones, and strong jawline. They call him a fine specimen. Females and males are drawn to him like moths to a fire, feeling his magnetic pull. His power.

Like a predator, he's meant to lure you in. Attract you. Right before he possesses your soul and strips away your morals, damning you to an existence of darkness and torture.

His violet eyes lift and lock onto mine, narrowing when he sees me standing here. I've always envied the color; it matches my mother's. A reminder they were once archangels.

"I will only be a few minutes," I announce.

"You sure you don't want me to come in with you?" Lev asks.

"I didn't tell him I was bringing anyone."

"Then why the hell am I here?" he counters.

"Because I said to be," I snap back.

Lev shrugs, nodding, annoyed at my poor attitude.

"You're late, Stolas. Why is it so fucking hard for you to be on time to meetings?" Lucifer growls, as I push open one of the glass doors and step into the conference room.

To anyone looking at this scene, it would seem like a typical business meeting. That is, until they look out the floor-to-ceiling windows onto the view of the Ninth Circle.

Below us, an ice-cold lake expands as far as the eyes can see. Dark souls who've committed severe sins are cast deeper in the lake, trapped within ice pieces that float. The Ninth Circle is divided into four rounds, or parts, depending on the seriousness of their sins. My father oversees this circle, which welcomes those souls who have committed fraudulent acts against those they share special bonds of love and trust with. It's rumored he designed this realm for my mother's soul after she betrayed him.

Giants guard this Circle, acting as towers and columns, but always watching and reporting back to Lucifer. Doing his dirty work when he is unable to. Filthy creatures.

To my father's annoyance, I don't answer. Bored, I grab a seat and drop into it with little interest about what is being discussed in the room. No doubt more torture tactics.

In my peripheral vision, I see Avi outside with Lev, whispering.

"Starvros!" my father shouts at the demon.

"Yes, my Lord?" he responds quickly.

Lucifer's eyes meet mine in challenge. "Where are we with the oracle?"

I remain calm and try to show I'm unaffected by his question. It's a test. You'd think, by now, I would be used to them. But I had no idea he'd call me out like this at the meeting.

"Did I stutter?" he barks, impatient.

I cock my head to the side, arching an eyebrow at my father's ill temper. His irritability appears to have a shorter fuse than normal. He seems less in control.

"Not one of my Seekers has located her soul," Starvros replies, like a good soldier.

Respect crosses Lucifer's expression. "You were telling the truth after all, Stolas."

"No shit." I hold his hard glare.

"Keep looking." The comment is directed at Starvros, but meant as a warning for me.

"Yes, my Lord," the demon answers.

After a few seconds, Lucifer snaps his glare away from mine. "And the Russian prime minister?" he commands. "Where are we with his allegiance to the Circles?" he asks.

"He has pledged his allegiance to the Circles," a female answers, "with some coaxing."

"Well done, Novilia," Lucifer compliments.

I look back and forth between Novilia and my father, before my stare settles on her. When I study her, she eyes me warily, knowing I'm not buying her lies. Even after all these years, my father's minions do not respect me, but they fear me. I despise their lack of respect, but understand why their fear is so prevalent.

I stand, placing my hands in the front pockets of my jeans, staring at Novilia.

"I've decided to make some changes," I announce, "now that I have accepted my birthright." It's time my father's minions learn to respect me more than him.

"What kinds of changes?" Lucifer asks, uninterested by my dramatics.

"My Lord, if you want to send a succubus out to fraternize with mortal leaders, I can't stop you. Personally, I'm over them spreading their legs for compulsion," I bite out. "What you did in Russia took no effort. And yet"—I lean into her face—"you've failed."

"Is this true, Novilia?" My father's furious voice booms around the room.

My jaw clenches, knowing I've just signed her death warrant.

But I had no choice.

"My Lord," she cries out. "I tried. I just need more time. To be frank, the prime minister's tastes are different than what I can offer him," she admits, her head bowed.

"Are you telling me that you had no idea he preferred incubus?" Lucifer tsks, unhappy.

"He hides his preferences well, my Lord," she whispers.

My father sighs heavily. "Stolas is now in charge of Russia. And your fate."

Novilia's eyes look up at mine, pleading. "Now that I know his preferences, I can approach the prime minister from a different angle. He will pledge his allegiance. I swear."

It takes everything in me not to accept her apology. "There are no second chances in the Circles," I reply, my tone cold. "Starvros, since you have proven to be trustworthy and competent, you will meet with the Russian prime minister," I state. "I know you will accomplish what Novilia could not."

"With all due respect, Prince Stolas, I am a Seeker, not a negotiator," he responds.

"I see." I slowly walk over to Starvros, standing behind his chair.

Knowing that my father and the members of his council—his most trusted—are watching, I slowly inhale through my nose and place my hands on the demon's shoulders, removing my dagger from my sleeve before I slit his throat and violently rip off his head. Once it's completely severed, I toss it arbitrarily onto Novilia's lap.

She tries not to flinch.

"Get rid of it," I order.

"I—" She looks around.

"Get rid of it. Or I'll fucking get rid of you."

Grabbing the head, she rushes out of the conference room.

I look around, meeting everyone's eyes. "Anyone else want to question me?"

The room falls silent as the demons avert their gazes.

Full of pride and glee, my father claps from the corner of the room. "Well done."

I motion to the black tar-like blood all over me. "I need to clean up."

My father nods and motions for me to leave.

By the time I push open the conference room door, my head is pounding. I walk through it and head into the elevator with Lev and Avi in tow. Once the doors shut and we're out of earshot of my father, I sink down on the ground, placing my elbows on my knees, resting my head in the palms of my shaking hands.

"Speak freely," I exhale.

"Shit, Stolas!" Lev sighs. "Aside from Vassago, Starvros was our best Seeker."

"Which is why I had to end his existence. He was ordered to keep searching for Hope. Given more time, I have no doubt he would find her soul and report back that she is alive," I reply.

"That was all a setup?" Avi asks. "To kill him? To protect Hope?"

"Yes."

"What about Novilia?" Lev inquires.

"Her fate was sealed when she lied to my father about the Russian prime minister."

Commotion from the hallway outside of the elevator has me on my feet as the doors open. I ignore my inner conflicting feelings as we walk past the two giants tearing Novilia apart piece by piece. Starvros's head lies on the ground, next to pieces of her skin.

I hate what I've done, what I've become, but Hope comes first. No matter the cost. Once we're outside the building and in my limo, I finally breathe and push away the result of my actions today, refocusing on Hope and the end goal of all this shit.

After a few moments of silence, I slide my attention to Avi.

"Did Kagami arrive in Switzerland safely?" I ask her.

"She did. She and Hope will be moving on from karate to kung fu practices this week." The demoness smirks. "Hope has been learning quickly. Who knew she had a knack for demon ass kicking?"

I shift my focus outside the window, watching the crimson raindrops fall from the sky in the Eighth Circle. "I'm pretty sure we all knew." I mumble under my breath.

"Why is Hendrix's chosen teaching her martial arts?" Lev asks, sounding surprised.

"Vassago." I keep my eyes trained outside the car window.

"Vassago?" Avi repeats, taken aback.

"He was right. If Hope and I have any chance of survival, she has to learn to take care of herself. Fend off the darkness. Learn to live with it shadowing her. Kagami is going to teach her how to do that, even if she doesn't know what, or why, she's learning." I exhale.

"She will rise to the occasion," Avi states with confidence.

"Hope has no choice," I reply.

"I hate to point this out, but the meds are masking her oracular gifts. What happens when they resurface and she can sense and read dark souls again?" Lev questions.

"She is being taught to center and manipulate her oracular gifts," I add.

Avi's eyes meet mine. "How long are we leaving her at Shadowbrook for?"

"As long as it takes," I state.

"That's cruel—" Avi trails off, lost in thought.

"Not as cruel as my father," I counter. "Where are we with the legion?" I ignore Avi's concern for Hope and turn my attention to Lev, as he's the chief lieutenant of my father's army. Talking about Hope hurts. Too fucking much. I don't want to be reminded.

"Half have agreed," he replies.

"And the other?"

"The other half are scared to defy Lucifer."

"We need a higher percentage than half, Lev."

"I'm doing my best to make that happen, my Lord."

"Up the ante if they show disloyalty."

"To what?"

"If they don't cooperate, then they cease to exist," I state, so he knows I'm serious.

"And just how many existences are you prepared to end for her?" Lev questions.

My eyes shift and meet his. "Every. Single. One of them."

8

ETERNAL DARKNESS

HOPE

When I bow to the petite, Asian woman, the silky dark waves that cascade down the sides of my face fall over my shoulders. Just as I return myself to my full height, she pins me with a sharp look. Annoyed with my loose hair, she wordlessly holds out a hair elastic.

With a sigh, I take it and put my hair up in it.

Shadowbrook is a mind-body healing facility, which means one of the required sessions for patients is private meditation in the Zen garden—it's part of our care. One day, after about an hour of channeling inner peace, I became bored and agitated. My Japanese instructor, Kagami, decided to teach me karate instead.

Oddly, I find the hits and sharp movements more calming and soul-centering than meditation.

"Thank you, Sensei." I say, before walking around the dojo.

Kagami likes me to feel the energy in the space before we begin lessons. When I come to the wall displaying the three horizontal swords, I allow my fingers to run over them.

She once revealed to me that she is trained in the ways of the shogun samurai. I have yet to convince her to teach me more about what that entails, other than that they are extremely disciplined warriors who live by a strict code of honor.

And there are some really badass swords involved.

I take in her small figure as she approaches me, knotting her black belt. Kagami is a slender woman, in her fifties—elegant and pretty. Don't let her size, quiet manner, age, and looks fool you; she'll kick your ass and have you on your back in a second flat.

I know this from experience.

"No!" She bats my hand away from the steel, scolding with her Japanese accent. "Here."

I follow her over to a stand of sticks. After looking them over, she plucks one up and throws it at me so I'm forced to catch it mid-air. Then she grabs one for herself and points it toward the center of the room.

We walk over to where she wants us and face each other.

"This is just a practice sword. It doesn't even have an edge," I complain.

"You must earn steel."

I lift my chin. "How do I do that?"

She lifts her stick and, without warning, she whacks it on the side of my face.

With a curse, I bend and clutch my throbbing cheek. "Ouch. What the hell?"

"That is what it feels like to have a practice sword hit you on the side of the face."

I look up at her with pinched brows and a swollen cheek. "That hurt."

She tilts her head. "Then you are not ready for steel. Now, get up and learn."

"Learn what?" I mutter under my breath, pushing myself to my full height.

"How to fight off the demons that hunt and haunt you," she replies.

With a deep inhale, I give her a sharp nod, understanding the meaning behind her words. She's been using martial arts as a way to help me focus and calm myself when my schizophrenic episodes are triggered and I have hallucinations or delusional thoughts.

For the most part, it's been helping. Then there are days, like yesterday, when the emptiness takes over and the urge to self-harm becomes so overwhelmingly strong and severe that even normal breathing feels like an effort. The strange part of it is that those are the days when the demons and shadows aren't present.

"When using swords, it's not necessary to use charging momentum," she instructs.

"Why not?"

"You will work too hard. Use too much external force. Weapon art is learning to master your internal force. Mastering silence. Mastering fear. Mastering your darkness."

"Yes, Sensei." I take a warrior stance.

"Derive your power by harnessing your inner force. Focusing your chi in a fight helps you overcome any obstacle or any being who attacks you. Physical or mental."

"Yes, Sensei."

"Now lift your stick and learn how to protect yourself against eternal darkness, Hope Annandale."

———

I GROAN as I shift my sore, aching body on the couch. My cuts and bruises from today's weapon-training session sting. Tazia hands me an ice pack and with a grateful half smile I take it and place it against my cheek. Dr. Foster is my primary therapist, but Tazia is my secondary therapist. She checks in on me once a week, like today.

She gives me her best disappointed and worried look as she stares at my cheek. "Honestly, I don't know what that unassuming tiny Japanese woman is doing. This is a healing facility. Not a kick-the-crap-out-of-our-patients facility," she huffs.

"Kagami is training me to control my emotions," I mumble.

"By beating you?" Tazia counters.

"She didn't beat me," I argue. "I just suck at weapon fighting."

"Weapon fighting?" Her surprised tone hits a high octave.

"Sticks. Practice sticks. It's okay," I ramble. "I'm learning a lot. It helps."

"Good lord," she sighs heavily. "That woman is insane."

I lift my gaze and meet her gentle violet one. It's so odd—I've never met anyone with violet eyes before, but hers are so striking they actually pull you in. She must think me strange, always staring, but there has always been something familiar about her.

Tazia is beautiful. The kind of beautiful that just doesn't exist. Otherworldly beautiful. It's not just her long dark hair, or exotic looks; it's also her accent. It lulls you. It's hard to place and explain. It seems old-world, from another time. I've never worked up the courage to ask her where she's from.

All I know is that I'm always at peace in her presence.

I cock my head, studying her.

"Are you comfortable?" She crosses her long legs after sitting next to me.

"I am." I look around the lounge area before my eyes land on the piano in the corner.

"Shall we chat a bit?" Tazia asks, starting our session.

"Why don't you have an office?"

An amused laugh falls from her pink lips.

"An office? For what purpose?"

I turn my head, meeting her warm stare. "I don't know. Meeting with patients. Displaying your pretentious degrees. Files. Phones. Isn't that what offices are for?"

Her long dark lashes touch her cheeks as she blinks and looks around the facility's common area. "I think you are confusing me with Dr. Foster. I prefer to meet with guests in a more casual setting. Somewhere they are comfortable. As for my degrees, I don't feel the need to showcase where I went to school to prove my listening credentials."

"You also never take notes," I point out.

Tazia shrugs. "If I'm listening to you, Hope, and becoming your friend, then why would I need to take notes to remember what it is you've said or shared with me?"

Unlike Dr. Foster, I enjoy talking and being with Tazia.

She doesn't judge or make me feel crazy.

"Hello, Hendrix." She smiles at one of the male nurses as he approaches us with a silver tray carrying a tea set filled with herbal tea, along with my paper medicine cups.

"Ladies," he greets. "And how are two of the three most beautiful women at Shadowbrook today?" he charms.

Tazia giggles like a schoolgirl at the compliment.

"We're lovely. And you?"

My gaze lifts as I take in the fair-skinned, middle-aged nurse. He's watching me with a sparkle in his pale eyes. His short blond hair looks even sharper today; he must have gotten a haircut recently.

The one oddity about Hendrix is his height—he's well over seven feet. I guess when you work in a mental facility, height is an asset.

"Oh," he winks, "can't complain."

He hands me my pill cup and I look inside before frowning.

"These are different."

Tazia takes the cup from me, turning it upside down so she can inspect the drugs. After a moment, she and Hendrix exchange a glance and she nods briskly at him.

"They're fine for you to take."

I take the cup back from her as Hendrix speaks, "I think these will make you feel much better. Less under water. This dosage and brand will help clear your visions a bit better."

"I agree," Tazia says. "They're a much better fit for your needs."

81

With that, I take the meds and accept the warm tea Hendrix has poured for me.

"Well, ladies. I'm off to flirt with a certain Sensei." He smirks wickedly.

"Have a lovely day," Tazia says, and I wave at him.

"He is so in love with Kagami," I mutter under my breath.

"That he is." Tazia smiles.

We share a brief moment of silence before Tazia breaks it.

"So, aside from the physical, how are you feeling?"

"Honestly?" I prep her.

Tazia nods with encouragement.

"Like I don't belong in this world," I admit.

She tilts her head, considering my answer.

"What world do you think you belong to?" she asks.

I take the cold pack off my cheek and play with the corners.

"Would you think me crazy if I said another dimension? A darker one? A place full of sadness, torture, and pain?"

"No." Her voice is kind.

I raise my brows at her answer. "Really?"

"Sometimes when we struggle in our own lives, it's easier to pretend we belong to another world. Another dimension," she replies. "It makes perfect sense to me."

"That's not what I'm doing."

"No?" She shifts on the couch. "Then what are you alluding to?"

My gaze shifts back to the piano. "I don't really know. It's strange. I feel like I have no memories. There is an emptiness inside of me, but it's not depression, or sadness."

"What is it, then?"

"Loss."

"Loss?" she pushes.

"Loss of love." I look at her. "This. . . black hole. A void that can't be filled."

"Love?" A small smile crosses her lips.

"What?"

"You were adopted, right?"

"Yes."

"Often when children are adopted, there can be a multitude of issues that can arise at different moments in their lives. Adopted children may feel grief over the loss of a relationship, cultural, or family connection that would have existed with their birth parents." Her voice is gentle. "Feelings of loss of love can be especially intense in closed adoptions, where little or no information has been provided. Grief and feelings of abandonment can be triggered at different times throughout the adopted child's life, leading to feeling as if you've lost love somehow."

"Do you think that's what is happening?"

"It's been a while since you've seen your parents.

Could you be feeling the loss of their presence? Perhaps that distance is triggering a sense of emptiness within you," she replies.

"Maybe," I answer.

"I know they were planning to rent a flat near the facility, but at the last minute, they changed their minds." She pauses, an odd look crossing her face before she continues. "Do you know why they decided not to do that?"

"Me."

"You?"

"I asked them not to."

"Why would you do that?"

I shrug. "They live in the States. It feels like a huge burden to ask them to sacrifice so much, put their lives on hold and come to Switzerland once a month," I reply.

"Do you normally feel like you are a burden to them?" She prods. "Or a sacrifice?"

"At times. Less when I was younger," I trail off. "I guess you wouldn't understand."

A comfortable silence falls between us again as my eyes drift to the large windows and I take in the sunshine falling across the snow-covered Swiss Alps. The air where we are is starting to warm, melting away the snow, revealing the green grass and buds on the trees.

"I have a son." Her voice is wistful, far away.

"You do?" I don't look at her; talking about him is clearly painful.

"It's been quite a long time since I've seen him." She clears her throat. "He, um, lives with his father." She pauses. "I understand the sacrifices parents make for their children."

"I had no idea." I watch her, surprised that she's never mentioned him before.

Tazia shifts on the couch again, and her eyes follow mine, fixating on the outdoors.

"What's he like?"

"He's beautiful. Created out of an intense love. You see, his father had this . . . magnetic soul—at one time, it was full of light and love. And when he spoke, it was as if Heaven was speaking directly to you. As if you were the only being in existence." Her tone is full of melancholy. "My son had the same allure. But, unlike his father, he wasn't full of pride or hunger for power. There was only light in him."

My brows pinch together. "What happened to him?"

She clears her throat. "Like his father, eventually, the darkness overtook him. His charismatic personality was snuffed out, leaving only a shell of who he once was. Who I, and creation, intended him to be. I tried"—she pauses—"but . . . his soul was unsalvageable."

"All souls are savable," I reply. "Maybe it just takes . . . a different kind of soul saving."

Tazia's eyes meet mine. "I hope you're right."

"Is that why you became a therapist?" I shift direction.

Her smile is sad. "Perhaps. I couldn't save him, so maybe I try to save others."

"If I may, what's your son's name?"

Tazia pins me with a look. "Stone."

My lips part as the name rolls around my mind, triggering something deep within me. An unmerited feeling of panic and something else simmers under my skin, heating it.

"Stone?" I whisper.

The second his name falls from my lips, my world tilts. Suddenly it's too hot in here and I can't breathe. Gasping for air, I hear shouting around me, but it seems to come from far away. On its own, my body begins to shake. My breaths come out in sharp, quick pants. Every forced gasp burns my lungs as I try to pull it in.

A sudden pain tears through my heart, ripping it with a fiery break. The pressure in my chest chokes me and tears fall. Everything around me becomes still as the darkness takes over. And I fall into a peaceful abyss.

9

WORD PLAY

VASSAGO

My demeanor changes as soon as she barges into my office. The goddess strolls in without any regard for privacy, or for the demon sitting behind the desk taking her in. Apparently, I need to fucking remind her who she is dealing with. In silence, I study her with a predatory regard, leaning back into my chair.

As always, she's guarded.

"You have heard of knocking, haven't you, goddess?" I cock my head to the side.

Lore's eyes narrow at my question.

My assistant runs in after her, out of breath.

"I'm sorry, my Lord. I—"

"Leave us," I order in a harsh, demanding tone.

He hesitates for a moment and then nods, closing the door behind him.

"I hope he enjoys the last ten minutes of his existence," I mumble, eyeing her up and down. "No one enters my office unannounced. Even you," I point out in a cold tone.

Lore rolls her eyes at me, as she steps toward my desk.

My eyes wander over her body, making her uncomfortable.

She hates being admired. Lore's exotic beauty isn't something she flaunts, which makes her unassuming presence even more attractive. Dark eyes look directly into mine, trying to stare into my soul. Too bad I don't have one. Not one that anyone would want, anyway. And for some reason, with her, that bothers me.

Without thinking, I trail my eyes down her long neck toward her heaving chest. Lore is like forbidden fruit. Gorgeous forbidden fruit.

Which is why I need to stop eye-fucking her.

Her pouty lips purse, conveying her displeasure with me. "What are you looking at?" she defies.

"Whatever the fuck I want. This is my office." I arch an eyebrow in challenge.

She sits in the chair in front of me, holding back her emotions, as always.

"Why are you here, Lore?"

She places a black box in front of me and gives a firm kick to my desk, jolting it. The box jumps toward me while she watches me with a blank expression. "Open it," she demands.

My eyes shift from her to the box before I quickly snatch it up and flip it open. The bright light gleams off the obsidian knife, which is cradled in black volcanic rock.

"Is this—" I trail off, in awe of the dagger's beauty.

"The Weapon of the Smoking Mirror," she confirms, finishing my thought.

I've heard rumors of the weapon throughout the Circles. It's something the pantheon had commissioned at the request of the sun and war god, Huitzilopochtli. I quickly snap the case closed, tossing it back at her.

"It's cursed."

Lore grins, like I'm amusing to her. "Aren't we all, my Lord?"

"Why the hell do you have it?" I bark.

"My father gave it to me."

That piques my interest. "Why?"

"I am its new protector."

"What the fuck?" I breathe out, peering around the room in confusion before meeting her gaze again. "Why the hell would the Aztec deities gift you a curse to wield?"

She shakes her head. "Not to wield. To protect."

"I don't understand."

"I am to protect the weapon until its purpose is fulfilled."

"Who is expected to use it, then, if not you?"

"You."

Time seems to stop, and nothing in the room moves, including me. "I'm a demon prince, not an Aztec god," I point out. "Why would the pantheon want me to wield a weapon created by the deities?"

"The oracle's creation tipped the balance. The gods have decreed it must be restored to prevent war," she explains. "According to my father, her divinity must be released. It is the sole purpose why you and I have been placed in one another's path. The destruction of the oracle's divinity is our predestined fate."

I rub the back of my neck. "We're supposed to kill my brother's chosen?"

"Not kill."

"Enough with the word play, goddess."

Lore tilts her head. "The curse states the red serpent must drain her of divine life."

"That is the same as ending her existence." A sharp laugh leaves me, considering her words. "Make no mistake, I have no attachment to the mortal. Or human souls in general, for that matter. However," I deepen my tone. "Stolas does. After all he's done to protect the oracle, do you really think he will excuse Hope's death at my hand? Or yours?"

Her eyes bore into mine, trying to convey understanding. "The deities do not require her death. Just her divinity gone, as it relates to upheaval within the Circles, Vassago."

I blink, trying to understand. "What the fuck are you talking about?"

"As long as Hope has divinity in her soul, she is a threat to the balance." Her voice quiets. "But if we release her divinity and replace it with a dark soul, she can continue to exist. To live on. Enjoying immortality here in the Circles. By Stolas's side," Lore explains.

I push back in my chair, contemplating her words, never taking my stare off the goddess. Slowly, she stands and walks around to my side of the desk, settling in front of me. With a lift of her chin, she crosses her arms and sits back on the side of the desk.

I envy her in this moment.

Seeing her control her power and emotions—it makes me crave her like a drug. I look into her deep brown eyes, trying like hell to restrain the desire to kiss her.

"The only way Hope can become a dark soul is if she breaks a divine rule," I ponder out loud. "And even then, she will be judged by Hendrix and sent to the appropriate Circle."

"There is another way."

"Which is?"

"A bonded soul transfer after a blood sacrifice."

"What is that?" I ask, tiring of her vagueness.

"Stolas has an established protection bond with her.

Meaning, if she is dying, he has no choice but to save her. By any means necessary. Even if he doesn't want to," she replies.

I raise my chin and cock my head to the side, starting to understand where she is going with this information. I flash her an arrogant expression and shake my head.

"He'll never agree to do it."

Lore bends at the waist, placing her hands on either side of my chair. Her lips are a sliver's breadth from mine as she looks me in the eyes. "He will if it's her only option to continue to exist."

"What you are suggesting is turning her."

"He won't have a choice," she argues.

My gaze falls to her mouth, watching as she runs her tongue over her bottom lip. She's testing my limits. Provoking me on purpose. And this isn't a power struggle I'm willing to lose. In one swift movement, I grab her ass and stand up. With one step forward, I lean her back on my desk so I'm hovering over her, looking down into her eyes.

"And just how the hell do you see us executing this?" I draw out.

"The mortal is a self-harm patient. In a mental health facility," Lore says, quietly.

I lean closer to her mouth, taking one of my hands and softly splaying my fingers over her neck. The pulse at the base of her throat quickens at my touch.

"Common knowledge."

"As long as you trigger her blood sacrifice, you have fulfilled the pantheon's order." She swallows. "A human blood sacrifice made with the Weapon of the Smoking Mirrors breaks a divine rule. If the mortal uses the knife, she will end her own divinity."

"And how am I supposed to trigger a blood sacrifice without actually killing her?"

"You and I guard her. We can recall her memories. Remind her Stolas is in danger." She shifts a bit under me as I step farther between her legs. "Remind her of how she feels."

My eyes fall to her lips. "And how does she feel?"

The loaded question hangs between us. Both of us know there is more meaning behind it than just how Hope feels for Stolas.

Lore doesn't move an inch as she holds my gaze.

"She loves him. She would do anything to protect him," she answers shakily. "He is her only reason for existing."

I swallow, understanding her words are meant for me. "Is that right?"

Lore sits up a bit, her face getting closer to mine. "When the mortal demands to see the prince, or return to the Circles, you hand her the Weapon of the Smoking Mirror."

"And she cuts herself with it?" I surmise.

"She'll break the rule by spilling her divine blood

with a sacrificial obsidian weapon. Stolas will have no choice but to turn her in order to save her—"

"By giving Hope his blood," I assume.

"And turning her soul dark so she can live," she finishes.

"What happens to her after she turns?"

"With a dark soul, she can return here to the Circles by Stolas's side, as his chosen."

"And my father?"

"Lucifer will be forced to accept that she's Stolas's mate," she trails off.

"And your father?"

"In the eyes of the pantheon, we will have fulfilled our duties. With her divinity gone, the divine realm will have no cause to start a war with the Circles. Everyone wins."

The goddess doesn't bat an eye. She's calm, cool, and collected. Displaying no emotion at all. That's one of the things that draws me to her—she is so in control of her surroundings, of her demeanor. Of me. Manipulating me to do what she wants without even trying.

And fuck if I don't want to please her.

"You are suggesting I betray Stolas." I watch her closely. "Even for you, goddess, the request seems foreign. What happens if I choose not to wield the weapon?"

"Then you seal my fate."

I keep my eyes connected to hers the entire time. "Which is?"

Her gaze hardens. "I cease to exist."

My heart jumps, my pulse quickening with each breath I take.

"Because you failed to protect the curse?"

"Because you failed to protect me."

I narrow my eyes at her statement. Of all the shitty things I've ever done, or will ever do to Lore, failing to protect her will never happen. My eyes take in her steady gaze, penetrating through all the layers of sadness and despair. Cutting through all the things that eat away at her as she sits in front of me, exposed as her words captivate me in a way I have never experienced before, in pure fear.

"Why would my failure end your existence?"

"Our fates are tethered."

"Our bond doesn't tether our existences," I point out, confused. "We can survive without one another."

"We have been cursed. The deities made it so that when we did share golden blood in our runes, my fate would be tied to yours by the curse. If you fail to fulfill your destiny and drain the oracle of divinity, your punishment is an existence . . . without me in it."

And there it is.

It's either Stolas's love.

Or mine.

TORTURE

LORE

Torture is an art form. A cultivated skill. One that Vassago has mastered over the years. A proficiency he applies to all aspects of his existence, especially when it comes to me. His silence causes a tortured unease within me as he ponders everything I've said.

I intentionally left out the part about the pantheon declaring war on the Circles. He doesn't need to know that yet, because there is still time to figure that part out.

We're always desperately walking this line. If we cross it, again, it will have dire consequences for both of us. Even so, no matter how many times he pushes me away, Vassago would never allow me to cease to exist. When it comes to us, the shield he's built around himself —in order to keep me out and at bay—is only there to protect his heart.

Lucifer's threats to my existence are meant to keep him loyal—to both his father and the Circles. Yet all they've done is make the demon feel trapped, as if he's screaming and drowning, but no one can hear or help him. Except me. I will pull him to the surface, every time. Even if it takes my last breath to save him.

And I will save him. Every time.

I love him. I lost him. And both hurt like hell.

The only escape from the pain is mortality.

An ironic impossibility for immortals.

I lick my lips as he stares down at me, his warm hands curling around my waist. At his touch, my desire for him stirs and the bloodthirst begins to burn at the back of my throat.

He watches me with a look that says he's two seconds away from bursting into flames, which causes my skin to heat with need. Sensing my distress, he leans closer.

Then his lips brush mine with the gentlest of touches.

And I'm gone.

"You will never cease to exist."

I exhale slowly, relieved.

"I will always make sure of that," he vows.

For the first time in a long time, I feel safe.

"Thank you." My voice is quiet, almost hard for him to hear.

"I will always choose you," he admits.

I soften my expression and study his face.

"My love for you is my curse," I murmur.

In one swift move, he tugs me toward him, leaning over me. Bringing his body on top of mine, he supports his weight with his arms on either side of my face. His mouth hovers over mine, teasing. My blood-thirst grows with my desire for him, becoming unbearable.

Uncomfortable, I shift and try to swallow away the dry, scratchy feeling in my throat. Seeing my growing ache and need for blood, he slides a hand down my body toward the top of the desk. Without breaking eye contact, he opens a drawer and pulls out his dagger.

With a wicked grin, he slowly brings the knife up my body, being careful not to cut me as he runs the top gently over the side of my leg, up my stomach, over my chest, and finally between us.

Unhurriedly he drags the tip over his lips, cutting them slightly so the blood slowly pools. When I don't move, he pushes against my mouth, encouraging me to take what I need. With restraint, I lift my hands, taking his face between them, commanding him to pull away.

He does, with questioning eyes. I peer up at him as I lean forward, brushing my mouth against his one last time.

"We need to stop," I purr, arching my back off the desk.

Within seconds, he kicks the chair behind him away. It crashes into the wall behind us with a thud. I don't jump or startle at the loud noise or unexpected outburst. I'm used to Vassago's mood shifts.

Dropping the knife to the side, he grabs my wrists with his hands and places them over my head as he grinds his hard length against my core.

My lips part and I lick the remnants of his blood off my lips.

"You're my death sentence," he growls.

Then he takes my lips with a harsh bite. Our kiss deepens and I become lost in the feel of his velvety tongue. I don't even realize that I'm biting his lip and pulling his blood into my mouth to quench my thirst until the burning sensation in my throat begins to fade, replaced by unrestrained need.

The darkness that surrounds him only drags me further and further into a pleasurable abyss. I exhale as he inhales. As if we're breathing for one another.

After a long time, Vassago pulls his mouth from mine. A nerve strains along his jaw as he stares down at me, his eyes burning into me.

He leans in, his breath curling down and across my cheek.

"Tell me you love me." I plead, needing to hear the words.

I sense the demon energy swirling under his skin.

I'm so wrapped up and consumed by the feel of him, I almost don't hear him whisper, "I'm not capable of fully loving you."

———

IF I'VE LEARNED anything from watching mortals over the length of my existence, it's that human life isn't just unfair; it is unjust, desolate, and forlorn. I've always thought mortals to be weak, bothersome creatures. They whine over insignificant things—mainly material—and walk around wearing friendly and cheerful façades. All the while, underneath their skin, their souls are lonely and vain. Most have no idea what true pain and suffering is.

Inhaling, I take in the humans sprawled around the grounds of Shadowbrook. I find it ironic that mortals send one another to places such as this when they are assumed to be broken, dark, or weak.

If you ask me, the mortals here are the strongest amongst their kind.

These beings are the souls who have endured what true darkness is, and yet, they survive. Fight. Continue to move forward. That is not weakness; that is true strength.

Sensing her approaching presence, I resist my sickened reaction whenever one of them is near. Even though Stolas's mother was exiled and turned mundane, the divine stench in her soul and blood lingers. She was originally created of fire; that never ceases to exist.

Tazia steps to my side.

"I thought I felt your immoral soul lingering, Lore."

I press my fingers into my arms so I don't kill her. Tazia and I have never seen eye to eye. Ever.

"You reek of humanity."

"Hope is under divine protection now. You shouldn't be here."

I keep my eyes on the oracle.

"It is not your place, mortal, to question my presence."

Tazia turns to face me.

"I may be human, but I can still sense dark souls."

"I've always wondered. What came first for you? Your courage? Or your fall?" I challenge, put off by her. "I recall you being more feeble when you had golden wings."

Tazia steps in front of me, looking down into my gaze.

"Why are you here?"

"Stolas requested I be."

"For how long?"

"As long as Prince Stolas requires me to be."

"The more demons Hope senses, the less the memory wipe will hold," she states.

"The mortal's magical wards are of no concern. My lord requested my presence."

"Stone needs to let her go," she whispers. "For Hope's own sanity and healing."

I press my lips, annoyed she used his divine name.

"Stolas doesn't care about her sanity. He doesn't care

about her humanity. He doesn't care about her. Or you. At all."

Tazia narrows her eyes. "If my son doesn't care for her, why are you here?"

"I imagine it has something to do with his distrust of Gabriel's word," I spit out.

"We will hold up our end of the deal."

"You'd better," I demand. "In Lucifer's hands, the oracle will be deadly to us all."

Tazia laughs without humor. "I know Lucifer better than all of you. He knows she is alive. He will come for her. And when he does, the divine will be ready for war."

I take in her words before stepping into her space. "You speak of things you no longer understand. You are mortal now. By your own doing. And while your memories of Stolas are intact, never forget, you now are a human pawn in a game of divine chess. You are nothing more than a silhouette of a pathetic being."

"Then why did my son trust me with her care?"

"Trust you?" I bark-laugh. "Stolas doesn't trust you. He hates you. Despises what you did. Gabriel's love for you was leveraged so the divine would agree to guard the oracle."

"Vassago sought me out himself. Brought me here to watch her," she argues.

I smile cruelly. "You were chosen because of your human emotions. Prince Stolas knew if it came down to it, you'd die saving the mortal because of your love for him and the guilt you feel at leaving him behind with the monster that is his father."

Tazia falls silent at the truth in my words. Her lips turn down, foolishly displaying her sadness, and I step around her so that I can watch over the oracle.

"Get used to Vassago and me being here."

HOLD ON

STOLAS

C onfused, I step into the dimly lit room. The blue and silver beams of light from the full moon shine through the large floor-to-ceiling windows to my left. After a few casual strides, I stop, distracted by her scent. My gaze drifts away from the picturesque view of Switzerland, which is bathed in nightfall and stars.

My attention shifts toward a corner where Hope is sitting at a piano.

Where am I? Shadowbrook? I look around.

Our eyes meet and, for a moment, I stop breathing at the sight of her. An ache builds in my chest. A deep-seated yearning to touch and be near her.

She's wearing a large, gray thermal shirt—my shirt. The one I purposely left in her room the night I walked away. I can't help but smile when I notice the holes she's cut in the sleeves so her thumbs can slip through. Her long, dark hair has fallen over her slender shoulders and I take in her thinning frame.

Hope looks as exhausted and as lost as I feel.

Without thinking, I take a slow, measured step in her direction. The fireplace ignites, coming alive in my presence, bathing us and the room in soft orange hues. That's when I notice she's barefoot. All that's covering her body is the cotton thermal, which falls to the middle of her thighs.

And fuck—her bare legs.

My hands twitch with the need to feel them.

Silence lingers between us as I slowly approach her. Without saying a word, she watches me, an unreadable expression etched on her face. The closer I get, the more her eyes widen.

It's as if she can't decide if I'm real or not.

Shadows from the fire dance across her face and my chest seizes at her sheer beauty. With a final step, I stand next to the empty seat on the piano bench. Holding my gaze, her lips part and she slides over, inviting me to sit next to her. We don't drop our eye connection, even when I sit. For the longest time, we just stare at one another, not speaking, soaking one another in.

Trying to figure out what is real and what is imagined.

"Am I dreaming?" she whispers.

My heart jumps in my chest at the sound of her

voice. It's raspy and dry. Like she hasn't used it in a long time. The thought infuriates me, and my runes begin to glow red.

I dip my chin, touching one of the piano keys with my fingers.

"Perhaps," I reply.

Her eyes fall to my hand and then my arms, where my sleeves are pushed to my elbow. She studies the charcoal smudges and swirling runes with an odd curiosity.

My gaze roams over her face and I watch the way she takes me in, the way her chest rises and falls with each breath she takes. I can't fucking help myself. I need to see if, like the piano, she is real. Really here with me. I reach out and brush my thumb over her cheek.

At my touch, she jerks away the slightest bit, and immediately I pull my hand back.

"I didn't mean to frighten you," I say in a quiet tone.

"You didn't." Her response is quick and firm.

My lips twitch, trying to form a smile. We stay lost in each other for I don't how long. All I know is that I want to grab the sides of her face and take her mouth with my own.

Hope looks deep into my eyes, intently searching for something in them. A trace of the being she used to know, perhaps. Trying to find a shred of the demon prince she fell in love with. It's strange, I've never seen her look at me like this before.

It's scary, unnerving even.

And pure fucking heaven.

Slowly, I move my thumb along the edge of her face, tracing her cheek from side to side, soaking up the feel of her skin against my fingertip. It's warm and soft. Silky and smooth, like porcelain.

She licks her lips and I run my finger down her chin to her neck, stopping over the beating pulse on the side of her throat, basking in the soft, steady pulse.

Her focus drops to her left hand, which is curled around the bottom of her sleeve, clutching something. My gaze follows hers and slowly she uncurls her fingers, revealing a piece of charcoal from the Circles that I draw with. The same one I used on her.

"I need something," she breathes out.

"Anything."

Hope's teary eyes hold mine as she reaches over to take my hand in hers. Her fingers caress mine, sending shivers through me that shake me to my core when she gently places the charcoal stick in my palm and closes my fingers around it. Before releasing my hand, she brings it up over her heart, which is beating a mile a minute.

She gazes into my eyes with a glazed look and speaks softly. "I hide away like a ghost from them here. Pretending not to know. Or remember. They're trying to make me forget you and the Circles. All of it. But I won't. I can't. I have to save and protect you, Stone."

At the sound of my name, I tense.

"My heart is missing," she continues.

I clench my jaw.

"When you left, you took it with you."

She shifts closer to me, leaving no space between us.

"I've lost my way," she exhales.

"No. You haven't."

"I'm stuck in the darkness that surrounds me."

I shake my head. "You won't be forever."

"You left me. Alone."

"You aren't alone. I'm here. Even when you don't see me."

At my admission, she inhales.

"I knew it," she says more to herself.

"Knew what?"

"Sometimes, at night, I feel you breathing on the back of my neck."

Hope slides her thumb out of the hole on her left sleeve and pushes the cotton material up to her elbow, revealing her unmarked forearm and wrist.

A single tear falls down her cheek. "They took it away . . . took away my—"

"Your what?" I cut her off.

"My heart."

My eyes narrow at the meaning of her words.

The charcoal heart I drew on her is gone.

"I need you to give it back. So when you leave again, I can be strong."

"I left you here to protect you. I didn't want to. To

leave. To love you . . . I tried to stay away. Despite all that, you've brought me to my knees." Her hand settles on the side of my neck and I close my eyes. "I wish I could, Hope. But I can't be your savior."

"I don't need a savior. I can save myself."

I open my eyes. "You can't save yourself from my world."

"I can. And I will," she says with conviction.

I shake my head.

"And then, Stone, I'm going to save you."

"I can't be saved. I don't want to be saved. Do you understand?" I drop my tone, lining it with seriousness.

"You do. You just don't know it yet."

"I didn't come here for you to save me," I argue.

"But, you're here. You came back to me, when I called."

"I don't know how I'm here. Or how you remember."

I watch as she ponders what I'm saying. "Hendrix once told me to call your name. If I did, he said, you would come. Tazia reminded me of your name earlier," she explains. "And then, I whispered it before I fell asleep tonight." Her eyes meet mine. "And here you are."

"Here I am," I whisper.

"Make me strong again." She moves her arm closer.

My hand lifts and wraps around her wrist. I brush my thumb over her pulse before guiding her arm down flat so I can draw on it. A quick breath emerges from her perfect lips when I press the charcoal to her skin. Quickly, I redraw the heart on her arm.

When I'm done, I lean over and press a light kiss over the design, as I did before. A single tear slides down my cheek, falling and landing in the middle of the heart. We both watch as her snow-white skin absorbs the tiny drop.

After a moment, I gaze up into her eyes and she looks down at my lips, taking in a deep, calming breath. With our gazes locked, Hope leans in, tenderly placing her lips on mine. For a second, I don't move. My lips are starved for her affection, because I haven't kissed her in fucking forever. Yet I'm afraid. Then, like a switch, our mouths begin to desperately move, dancing over one another.

Devouring her, I pick her up. She wraps her legs around me and I gently place her on top of the piano's keys, never breaking our heated kiss, even when the keys bang erratically.

Once she's seated, I grab her hands and pin them behind her back, holding them together with my fingers wrapped around her wrists. With my other hand, I reach for the hem of the shirt, pushing it up a bit, revealing her white cotton boy-shorts, which I proceed to tear off her in one motion, like a savage animal, tossing them to the side.

When her tongue meets mine again in a frantic sweep, my heartbeat accelerates and I swear the sound echoes through the room. Quickly, I undo the button on my jeans, pushing them down with my boxers. Without giving either of us a moment to think, I slam into her and still. The piano's rough sounds echo my emotions.

Unbalanced.

Wild.

Needing air, I release her mouth and Hope shuts her eyes. When she reopens them they're filled with tears. Seeing her break is my undoing. Fearful I've hurt her, I grip the sides of her face with my hands so she looks at me, while I remain buried deep inside of her.

"Did I hurt you?" I breathe out against her lips.

She ignores my question.

"If I ask you to choose me—to choose us—would you?"

I lean back, staring into her teary eyes, and wipe away her tears with my thumbs.

"I did choose you. Now I have to protect you."

Hope's hands land on each side of my face, pulling me back to her lips. My forehead rests on hers as I slowly begin to move in and out of her, basking in every sensation, reclaiming what is already mine. Every part of me strains against her as I slide in and out.

Each thrust goes deeper, becoming something more. The feel of her body gripping me, clinging to me with each movement, has me losing control. The demon takes over and I begin to reach my limits seeing her writhing in front me. A low rumble erupts from me as our movements become more frantic and savage. Hope's body reacts just as violently as my own, causing me to slam into her, over and over again. She matches my ferocity as we punish each other, unleashing all the built up hurt and anger that lingers between us.

Each time I plunge deeper into her, I try to imprint myself onto her soul. My hand reaches between us and rubs her as I bite down on her lip and we each reach our climax.

When she pants out my name in a deep moan, I feel myself lose control completely; my cock throbs and empties itself inside of her.

After what feels like an eternity, our heavy breaths sync while reality begins to slip back in again, along with the hard sound of piano keys banging as she shifts.

The red coloring in my runes fades along with my emotions.

I remain inside of her, not ready to pull out.

I push away the hair from her face, looking deep into her satisfied gaze. Needing to be inside her, I rushed this. Now, all I want is to feel her. I run my hands down her face, neck, and eventually up her bare legs and thighs before grabbing both her wrists, bringing her palms to my mouth and placing a kiss on each.

When I do, the moon's light bounces off a fresh scar on her wrist. Not one of her old ones, but one that is new. It's an angry red color and raised.

Taken aback, I release one of her arms and push up

the sleeves on the shirt she's still wearing, examining the remains of the long, thin cut on her wrist. Pissed, I grab the other wrist and do the same, only to find a matching one. My eyes lift and meet hers. Her lips tremble and whatever piece of peace I thought I had a few moments ago crumbles beneath me as I gently pull out of her and get dressed. Unmoving, she watches my every move.

I lift her off the piano and sit on the bench, pulling Hope onto my lap, holding her shaking body to mine. "What the fuck happened?" I don't hide the harshness in my tone.

"They say . . . I tried to commit suicide."

"Did you?"

"I don't remember."

My thumb brushes over the raised scar.

"The doctors said I freaked out about a book in the library."

"Who found you?" I snarl.

"Sto—"

"WHO!" I shout.

"Hendrix."

I tilt my head. What the fuck is Hendrix doing?

As her eyes hold mine, without warning, the room begins to dissolve around us. My fingers tighten around her, but it feels like I'm gripping air, not her. Just before she disappears, I hear her whisper.

"I'll save you, Stone. Just hold on."

SCARLET TEAR

HOPE

White light pierces my eyes. I struggle to keep them open as Dr. Foster flashes his tiny flashlight in them, checking my pupils. I try not to blink. After a few moments, he shuts off the light and steps back, tilting his head as he stares at me, assessing my health. He's giving me this odd, half-determined and half-tentative look.

He stands there for a moment, before turning and walking behind his desk. After taking a seat, he tosses the light onto his desk with a deep, worried sigh.

Relieved that he's not hovering, I settle back onto the chair, pulling my legs up underneath me as I fiddle with the sleeves on my gray thermal. When I'd fallen asleep last night, I was wearing it. And then, when I woke up, it smelled of something familiar.

Something comforting and masculine. Like warm

citrus with notes of sweet cinnamon and smokiness. For some reason, the smell of the shirt makes me feel safe. Happy even.

"I can't explain it," he states, sounding confused. "Yesterday, you were ten pounds lighter. Your skin was gray, and the dark circles under your eyes seemed permanently etched onto your skin. Today, your eyes are bright, your weight is back up to a healthy level, and your skin is glowing."

Not to mention the angry scars on my wrists have healed, completely. Though I don't dare mention that out loud to him.

"Hendrix and Tazia changed my medicine a few days ago. Maybe that's it?"

"Overnight?" Dr. Foster's deep brown eyes hold mine.

Swallowing, I drop my chin.

He's right.

Yesterday, I felt hopeless and tired all the time. Today, I woke up with a renewed sense of purpose and energy. For the first time in a while, I feel like my old self.

"I'd like to set up an appointment for you with the physician. If it is a delayed reaction to the medicine dosages and changes, I'd like to be sure there aren't any lingering health issues or side effects," he says.

"Okay."

"Do I have your permission to do so?"

"Yeah. That's fine," I agree.

Dr. Foster watches me, baffled, as I pick at my sleeve. When I meet his eyes again, there is an odd look on his face before it's gone.

He clears his throat. "Appearances aside, how are you feeling?"

"I woke up today feeling better than I have in a long time."

"I'm glad to hear that, Miss Annandale." He looks down, tapping on my folder.

I narrow my gaze. "Why do I sense an underlying but coming?"

With a long exhale, he meets my eyes again. "Depression can trigger mood swings, ranging from low, depressive episodes to extreme euphoria. It would be normal for you to feel hopeless and helpless one day, and ready to take on the world the next," he says.

"That's just it—I don't feel euphoria."

"No?"

"I feel . . . whole again. Stronger."

Dr. Foster nods, considering what I've said. "Well, that is a good start. Still"—he pauses, watching me carefully—"it doesn't happen overnight. So let's just go slow here."

"Slow is my middle name," I quip.

Dr. Foster gifts me a small sad smile before standing. "If you'd be so kind to give me one moment," he says, "I'll go check in with Dr. Wang across the hall and see if she can see you soon for some blood work and a medical evaluation. Sound okay?"

Nodding, I play with my sleeves while Dr. Foster slips out of his office. Feeling warm, I take my thumbs out of the holes and push up the sleeves. The second I do, my brows pull together. Leaning in closer to get a better view, I notice that over the tattooed ink lines of my heart there is fresh line of charcoal. Like someone drew over it.

Even more strange is that centered in the middle of the heart is a raindrop, glowing scarlet.

"What the fuck?" I whisper into the empty office.

With my thumb, I try to rub it off, but it's branded on my skin. After a moment, the red glow somehow seeps into the heart tattoo and the outline begins to swirl as it lights up in the same deep scarlet color.

Frowning, I watch as the glowing brightens and the lines crawl in hieroglyphic flame shapes up my arm before fizzling out just as fast as it started.

"Hope?"

At the sound of Dr. Foster's voice I startle and yank my sleeve down. Quickly, I jump to my feet and watch him as he stares at me, while I nervously shift and act jittery.

"I'm sorry, what?" I manage to force out.

"Everything okay?" He looks around the office before his eyes land back on me.

I nod and swallow, unable to speak.

A cold chill has seeped in under my skin.

"Dr. Wang can see you tomorrow afternoon. Does that work?"

"Sure. That's fine," I answer, not really paying attention.

Dr. Foster frowns and takes a step toward me.

"You sure you're okay, Miss Annandale?"

Inhaling through my nose I manage to force a smile on my face and meet his eyes. "Yeah, just tired. You were right, um . . ." I pause. "I, ah, I'm feeling tired again."

His lips press together as he studies me. "The mood swings are all part of it." His voice is calm and resolved. "Why don't we cut our session short for today. You can head back to your suite and get some rest before lunch. I'll have Tazia check on you later."

"Sounds good." I rush past him to the door.

Just as my hand finds the knob and turns it, Dr. Foster's voice stops me. "Do not abandon all hope." I don't turn around, even though the words cut through me for some reason. "You won't live in darkness forever. Just . . . hold on for a bit."

I make quick work of opening the door and slipping out, rushing back to my room. Closing the door to my suite, I push my sleeve up again and run my finger over the fresh lines of charcoal that cover the heart tattoo underneath it. The moment I touch it, it glows scarlet.

Panicked, I run to the bathroom, turn on the faucet, and grab the soap. Once the water is hot enough, I scrub and try to remove it, but all that comes off in the soapy water is the charcoal. The rest continues to glow, seeming to darken with my anxiety.

After what feels like hours, I give up and throw the soap into the sink, shut off the water and look up into the mirror.

As I meet my own eyes, my lips part and I spin around.

"Holy shit!" I blow out, taking in the bathroom. "What. The. Fuck?" I drag each word out.

Written all over the walls, the door, the toilet, the shower—everywhere, actually—is the word Stone in black chalk. I take it all in. It's written over and over again, covering everything.

Stepping closer to the wall, my hand lifts and my fingers brush over the word. They're all written in my handwriting.

Every last one.

Why would I have done this? I bite my lip. The scent from my shirt floats around me and the scarlet on my arm glows brighter when I read the word out loud in my head. After a few moments, the scarlet glowing fades, leaving only the soft inky black outlines.

"Stone," I whisper out loud.

Suddenly the room brightens and becomes white before the light dims. When it does, a man is standing in the doorway, across from me.

Everything around me feels like it's moving in slow

motion. The raven-haired man is dressed in a sharp ivory tailored suit. With a causal self-assurance he cocks his head, assessing me. As he watches me, I feel overwhelmed and humbled to be in his presence.

"Who are you?"

At my question, his violet gaze softens. "Gabriel."

I stare into his eyes.

Sudden recognition hits me—the color matches Tazia's.

"What do you want?" I confront him. "Why are you here?"

"To deliver a message."

I have no idea why, but in his presence I feel threatened.

As if he read my mind, Gabriel's expression falls, becoming concerned, and he softens his hard warrior pose, taking a step back, away from me, giving me some breathing room.

"Deliver it, then." I bark in a shaky tone.

"It is time for you to face your destiny, Hope."

13

BLIND TRUST

VASSAGO

Uninvited, I stroll into the penthouse and make my way into the sunken living room. Before Hope, none of us were ever allowed in my brother's home. Now, it seems this is the only place he wants to discuss business—in the presence of her ghost.

Neither Stolas nor Leviathan bother to get up as I enter. They both fall silent and watch me with curiosity. With a smug look, I approach them and sit in the empty chair next to Lev and across from Stolas, waiting to be addressed.

"Do you need something?" Stolas asks me.

"My Lord." I sigh.

Annoyed at his cockiness, I slide the obsidian box across the coffee table.

"What? No gift for me, Vas? I'm hurt." Lev feigns heartache and winks at me.

I don't acknowledge his idiocy. Since day one, there's always been something about Lev—let's just say I tolerate him. Some days, he's entertaining. Others, he's a complete prick. And right now, I don't have the patience for his shit. The last thing I need is to babysit another demon who thinks with his dick instead of his head.

My plate is full with Stolas.

"What is this?" Stolas asks, eyeing the box.

"A complication," I reply.

"Another one?" Lev sits forward, shifting to business mode.

"What kind is this one?" Stolas inquires.

"The cursed kind," I answer.

"Cool," Lev exclaims, excited.

"It may require an inducement," I add.

Stolas narrows his eyes at me, cocking his head to the side.

"More bribes?" he asks.

"Shit," Lev mumbles around his unlit cigarette.

"What do you mean more?" I question.

"We've been incentivizing legionnaires," Stolas answers matter-of-factly.

"Why are we being unwise by bribing low-level demons?" I ask.

"Only half of them pledged their allegiance. The other half needed incentives," Lev replies.

My eyes slide to his. "And those who don't want to accept the enticements?"

"Punished for disloyalty. Indefinitely," Lev responds proudly.

Regardless of his charming, surfer-boy good looks and overall casual appearance, Leviathan has some brass balls. I guess you'd have to, being best friends with the Devil's son. I've always envied their friendship. He and Stolas are close. The kind of close where they can communicate without words—like they're doing now, giving one another sharp, knowing glances. It's fucking annoying.

I sit back in the leather chair, watching my brother with an unamused expression on my face. "Inducements to legion members is a big risk that you're taking," I point out.

"Big risks, equally big rewards," Stolas counters, bored.

We stare each other down.

"Shall we chat a bit more about the latest enticement needed?" Lev breaks the silence.

Stolas leans forward on the couch, elbows on his knees, the box sitting in front of him as he stares at me. Waiting. Reading me.

Trying to figure out my angle.

As I study him, I notice he looks more relaxed today. Even his temper seems to have mellowed out today. The color has returned to his cheeks and he appears more in control.

"Want to tell me what you were doing last night?"

I query.

Silence.

"Or whom?"

"It's none of your fucking business," Stolas hisses.

And there it is. "If it was the mortal, it is," I goad.

Lev's eyes slide between the two of us before landing on Stolas.

"Are you fucking kidding me?" Lev bites out. "I thought I smelled mortal sex all over you."

Stolas inhales deeply. "Hope is not up for discussion."

"I knew you couldn't handle it," Lev sneers.

"What the fuck are you doing?" I bark out.

"It's not like I went to her of my own accord," he argues.

"Did the mortal suddenly turn vampire and compel you?" I taunt in a sarcastic tone.

Stolas picks up the box and shakes it at me. "What is this?"

With an arrogant look, I ignore what he did last night and focus my attention back on the reason I'm here in the first place.

"That"—I point to the box—"is not legion business."

"Then who?" Stolas asks.

"The pantheon."

Stolas grins, tapping the charcoal-stained fingers of his other hand on the table, one right after the other as he considers my words.

"The Aztec deities?" He sounds doubtful.

I dip my chin in confirmation.

He opens the top and pulls out the knife.

After a moment, his eyes meet mine in question.

"They've gifted you . . . a weapon?"

"A curse," I counter.

"Why would a knife be a complication?" Lev asks, reaching over and taking it from Stolas to look at it more closely. "Don't get me wrong, it's a kickass dagger. Is it obsidian?"

"It is," I confirm. "Obsidian mirror."

"Tezcatlipoca give it to you then?" Stolas inquires, picking up on the mirror part.

"Yes. It's the Weapon of the Smoking Mirror. And it comes with an ancient curse."

"What kind of curse?" Lev probes.

"Smoke. Mirrors," Stolas mumbles, repeating the words. "Shit."

"What?" Lev looks up.

"It's a symbolic relic meant to be used for battle and sacrifice." Stolas meets my gaze. "Black mirror obsidian, Vas? A reflective and a vital part of human blood sacrifice."

Once again, I dip my chin in confirmation of what

he's figured out. "The curse is that Lore has been assigned to protect it until it's used. Her existence is tied to the dagger."

"Meaning?" Lev prompts.

"If the dagger isn't wielded as the deities desire, she ceases to exist." I inhale, trying to hide my displeasure.

Stolas blows out a hard breath. "And the weapon's purpose?"

I can feel Lev's gaze burning a hole in the side of my face as I meet Stolas's eyes again.

"To spill the oracle's divine blood."

Lev releases a low whistle, causing the cigarette still dangling from his lips to bounce between his lips.

"What the fuck do you mean, spill her blood?" Stolas growls.

"Hope's divinity must to cease to exist."

"Why do the deities care whether she is divine or not?"

"They feel your mortal is a threat to the Circles' balance—"

"Oh, for fuck's sake," Lev cuts me off. "Who doesn't at this point?"

With a sharp snap of his gaze, Stolas pins Lev with a hard look.

"Don't do that. Don't give me the don't fucking talk about her like that look, Stolas. Your mortal is causing us more grief than she is worth," Lev sulks.

"If I wanted your fucking opinion about Hope, I would've asked for it," Stolas bellows.

Lev places the knife back in the box. Leaning back, he slips his hand into the front pocket of his jeans, pulling out his lighter. With an amused shake of his head, he lights his cigarette and inhales.

Holding my brother's gaze, he says, "Now." He blows the rest out on the dark cloud of smoke he releases. "Now, you sound just like your father, my Lord."

"Fuck off!"

Lev laughs, pinching his cigarette between his fingers as he sits forward. "We're taking a huge risk in protecting your little human pet. If everything goes to shit—and it will—our risks are not only going to cost you and the Circles, but us too. Remember that."

The prince's jaw clenches. "Do I need to remind you that you work for the Circles, Lev? Not the other way around. Friend or not. You don't make the rules, I do."

"I may not make the rules, friend, but I fucking protect the Circles. And your sorry ass," Lev counters.

"Enough!" I interject. "You're both acting like children instead of demon lords."

"He started it." Lev juts his chin in the direction of Stolas.

Stolas responds with a tight, displeased expression.

I sigh. "The deities are firm on this, Stolas."

"Why?"

"When the pantheon agreed to assist Lucifer, it was in the name of offering free will to all beings. Over the past few centuries, they have seen what Father's vengeance has turned both him and the Circles into. They don't like what they see."

"What the fuck does this have to do with Hope?"

"I assume, they think if Lucifer gets his hands on Hope again, he will start a war with the divine," I guess.

"So? The deities want peace between the dark and divine dimensions?" Lev asks.

"No. But they don't want upheaval either."

"Then what do they want?" Stolas asks.

I sit forward. "They want you to reign."

Stolas nods. "And in their eyes, her continued existence is a threat to my reign and the Circles' endurance."

"The deities commissioned the weapon after learning the oracle was created. It's their way of protecting their interests in the event of war. The divine blood that runs through Hope's veins and her soul require celestial protection. If Lucifer were to take her again, now under divine protection, the divine will attack. To protect her. At any and all costs," I add.

"How did you come into all this . . . knowledge?" Lev inquires, finishing his cigarette.

"Some of it came from Lore." I exhale slowly. "The rest I'm taking a stab at."

Stolas's gaze narrows at my response. "If I'm following you, Vassago, you're saying that the pantheon has ordered my chosen's blood spilt, at the hands of the goddess you love?"

"If Lore is to continue to exist, she must execute her part in all of this," I respond matter-of-factly.

Stolas stands abruptly and begins to pace. In deep thought.

"There has to be a way to save them both," Lev interjects.

Stolas inhales deeply, his focus sliding between us.

"There is." I offer.

Standing I walk toward him.

"And what is that going to cost me?" Stolas asks with a cool tone. Apprehension radiates off him as he looks me over, reading my body language.

I stand in front of him, holding his gaze. "Your trust."

"My trust? Is that all?" Stolas asks through a tight jaw.

"That is all."

"And if I give it to you?"

"Then, my Lord, we prevent war."

"And your mate lives."

"And Lore continues to exist." I lift my chin.

"And Hope?" he prods.

"The mortal . . . will end up by your side. You have my word."

"Care to share how you are producing this pretty bow?" Lev asks, approaching us.

"No," I clip out.

"We're just supposed to have blind trust in you?" Lev scoffs.

"Have I given you a reason not to?" I fire back. "For centuries, the three of us have been working to remove Lucifer from power. I have been aligning us with the pantheon all this time, as requested, Leviathan." I look at my brother. "And even after I protested, I still guard the mortal with my life. I think I've shown my loyalty and trustworthiness."

Silence falls between the three of us.

Stolas steps up to me, pinning me with a look. "Betray me, brother," he seethes, "and not only will I end your dark-souled existence, but I will torture Lore for the rest of hers."

My body goes rigid at his threat; it's unusual for him to threaten one of our mates, which can only mean he's scared for Hope.

"Let me handle it, my Lord," I implore.

"Handle it. Just remember, at my hand, the goddess will cry a river of tears knowing that you are the reason she suffers if you fuck me over," he adds.

I don't reply.

My silence is my agreement.

In his shoes, I would do the same.

Stolas nods toward the door for me to get the fuck out. And I do, without another word.

The irony in all of this?

I'm about to save two women, in the name of love.

14

RIVER OF TEARS

LORE

Darkness blankets the earth as I walk along the stone pathways, listening to the sounds of the night. Unlike in the Circles, here in the mortal realm, crickets call to one another and the night sky sparkles with thousands of twinkling stars. Tonight, the moon appears to be larger and brighter than when I am normally here.

It's mesmerizing and awe-inspiring.

A part of me feels lucky. Most dark souls are not allowed to cross dimensions or leave the confines of the Circles. And yet, the taste of freedom chokes me. The ability to move freely through the human realm is suffocating. The fresh air is a shroud, deep and impenetrable, encircling the creatures that prowl during nightfall.

Dawn is hours away.

I stop walking when I see the mortal sitting in the

Zen garden with her knees pulled up against her body and her eyes on the sky. Sleep does not come to her anymore; her mind is crowded with sinister thoughts. I can hear each one. They rattle around in her head, taunting and worrying her as she sits motionless, trying to be unseen. Except I see her. Hope looks the way I feel—lost.

Like me, I sense she longs for something we can't have.

I shouldn't venture near her; direct contact isn't allowed. But tonight, there's something about her sadness that calls to me. It's like a magnet pulling me toward her.

A chilled breeze sweeps through both of us. She rubs her covered arms briskly, trying to ward it off. With one final look around, I notice that even with the wind, nothing moves in the darkness. The mortal takes in a deep breath and closes her eyes as I soundlessly approach.

"You're back?" she whispers, opening her eyes.

The moment they lock onto mine, I become still.

Panicked that she addressed me.

She watches me with a smug expression. "I can see you."

"Most can't."

A small smile plays on her lips. "I'm not like most."

A part of me appreciates her response. It's fierce.

We stare at one another in silence for a moment.

"Why aren't you afraid?" I question.

"Your friend asked me the same question the other night."

"Friend?"

"Red serpent tattoo. Angry demeanor. Buzzed hair." I cross my arms and lift my chin. "Vassago?"

The mortal smiles as if she's learned a secret. "So, you do know him. Are you two friends?"

My lips press, betraying my annoyance at her discovery.

Hope studies me with a knowing look. "Therapy and antipsychotic medications don't seem to make you guys disappear." Her eyes dance with amusement. "As a matter of fact, there seem to be more of you visiting."

"You guys?" I prod.

"Demons."

I don't acknowledge her accuracy.

"Even stranger, it appears you know one another."

"You shouldn't refuse the meds." I try shifting the topic of conversation.

"I don't," she replies. "And even if I did, it wouldn't change the fact that I see you, demon."

"It is your fate. Nothing can change that."

Instead of answering, Hope watches me in a calculated manner. It's hard to tell, but it feels as if she knows something about me. Something I have yet to uncover about myself. It's unnerving. I shift on my feet, feeling uncomfortable, an odd response for me.

"I can tell by your stance that you're a warrior," she gauges.

"Impressive."

"Here to kill me?" she taunts.

"You are dangerous," I reply sharply.

"To whom?" The mortal pauses, tilting her head. "You? Or me?"

"Both of us."

After a few seconds, she pushes off the ground and stands.

"Do you have a name?"

"Lore."

"Hope."

All I can do in response is dip my chin. Vassago doesn't want us to force or trigger her memories until he's spoken to Stolas.

It's clear that she has no clue who I am.

She tucks her hair behind her ears, watching me as she steps in my direction. "I get the feeling that you don't like me." It's a statement, rather than a question.

"I never have."

Her eyes blaze with excitement. "My instincts were right. We do know one another."

I don't flinch, even though I'm taken aback at how assertive she is being tonight. I knew better. I never should've approached. I should have stayed hidden in the shadows.

"How?" she questions.

My gaze snaps to the building behind her, but Tazia and Gabriel are nowhere in sight. Noticing my focus has shifted, Hope follows my sightline before facing me again.

Realizing I walked right into her trap, I ask, "Were you waiting for me, mortal?"

Her smile turns shrewd. "On your nights, you watch me from outside. Your serpent friend, he does his time inside, where it's warmer. Plus, he likes to eat my grapes."

"Vassago," I bite out, irritated that she keeps referring to his branding mark.

The mortal tilts her head at my tone. "Ah. I see."

I narrow my eyes at her in challenge. "You see what?"

A smug expression crosses her annoying face. "You're in love with him."

At her accusation, my runes begin to glow.

"Do not speak of things you know nothing about," I snap, but she doesn't hear me at all.

Her gaze is fixed on me. Ignoring my irritation, her eyes stare at the golden liquid running through my hieroglyphs. The luminosity is radiating off my forearms in the dark, as the demon energy swirls through the bow and arrow design, crossing in the center with a circle.

Hope steps closer, her lips parting as she obsesses.

"What are those?" she whispers.

I stand immobile, confused by her reaction. "My runes."

Her eyes widen, meeting mine with a final step into my space.

"What do they do?"

With a calming breath, I remind myself that she forgets she has seen them before. "My demonic magic is attached to them. The design is the reason I was created."

Her breath catches. "It's a symbol for a warrior?"

I roll my eyes. "The bow and arrow is a tribal symbol of my Aztec heritage. I am the daughter of the earth god."

"And, th-they—" She swallows. "They glow?"

"When my emotions are high, or I need to call upon magic."

"What is the tree in the middle of the circle?"

I sigh. These ceaseless questions are infuriating.

"It is a symbol of the Seventh Circle."

"The Seventh Circle?" She searches her mind. "It's a place with a black forest, right?"

I don't confirm. She shouldn't recall that. The memory wipe should have removed that from her mind. "The tree is a mark, to show that I belong to that particular Circle."

The mortal nods as if understanding. "A branding."

"Yes."

"Who gave it to you?"

I take a small step back. "You speak incessantly."

"Who?" she asks again.

"Why so many questions about this?"

Disinterested, I watch as she fumbles pushing up the sleeve of her sweatshirt. Turning her arm over, Hope runs her finger over a heart tattoo etched onto her smooth pale skin.

I regain interest when she speaks softly under her breath and says the prince's divine name, Stone. As she does, the tattoo comes to life and scarlet liquid runs through the lines.

With a step in her direction, my hand snaps out and I wrap my fingers around her wrist and harshly bring her arm up to inspect it.

When I do, my breath escapes me.

At my response, she tries to pull her arm away, but I don't relinquish it. My grip turns harder and more painful as I study the goddamn mark Stolas left on her. Holy shit!

Once she realizes I am not going to let go, she stops fighting my hold. "Can you help me understand what this is? Does this tattoo tie me to where you come from? The Circles?"

"No," I lie.

"Do I have demonic magic?"

"Stop!" I shout, and drop her arm, taking a step back, needing space from her chatter.

"What does the raindrop in the center mean?"

"It isn't a raindrop." My tone snaps with anger.

"Then what is it?"

I inhale, trying to control the bloodthirst rising along with my anger before I lash out and kill her. "It's a blood tear. A symbol of the Eighth Circle," I manage to reply.

She shoves her arm back at me. "Why the hell have I been marked by the Circles?"

I rear back and pin her with an annoyed look. "I have no idea."

With a huff, she tugs the sleeve back down and paces.

"Why is it red and not gold like yours?"

"I am a goddess. Mine are gold. I do not know why yours are red," I lie again.

"Guess." Hope grinds out through a tight jaw.

"Maybe it's because the River of Tears in the Eighth Circle is stained crimson," is all I offer.

"For what reason?"

"To remind the souls of their sins."

"Blood and water?" she mumbles under her breath, as if trying to figure out a riddle. After a few moments of talking to herself, she stops pacing. "None of this makes sense."

"You are a mortal. The inner workings of the Circles should be illogical to you."

Hope clears her throat. "Where exactly do the tears come from? How are they red?"

"The dark souls, before they flow into the river and

turn crimson. After, they fall endlessly from the sky in the Eighth Circle. It is a vicious, never-ending cycle."

Her frown deepens. "The dark souls . . . they . . . cry?"

I press my lips together, because she can't be this moronic.

Then again, she is human.

"Yes, mortal. They live in a constant state of despair."

"Like I do?"

"Despair in the Circles is nothing like what you suffer from."

Hope pins me with a look. "Isn't it?"

Tired of her, I cross my arms over my chest. "Enough," I growl.

Her expression is one of determination as she stares at me.

"I am done with all of this exasperating banter. You are a mortal. A mentally unhealthy and unstable human, which is why you are here—as a patient."

"Low blow," she bites out.

"This is your mind playing trickery."

She scoffs at my attempt to dissuade her. "If that is really true, and I'm so mentally unhealthy, then why are you and Vassago here? If not to kill me, then what? Protect me?"

At my silence, a light dawns.

Her eyes become brighter with each passing second.

"That's it. You and he are protecting me."

My jaw clenches at her newfound strength of mind.

She looks around. "From what?"

"Vassago and I protect something greater and far more valuable than your existence."

"Such as?"

There are a thousand answers I could give, but I no longer feel like wasting my breath on the mortal. I lift my hand toward her, allowing my magic to flow through the runes. None of this even matters. In a few seconds, she won't recall this conversation. Or me.

Unaware of the memory-wipe threat, she steps closer.

"Why am I marked?"

"We're done."

"You're giving up? I thought those glowing runes meant you're a fighter. A warrior."

"They do," I snarl. "As it is my destiny to be."

She exhales. "Then what if mine is to protect the Eighth Circle?"

"Impossible. You are human."

I keep my palm out to her, ready to free the magic. Hope is unfazed by the threat.

"The blood tear is in the middle of a heart. You said it yourself—the middle symbol is a branding of the Circle you belong to. The outside design, your fate."

"Don't twist it, mortal. Those rules do not apply to you."

"What if they do? What if there is something in the Circles I need to protect and love?"

"There isn't." My bitterness fills the air around us.

"You and Vassago come every third night to watch over me. By your own admission, you are a warrior, which means someone higher in command orders you to do so."

"Stop!" My anger grows with each of her words.

With a step in my direction, she continues, "Stone?"

"What?" I ask, taken aback at her memory of his divine name.

"Is that the being in command?"

"ENOUGH!" A deep voice booms around us, startling us.

Hope jerks away and I drop my arms as my magic fades. When it does, I exhale. Relief washes over me that someone has ended the mortal's relentless demand for answers.

At the same time, indignation rises in the form of warmth in my cheeks when I glance at the being whose enraged voice still echoes around us and throughout the Swiss valley.

Vassago stares at me, his face expressionless as the tension rises between us. When our eyes meet, he inhales sharply, his arms crossing over one another. His shoulders are rolled back in a protective legion stance when his gaze slides to and narrows at Hope.

"Lore doesn't have to explain the Circles to anyone, especially an irrelevant human," he snarls out.

Hope flinches at his insult, but keeps her head high. "If I'm so fucking irrelevant, then why are you two going through such a big production to protect me?" Her voice is low.

"They do so on my orders."

Stolas steps into the moonlight, standing next to Vassago. Releasing a quick breath, I shift my eyes from Vassago to Hope. Her face has gone pale and she has become completely immobile and quiet—finally the mortal is speechless.

15

ENCHANTED

STOLAS

The ground feels as though it begins to dissolve underneath my feet as Hope stands inches from me, confusion etched on her beautiful features as she studies me. Her sparkling cobalt gaze takes me while she searches her mind for some spark of recognition.

With her eyes locked onto mine, a low growl pulsates from deep within my chest as my demon recognizes her as his. I inhale through my nose, trying to calm the beast within me.

Seeing her again evokes an unexpected powerful reaction. One I haven't felt before in her presence. It's this overwhelming need to say fuck it, grab her, and keep her by my side, always. No matter what.

I didn't expect such an intense response when I was forced to appear tonight. As I watched her beat down

Lore with questions, it filled me with a profound sense of pride.

And so much fucking yearning. I miss her so goddamn much.

"D-do I know you?" Her voice is quiet and thoughtful.

"Leave us," I order.

With a sharp look, but without a fight, Vassago dips his chin and saunters toward the woods, ire pent up in his clenching fists as Lore shadows him into the darkness.

Hope takes a small step in my direction.

"Who are you?" Her voice is stronger.

Standing to my full height, I deepen my tone. "No one of consequence."

Her gaze narrows. "If that were true, your demon minions wouldn't have scattered like frightened animals in your presence." Her tone confirms she doesn't believe me.

"Perhaps I'm the Devil. Here to lure you to Hell," I challenge.

"I don't lure easily," she counters.

"Is that so?"

"That is so. If you want my soul, you'll have to steal it."

I can't help but be entertained at her statement.

"Consider it stolen."

My gaze falls across her—she looks good. Healthier. Better than when I last saw her. Her weight is back to normal, her cheeks are flush with color, and her eyes are clear, less drug-addled.

I need to thank Hendrix for switching her meds to placebos instead of the fucking pills that asshole of an idiot doctor was forcing down her throat.

An amused smirk kicks up on her lips.

"Then you're here for me?"

"No." The word comes out quick and sharp.

We stare at each other for a moment before she finally speaks.

"If not me, then who?"

"For him." I motion with my chin behind her.

Her brows pull together in confusion before she looks over her shoulder to where the archangel is standing, behind her. Her focus is on Gabriel before she turns it back to me.

After a quick second, she steps to the side, making room for him to approach me. As he does, the mortal world slows around us, time almost stopping as the archangel shields us from human eyes but leaves Hope unaffected. The angel's violet gaze pins me with a hard look as he glides toward me with a casual self-assurance.

Tonight, his suit is ivory, a stark contrast to his raven hair and shadowed tight jawline, which flexes when he feels the energy of the Circles radiating off me.

A cool divine breeze radiates off him as he gets closer and takes on a warrior stance with his golden wings spread wide, ready to attack if need be. While the archangel may look menacing to some, to me, he's just an ever-present, fucking annoying nuisance.

"You are not supposed to be here, Stone." Gabriel's voice echoes in the darkness.

"Stone?" Hope repeats, before her eyes snap to mine in question.

I try not to flinch. Gabriel isn't permitted to use my demonic name, only my divine one, since it was given to me at my creation by my mother, who was also an archangel.

"You've broken our agreement, Gabriel," I seethe. "Therefore, here I am."

"As an archangel, I'm bound by my vows," he counters. "None have been broken."

"No. Contact!" I yell, startling Hope. "You weren't to go near her. Yet you did."

She takes a step away from me, but I can sense it's because she's confused, not scared.

"Let us not play these games, Dark Prince. Your presence was sensed the night prior to my interaction with Hope. Your name was written all over her bathroom, in charcoal."

I scoff. "That's your justification? A mental patient who wrote nonsense on her walls?"

"Hey," Hope snaps, her lips curling into a frown. "Don't insult me."

The archangel and I both ignore her; instead we stare at one another in a standoff.

"It was confirmation. Neither you nor I were to interfere with her healing," he adds.

"Her? Meaning me?" Hope asks, interjecting again.

Again, neither one of us pay her any attention.

"I didn't break our agreement."

"Shall we argue the merits of the arrangement?" Gabriel disagrees.

"You know there is a protection bond. If she calls to me, I have no choice but to appear to her."

A slight frown mars his lips before he speaks. "Is that what happened?"

I dip my chin, hating that I have to admit she has control over me. "I believe that is how I materialized that evening in her presence. Regardless, she has no memory of it."

"And yet, she is marked." The way he announces it is an accusation.

Not liking what he is implying, I growl, "She isn't marked."

I stare at the archangel with no fear. Only complete disgust and hatred for everything he symbolizes. Gabriel was the one who convinced the council to allow me to fall with my father. He is the reason my mother is human instead of still divine. Because of his unrequited love for Tazia, Hope, the oracle of lost souls, was created with his approval in order to protect me and remind me of my divine blood once I fell. And the protection bond I am now cursed with is his fucking trickery, done under the guise of divine protection.

"She is right here," Hope seethes.

My eyes meet hers briefly. "We see you."

Anger crosses her face. "Screw you, because I am marked."

I swallow, my throat dry as I peer at her.

"What do you know of it?"

Hope's lips pinch. Her eyes search mine as she pushes her sleeve up, revealing the heart I drew on her. It's glowing scarlet, exactly like my runes. I breathe out methodically and look at her, taking a step closer. Once I'm next to her, I grab her wrist, yanking her forward so I can inspect the design.

A crimson teardrop sits in the middle of the heart, also glowing.

A mark signaling she belongs to the Eighth Circle.

To me.

"How the fuck?" I blow out and snap my focus to Gabriel.

The archangel falls quiet for a moment before looking around. "The mark means I can no longer protect her. Her soul belongs to the Circles. Our agreement is null and void."

"I can't return her to the Circles. It's too dangerous. She doesn't belong," I snap back.

"You should have thought of that before you marked her," Gabriel retorts.

"I didn't mar—" I fall silent.

Motherfucker. Realization sets in. How could I have been so fucking stupid and careless the other night?

I look Hope over one more time and growl in frustration as realization hits me hard. There is truth in his statement. As much as I don't want to admit it, her renewed healthy appearance has nothing to do with the placebo pills. It has everything to do with the fact that I've inadvertently tied her existence to mine.

Understanding clogs my throat.

My demonic magic runs through her now.

Healing her. Mirroring my DNA.

No wonder I had such an intense reaction to her tonight.

We're mated.

As if she burned me, I drop her arm and take a step back.

"What's wrong?" Hope questions, taking a step toward me.

"For a mortal, she seems calm about all this." The statement is directed to Gabriel.

"I've given her back some of the memories you took," the archangel says quietly. "The rest need to be returned to her mind by you. It's time for her to face her destiny."

A chill runs through me. "Why the hell would you do that?"

Gabriel sighs. "Tazia mentioned your visit, and I had

no choice but to come see for myself. I found her in the bathroom, chanting your name. When I realized what you'd done, I returned some of her memories to her and guided her thoughts back to you."

"This is what you wanted all along, isn't it?" I bite out. "Your loophole to control me?"

"We may have created the oracle, but we never intended for her to be marked," he replies

"But she is." I darken my tone and step toward him, with Hope watching me.

"You asked for divine safe haven. I provided it. You marked her, severing it," Gabriel points out.

My heart jumps a notch at the consequences of my actions. She wears the mark of the Circles. Any divinity left in her will no longer exist, which means Hope is a dark soul.

"How long until all divinity is gone?" I grind out.

"One, maybe two mortal days."

Numbness falls over me.

I turn and face Hope, her lashes lower as she glowers at us.

"Are you two done ignoring me now?" she snaps.

"You do understand that I am a demon, right?" I ask her in a mocking tone.

Hope's glare narrows with more contempt. "Yeah. I got that."

I step closer, lowering my voice. "Remember it, the next time you choose your tone."

A glint flickers in her eyes. "Fuck off, demon."

I stare at her for a moment, overtaken by her strength and lack of fear. She should be terrified of me. Of the way I live my life without consequences or remorse. Even now, she isn't impressed by me. Even though I am terrified of her. Even more, of what will happen to her if I turn my back on her. I've never been so acutely aware of another being.

"Excuse me?" I sneer.

"I'm not entirely sure what is going on here, but somehow I know that you need me. And it sounds like because of this mark, I need you. Demon or not, I have a feeling that we're stuck together for a long time. So"— her face softens—"don't ignore me."

It's all I can do not to take her face and pull her lips to mine, kissing the snark out of her. Raw hatred and disgust at Gabriel for entrapping me twice with Hope shakes me to my core. Pure rage washes over me as I look deeply into her gaze but speak to the angel.

"I warned you, Gabriel, that if you betrayed me, or didn't keep her safe, I would come for you and the golden gates. That was not an empty threat. You've failed to protect her."

"I didn't realize that meant from you." His voice drips with condescension.

I turn and walk toward him with a menacing gait, staring him down. "You angels are worthless pieces of shit. You act high and mighty. Force morals and rules onto others that serve only your purpose. You think of dark souls no better than we think of mortals. Even though I have divine blood in my veins, you've always thought me inferior, uncle, and because of that, I don't fucking believe for one second that you didn't think your precious oracle of lost souls, a divine creation, needed protection from the Devil's son!"

"At least we act for the greater good."

I scoff. "Please."

"What do you do for it?" He fires back.

His words stop my movement and I lift my chin.

"I guess we'll find out."

"Is that a threat, Stone?"

"A promise."

"We're done here," Gabriel states, and walks around me. With a heavy sigh, he takes Hope's hands in his and dips his head toward her. I watch, forcing myself not to rip him away from her touch.

"Hope, it's been enchanting knowing you. Sadly, our time has come to an end because, Oracle of Lost Souls, your time—your destiny—is just beginning."

16

JUST HOW FAR

HOPE

I keep silent as Stone paces in front of me. Gabriel disappeared a while ago, his final words leaving a chill within me. I'm not sure what the full weight behind them is, but I have a feeling it has something to do with the demon in front of me who looks like his head is about to explode.

Stone pinches the bridge of his nose as Lore and Vassago approach us.

"You heard?" Stone asks them.

"Every. Fucking. Word," Vassago exhales.

"Twice," Stone bellows. "This is the second time the archangel entrapped me and sucked me into his games, tying my existence to hers." His hand motions to me.

"I've learned with angels never to doubt what they are capable of," Vassago replies.

"We can't bring her back to the Circles," Stone rants.

"Without divine protection, he will find her, especially if she is marked. She's like a fucking beacon for Seekers now."

"She is still here," I remind him, gaining his full attention.

Stone stops pacing, looks at me, and presses his mouth together, displeased.

I stare at him, a bit overwhelmed and confused by what I just witnessed. I'm not sure if I fully believe what just went on was real—I still don't trust my mind. My heart, though—it knows. Gabriel is real.

Vassago and Lore are real.

And Stone . . . he's real without doubt.

"Aside from the mark, does she have powers?" Vassago asks.

"If she did, we would know," Lore answers.

"How?" I interject.

Stone tilts his head at my question. "It's instinctual. They come out with extreme emotions. Sometimes they're uncontrollable when you're first learning to use them."

My gaze falls to my arm and I push the sleeve up. "This glows when I'm emotional."

Closing his eyes, Stone inhales, as if he's willing me to disappear. When his eyes open, my breath catches. Our gazes lock and, like a movie, images flash through my mind.

Stone sitting on a chair in the Zen garden, while I watch him draw from my window.

Me next to him at the piano in the lounge, my fingers brushing over his tattoo.

Hendrix's voice saying, "Ancient legend states you will make his heart your own."

Stone drawing the heart on my arm in a studio, before making love to me.

The Circles. His father. Lilith. Vassago. Lore. Avi and Leviathan. All of it.

With my sharp inhale, one final image runs through my mind. Only this one is in slow motion. Stone securing the restraints on my wrists as he ties me to the metal bars on a hospital bed here at Shadowbrook and turns away from me, walking away without another glance back. Letting me believe that all this time I was alone. Lost.

Tears sting my eyes as the vision dissolves and I'm left staring at Stone. I pull in a few quick breaths, trying to stop the world from spinning around me as I stare into the torn depths and layers of the demon prince's hard gaze. My stomach churns and I have to blink a few times in order not to vomit, glancing at Vassago and Lore as my memories return.

Catching my breath, I stand motionless and stare at Stone for so long, I don't even realize how much time has passed. It's as if the world has stilled, stopped around us. It's just him and me. The entire time, I let myself experience all my erratic emotions: relief, anger, love, betrayal, protective-ness, sadness, happiness, and finally pissed the fuck off.

Lifting my chin, I take a step in his direction. As I do, Vassago moves toward me, but Stone stops him by holding up a hand. Stone looks right at me, moving toward me because he can't help himself—I can feel it through our link. Crap, the link.

We're still bonded.

With each shaky step toward him, my fists curl. I don't know what to do or how to feel about all of this. Stone holds his breath the entire time, watching me with unwavering focus. When I take the final step to him, his scent assaults me and the world tilts again.

Sorrow and pain are clear in his eyes as he fights to hold himself together. His lips are not more than a breath from mine when he speaks, and I swear I taste his words.

"I'm sorry."

The sound of his familiar voice makes me shudder, while my emotions scramble to keep up. Recognition surfaces within me as I remember every second, every breath, everything we've shared. Tears fall down my cheeks. He lifts a hand, brushing them away.

Overwhelming passion and hunger for him takes over. I make a noise in my throat and clench my fists. My hand comes up and I punch him in the jaw, causing him to jerk away from me. Anger boils over when he lifts his hand and rubs the spot where I hit him.

"Holy shit," Vassago whispers, and steps away, next to Lore.

"Fuck you, Stone!" I shout, and charge at him, punching and swinging.

He stands in front of me, taking each blow until I become exhausted. When I do, he gently takes my wrists and holds me upright, pulling my body against his, holding me.

I feel his touch all the way through me.

It takes away that huge ball of pressure that only moments ago was in the center of my chest. I can finally breathe normally for the first time in weeks. Sobs wrack my body.

"Shh," he coos in my ear. "I've got you."

"I hate you," I sob. "I hate you so much it hurts."

Stone doesn't say anything; he just holds me while I fall apart in his arms. After a while, I pull my head back to look into his eyes, and when I do, I slam my lips onto his, soaking in his familiar taste as memories of us together explode in my head.

When his lips dance across mine, everything becomes right in my world again. Stone's hands come up, taking my face between his palms as he pulls me closer and our lips fight for dominance.

My fingers find their way into his hair, tugging,

causing him to groan, and I decide right here, I never want to be without that sound again. Without him again.

I melt against him, whimpering as our kiss lingers, before the sound of someone clearing their throat resonates through the wanton fog that seems to surround us.

After a moment, I pull away, trying to catch my breath.

"We all need to talk," Vassago spits out.

Stone glances around and shakes his head. "Not here."

Within seconds, the four of us suddenly appear in my suite.

I glance at Stone's runes. The scarlet liquid flowing through the flame design brings me back to the present and out of my emotional turmoil because suddenly, I remember the conversation with Gabriel.

"You left me here," I snap at Stone, "and then marked me?"

He stares out the window for so long, I think he's ignoring me.

"I had no choice but to leave you here." He turns and faces me. "It was for your own protection."

I suck in a sharp breath. "And they say I'm the one who's crazy."

"Hey," he snarls, taking a step toward me. "You are not crazy. Stop saying that."

"Don't even. You returned me here. It's presumptuous of you to think I need your protection," I snap. "Especially since now I know just how far you'll go."

He watches me a moment, then laughs darkly.

It's a deep, sexy, rumbling sound.

With anger radiating off him, he prowls across the room until he's directly in front of me. "I get you're pissed," he says, staring down into my eyes. "I do. But you have no fucking clue, Hope, just how much danger you are—or were—in. No clue," he reiterates. "My word is binding. I promised to return you to your parents. I did. I promised to protect you and keep you safe. I did. So back the fuck off."

I swallow at the dark shadow that has passed over his face as he speaks. A tremble runs through me at the intensity in his gaze.

No matter how pissed I am—and I am—I can't help but react to his fierce protectiveness.

"Fine. For now." I stand down.

A deep knock at the door snaps us both of us out of our trance. Vassago strolls over to it, swinging it open to allow Hendrix and Kagami to storm in. They both look as enraged, and at the same time as confused, as I feel inside. I inhale as they crowd into my suite.

"You requested my counsel, Stolas?" Hendrix inquires roughly.

"Hope doesn't look surprised by our presence. She has her memories?" Kagami asks.

"No thanks to you two." I hiss, with a tightness in my tone.

"Enough," Stone says, standing next to me.

"Don't tell me what to do," I counter.

"They were under my orders."

"Seems like everyone does your bidding around here," I snap.

Kagami bows to me. "Apologies, Hope, for misguiding you."

"It was for my protection, right?" My tone drips with sarcasm.

Hendrix sighs heavily, meeting my gaze with a frown. "If Hope has her memories, I'm assuming the divine have reneged on her continued protection here at Shadowbrook?"

"They have," Stone answers.

"Why?" he asks.

"My Lord has marked Hope," Vassago answers.

"That is unexpected," Hendrix mutters under his breath.

"How long?" Kagami's accent thickens with worry.

"One, maybe two days before her soul turns dark," Stone replies. "Gabriel was unspecific."

"The monks cannot judge her. She will go straight to the Eighth Circle, bypassing the City of Weeping and my assigning her. Do you understand?" Hendrix implores.

"I never intended to mark her," Stone sighs.

"But you did, my Lord," Lore points out.

"Can she be unmarked?" Stone asks Hendrix.

"Hey!" I step between them, facing Stone. "First you mark me without my permission, now you want to unmark me. How about actually asking me what I want?"

"No."

"Why not?"

"I know what you want. I will not give it to you."

I step closer. "You don't have a choice. It's my decision."

"She stays here," Stone announces, ignoring me.

"What?" I mutter.

"Stolas, Hope is marked. She cannot ignore the call of the darkness," Hendrix replies.

"We have some time to figure out a way to reverse the mark and sever the bonds."

My heart sinks at his words. Stone's anger and rejection suffocates me, throwing my mind and heart into panic mode. An edgy and frightening chill seeps into my bones.

"You're just going to leave me here? Alone? Again?" I whisper-shout.

Stone's grassy eyes drop to mine and for the slightest second, I see regret before he blinks it away, clearing his throat. "Vassago and Lore will remain to watch over you."

I cautiously glance toward the two of them, both narrowing their eyes at me. Lovely.

"Hendrix, you and Kagami will return to the Circles with me. We'll grab Leviathan and Avi and figure out what our next steps are. In the meantime, all things remain as is."

My breath hitches. Avi and I had become friendly. I didn't even realize how much I'd missed her until Stone just said her name.

Looking around the room, I wish she were here.

More talk ensues, but I tune it out, walking slowly into the bedroom. The darkness hangs in the small room. The only light comes from the moon from outside the window.

Exhaling, I just stand in the middle of the room, feeling lost and alone. Over the past couple of years, I've gotten used to it, but this time, it hurts. Like I'm being torn in two.

"This is for the best," Stone utters through clenched teeth as he approaches me.

When his chest brushes my back, I freeze at the contact. Even in the dark, I can feel him—sense the struggle inside of him. It bubbles under the surface, ready to boil over.

"You aren't the only one afraid of losing someone," he whispers next to my ear.

I turn and stare at his chest. "Then why are you leaving me?"

"We are safer apart." His breath caresses the top of my head.

I want to retreat; the intensity of his nearness causes an ache within me.

"No. We aren't."

"I am protecting you," he whispers.

"You aren't the only one who made a vow of protection."

His fingers curl under my chin, lifting it so he can look into my eyes. "I am a demon prince, I don't need protection for a mortal."

"I will protect you. From the Circles. Regardless of how many times you push me away, I will always find and come back to you." Both his and my runes begin to glow, swirling in the same patterns, in sync with one another. "The marking is proof."

"You don't even remember the marking."

"You came to me and I asked you to give my heart back."

His lips press together as he stands in front of me for a long time, staring into my eyes. With measured shallow breaths, I step closer, placing my hands on his chest, allowing my lips to lift within a sliver's breadth of his.

They almost touch as I speak softly into the room.

"If you leave me here again . . ." I let the threat go unvoiced.

"You'll what?" he matches my tone.

My voice goes low. "The torture I'll cause you will be

so horrific, the heartache so acute, you'll beg me to end your dark-souled existence." I breathe across his lips.

The tiniest of smiles crosses his lips.

"Vassago and Lore will watch over you in my absence."

"Stone," I warn.

"I've been enchanted by you twice now." His knuckles brush my cheek. "I'll fix it. I'll fix everything. I promise."

At his touch, my eyes close and a single tear escapes.

"There is nothing to fix. I belong with you."

"You don't belong in my world, Hope. It's too dangerous."

"Please," I beg in a whisper.

"I love you," he whispers before his lips press against my forehead.

"Don't leave me in eternal darkness again."

Silence.

When my eyelids flutter open, he's gone.

17

CHOOSE NOW

VASSAGO

I pop another grape into my mouth while watching Lore. She's sitting on the couch in Hope's suite ignoring me. Years of training in the Circles instilled natural instincts in me. With demons, you have to be on guard, ready to act, to defend. You always need to be aware of your surroundings and opponents. Unless your opponent is a flesh-eating goddess who despises mortals. Then, you're shit out of luck.

Frustrated I can't get a read on her emotions, I drop the bowl onto the counter. The glass clanks against the marble just as Hope steps out of her bedroom, showered and dressed. It's been hours since Stone left. The sun has already risen and it bathes the three of us in its morning rays. Lore ignores Hope as I motion my chin toward Stolas's chosen.

"Going somewhere?" I ask.

Hope's attention shifts from me to Lore and then back.

"I have a therapy session with Dr. Foster."

"You do know you don't need therapy?" I pose, and she bristles. "You have your memories back. Haven't you realized that you are not mentally unhealthy?" I challenge, staring at the dark circles that have etched themselves under her eyes again. "You also don't need meds, which I gather are the reason for your dark circles again."

"They're not from meds," she says, when she sees me staring at her eyes. Her tone isn't as strong as it was yesterday. "I tossed and turned all night."

"I will escort you to your appointment, mortal," Lore states.

Hope shakes her head. "Not you. Him."

Lore's eyes narrow as her gaze meets mine. After a moment, she growls in frustration at being dismissed. With her lips pressed together, she sits straighter on the couch.

"Pulling rank? Maybe you aren't such a waste of a mortal after all," I compliment.

"I need food," Hope announces, walking toward the door.

"So?" I question.

She opens the door waiting for me. "So, dining hall first."

Five minutes later, I watch her lay her pills out next to her plate.

"Those are poison."

"What they are is medically necessary."

She puts one in her mouth and swallows.

"I thought you were hungry." I motion to her plate full of eggs, fruit, and bacon.

She takes a long sip of water before speaking.

"I need to take them with food."

"None of which has entered your mouth," I point out.

"Why do you even care?" she asks, picking up another large pill.

"I don't."

"Then shut up and let me take my meds."

"You don't need them."

She swallows and sits back in the booth.

"You aren't real. Last night wasn't real."

I sneer at her statement. "Then how do you explain the fact that I am sitting here?"

She shrugs. "Either I dreamt you up or I'm having some sort of breakdown again."

My glower grows intense at her words.

"What?"

"That what you're telling yourself this morning, mortal?"

A server comes over and refills her water glass before disappearing without a glance in my direction, since they can't see me. The dining hall smells of coffee and feels like a small-town diner. All part of the facility's façade, to create normalcy for its guests.

Hope picks at her muffin, placing small bites in her mouth.

"Just eat it," I order.

"I hate muffins," she whispers.

"Then why did you order one?"

"They make me feel . . . something. Even if it's hate."

"Well," I scoff. "So long as you feel."

"And what is it you feel, Vassago?"

"Don't try and bait me," I growl, and look around.

Hope just frowns, shaking her head.

"What time is your appointment?"

"In half an hour."

"Fucking fantastic."

"Why are you so uncomfortable with me?"

"Why aren't you afraid of me?"

Her eyes narrow with annoyance at the question-answer. "You've been around me for weeks now. If you were going to hurt me, or worse, you would have done it by now."

"You shouldn't let your guard down," I warn.

"Is that so?"

"Especially around demons."

"You know"—she tilts her head, smiling—"I think you like me."

"Don't flatter yourself."

"Demons aren't real. They exist only in my mind." Her eyes narrow in a challenging manner. "Just like you."

I tighten my jaw. "Your refusal to believe all this is infuriating."

Hope lifts her chin and deepens her tone. "The lines, my lines, between reality and fantasy are blurred. On a good day. If I allow myself to believe—like I did for the briefest moment last night—that the Circles are real, that you and Lore are real, or even that Stone is real . . ." She pauses. "Well, it means that someone I love more than anything else in this world has turned his back on me. Twice."

My gaze falls back to her muffin.

As annoying as she is, and she fucking is, I get it.

"He's trying to protect you, Hope."

"Do you know what that feels like, Vassago? To feel for someone, so deeply, so completely, that you're willing to give up your very soul for them? To yearn for their touch, even if it's fleeting?" she whispers. "It was easier not remembering he existed."

I clear my throat, sitting forward, lifting my gaze, and locking my eyes with her. "I know what it feels like to give up everything in order to keep someone you love safe."

"Real or not. I'm in deep . . ." she trails off.

"You're going to have to trust that Stolas knows what he

is doing. I live in the Circles, Hope. He and I share the same father—Lucifer. But unlike Stolas, I am haunted, every fucking minute, by what my father did to Lore in order to keep me in line. I don't wish that on him. Or you. Even if he was foolish enough to bring a mortal into our world."

"I'm strong enough to handle your world," she fires back.

"No. You aren't." I shake my head. "Lore is a goddess. A warrior. What was done to her—it broke her. You? You are a mere mortal. One who is trying to convince herself that none of this is real or exists outside her mind. There is nothing in this world, or any other, that would make you strong enough to survive Lucifer's wrath. Or the Circles' torture."

"If it's real, then you and Lore can teach me."

"What are you rambling on about, mortal?"

"Show me how to survive your world."

I fall silent, not moving an inch or uttering a word.

"What?" she asks, watching me.

"I was wrong."

"About?"

"You are mentally unstable."

Hope clamps her jaw closed and leans over the table. "Name calling? Seriously?"

"No being in their right mind would ask to be sent to the Circles."

"I'm not asking to be sent to the Circles. I'm asking

you how to survive them, so that I can protect Stolas from his father, and whatever else threatens his very real existence."

Staring into her sharp gaze, something in me twists. It isn't what she is saying, it's how she is saying it—with a final resolve.

With or without my help, she is doing this.

Her determination has nothing to do with the divine; it has everything to do with her unwavering love for my brother. Reckless mortal. Given what has transpired over the last twenty-four hours, her soul will eventually become dark, regardless of whether I help her or not. She's marked.

Even more relevant to me, Lore's existence depends on Hope losing her divinity for good. At my hands. For that reason, I am going to help her, to save the goddess I love.

With a final sigh, I slide out of the booth, grabbing her elbow and forcing her out of her side. She tries to pull out of my grip—unsuccessfully—causing me to tighten my hold.

"Come on." I drag her out of the dining hall and into the hallway.

"Where? I have an appointment."

Once we're in the hallway, I whirl and push her against the wall, getting into her face. "Choose. Now."

Hope's brows pinch together. "What?"

"You want to learn how to survive the Circles? Protect Stolas?"

"Isn't that what I just said at breakfast?" she counters.

"Then decide which reality is the one you want to exist in. The Circles or Shadowbrook."

Her eyes dart around. Considering my words, she looks everywhere but at me. After a few moments, her gaze lands on my arms, focused on my runes. With my annoyance at her, they've sparked to life, the golden liquid swirling throughout the design. I take in a breath and push away from her slightly.

Hope swallows, her resolved gaze lifting and meeting mine.

"Will you and Lore help me?"

"Pick. A. Reality."

"The Circles."

"No more meds. No more doctors."

"Fine."

"And no more talk of mental instability."

A tortured smile works up to her eyes. "Got it."

"It's real. Say it," I demand.

Her eyes close, almost in silent prayer. I know she's fighting a war between her heart and mind as she says goodbye to her old life.

"I need to hear the words, mortal," I demand.

"It's real," she whispers.

When her eyes reopen, they're sharp and focused.

She has a determined expression.

"Let's go." I drag her to the elevator and up to her suite.

When we enter, Lore is standing in the kitchen, a hot mug between her hands. Her gaze shifts from me to Hope, her expression turning from soft to hard within seconds.

"What's going on?" Lore asks.

"We have two days," I announce.

Confusion fills Lore's eyes as she looks between us. "For what?"

I pause. "To protect the ancient curse."

Lore tilts her head at the meaning behind my words. "Are you sure?"

"She carries the mark of the damned. She'll need formal instruction. And we're going to give it to her."

"Instruction?" Hope parrots.

"In order to become a formidable mate for Stolas," I point out.

"Mate? For Stolas?" Lore repeats.

"Will you two be repeating everything I say, goddess?"

"Only the stupid parts." Lore responds.

I can see the fear in Lore's eyes.

"It's time," I reply.

Lore frowns. "Our involvement is dangerous now."

"I know."

"On so many levels."

"It always was," I argue. "Now, we just have a ticking clock."

Lore inhales and dips her chin before turning to Hope.

"Are you sure?" Her tone is harsh.

"Yes." Hope's response is quick and resolved.

I turn and face Hope, pushing my shoulders back and turning my expression vicious. If Hope wants to be a dark soul, and play in the Circles with the demons, Lore and I are going to give her exactly what she wants.

I walk over to her, every step precise and calculated, stopping right in front of her, forcing her to look up into my eyes. "Say goodbye to your mortal life. It's over."

18

HUMANITY IS WEAKNESS

LORE

O utside, the rain falls heavily onto the Swiss landscape. Every so often, through the large open shoji windows and doors, a cool breeze floats into the dojo, covering us in a light mist. I stare at the back of Vassago's form as he teaches Hope the art of kendo—the way of the sword. Vassago is a skilled swordsman and Hope is an eager student.

I become enthralled studying their precise movements. They defend themselves against each other's attacks. Their steps are fluid and both wield the bamboo swords in strong, sharp movements.

It's like a finely choreographed dance between them. The focused determination coming from each of them is captivating. Maybe it's because they're fighting for the same thing. Vassago tests her with each blow, trying to see what, if anything, Kagami has taught her. I can't help but be impressed by the mortal. Her sensei did an excellent job. Hope is smart and agile, fighting and protecting with a keen sense and understanding of dark souls, a rare trait in a humans.

Then again, when you fight for love, you fight hard, dirty.

Hope may not have been aware of what she was being trained for, but the mortal's mind has been acclimatized to think like a demon. She has been conditioned to push away the darkness and focus on protecting both her mind and her soul, a skill not easily mastered, even by our best legionnaires. It's remarkable and a bit shocking.

After a few more rounds, Vassago suggests a break. Grateful, Hope makes her way over to her water bottle across the room while the Seeker walks toward me with his eyes on mine. I can tell by his expression, he's impressed by her skills too. Her mental and physical proficiencies match our own. For a mortal, it's notable.

And unheard of.

Today's lessons are physical. Yesterday's were mental. Through meditation and mind transference, I showed Hope the layers of pain and suffering that occur in the Circles. The torture. The rules. The way life will be when she enters. She didn't even flinch.

Image after image, and nothing fazed her or even made her pause. It was almost as if she didn't see of any it. For a moment, I thought her human mind was too broken, too lost, for her to understand the depths of darkness, because she didn't shy away from any of it. Until it came to those containing Stolas. His past and present situation. What he's dealt with.

When I showed her what his life is—what he goes through every second—tears filled her eyes. The raw, agonizing burn in her gaze for him, it was a pain that no one else could understand, or even recognize, unless they'd lived through it themselves.

In that moment, an unspoken connection passed between us, brought on by pure evil and darkness. Even after seeing those visions, she woke up today more determined than before. Craving more knowledge about the Circles' dynamics and rules.

The mortal's soul is beginning to darken.

"Has Stone reached out?" she asks, approaching us.

"No," Vassago replies in a curt manner.

"Dr. Foster hasn't looked for me," she points out.

"Why would he?" I ask.

"I've missed my appointments."

Vassago finishes off his water bottle before answering her. "He thinks you're in Geneva, attending a mental health conference that Tazia and Hendrix are speaking at."

Hope arches an eyebrow.

Mind control makes her uncomfortable. But it is necessary.

"Must you always play around with people's minds? It's rude."

I glare at her for a moment, trying not to lash out.

"If you have something to say, Lore, say it," she says.

"Your humanity and vulnerability radiates off you. You must learn that holding on to your human morals will make you weak; you'll feel out of control in the Circles," I huff.

Vassago growls with disdain at my words.

I take a deep breath, trying to ignore him.

"As if I can help it," she snorts, and takes a sip of water. "To be fair, I am human."

"Fair." Vassago bellows. "What the fuck does that have to do with any of this shit?"

Every muscle in him tightens as anger swells and seeps out of his pores. In the past few days he has become even more agitated than normal, trying to deal with the curse and the mortal. She watches him with a guarded look as he storms away.

I want to smile at her reaction to him, but I hide it.

Hope clears her throat, shaking off his words.

He makes her uncomfortable, no matter how much she tries to hide it. I can see and feel it. Nonetheless, he's right. Fair isn't a dark-souled word. As much as Hope hates the idea of pushing her humanity away, she has to, if she is to survive. Like he does.

———

I'M ATTUNED TO HIM. His scent. The beat of his heart. We share a bond, so there is no hiding from one another. No matter how many times we try. I move through the room without a sound. My eyes shift to the window, watching the rain pour down from the night sky. It's not a soft and gentle rain; it's hard and unyielding—like Vassago.

He doesn't look at or acknowledge me, but that doesn't mean he doesn't know I am here. The lights are off, bathing him in shadows as I approach. He is silent as I take in his shirtless form seated in the chair. I study the black tattoos that climb up his arms and chest. My fingers itch to reach out and trace the branches, to feel the raw power beneath his skin.

When my eyes connect with his face, I notice a tortured expression as he twirls the obsidian box in his hand. The one that contains the Weapon of the Smoking Mirror.

Through our bond, I can feel him slipping away. Lost in thought. Fighting with shadows and cruel memories that haunt him—haunt us both. Reasons why he pushes me away, which scares me more than anything else, because I am so deeply in love with him.

Vassago doesn't look at me as I crouch down in front of him, keeping my eyes on the box. It's the reason for the shadows that have settled in his mind, more than usual. I take in a deep breath, stretching one hand out over his. His body goes even more rigid than before as anger swells in him.

Even though he wants me to, I don't cower, or leave.

I stare at him, challenging his displeasure with my silence.

"Stop that, goddess," he growls, his expression full of warning. His other hand runs over the serpent tattoo on the back of his neck. "Stop fucking looking at me like that."

"Like what?" I whisper.

"Like you understand what I'm thinking, or feeling. You have no fucking idea."

"Then enlighten me," I say softly.

His eyes snap to mine. "I'm just like her, you know."

"The mortal?"

"My mother is human. My humanity, while over-shadowed by malevolence, still lurks beneath the surface." He nods to her closed bedroom door. "Like her, I'm trapped between two worlds. Constantly struggling with and blurring the lines of both. There are days when I think I've become so depraved, so evil, that I don't think the light will come back."

"None of us are righteous. It's how we endure."

"The only difference between Hope and me is that I've seen the torture firsthand." The hurt laces his voice as he speaks. "She'll never last. We're giving her false courage."

"It's her choice. To fight for him. As it's mine. To fight for you."

"You don't see it. Love has blinded you." His eyes meet mine. "You will always be out of my reach. Close enough to taunt me, but never to have. It's a torture I live with, because I have no fucking choice. She does. There are times when I think maybe things could be different, if we are successful in overthrowing my father and controlling the Circles. But they won't. I know. Hope isn't secure in our world. Just like you're not safe in mine."

"Neither are your decisions to make. I choose to love you. Unscathed or not."

"I can't love you back. I'll save you, protect you from the curse, but then you need to leave my Circle. Leave the legion. I'm begging of you. Free me. Show me mercy."

"Stop being afraid."

"Afraid?" he rumbles, slanting his head.

I hold his gaze.

"Do I look like I'm fucking afraid?"

"Yes."

"Of what?"

"Me."

His jaw flexes and tension settles between us as he pins me with an unreadable glare. "I'm not afraid of you. I'm afraid of an existence without you," his voice is quiet.

"Is that why you've pushed me away? Ever since that moment Lucifer found out—"

"What he did to you, I see it. It's written all over your face, Lore."

"What?" I urge. "What did Lucifer do to me?"

"He broke you."

"No. He didn't." I grab his arms and climb onto his lap. He drops the box on the cushion, his hands fisting the sides of the chair. "You act like I don't exist. Like you don't care about me. I know you think you are going to great lengths to protect me, but stop. Do you know how hurt I was that you rejected me after all of that? Like I was tainted or ruined. Your father, what he did, that was hurtful, but you . . . you annihilate me, daily."

"How can you still want me?"

"It's simple, Vassago. I love you. Unconditionally."

His dark gaze settles on mine with distrust. "You haunt my every waking hour, to the point that breathing is impossible. I can't show you that. Every day I am threatened. I can't show weakness. And my love for you is a weakness. One that will destroy us both."

"I am a goddess. The only thing that will destroy me is your continued denial of what we are. How we feel."

A deep, primal growl reverberates from his chest at my words, and our runes glow. I lift my arm to his, showing him the matching swirls.

"Your blood and soul flow through me. Nothing will ever change that."

"Don't—" he starts, but I cut him off.

"Don't what? Speak the truth?"

"There is truth in lies."

"You've claimed me. I am yours, eternally."

"There's no changing where I come from or who I am."

"I don't want to. The darkness. The Seeker. The humanity. I want it all."

Vassago pauses for a moment, staring into my eyes, his hands grabbing my face, before pulling me to him as his mouth crashes down on mine, capturing my lips hungrily with his. His tongue parts them, demanding more as my fingers claw at his shoulders, pulling him closer. Our lips fight for control. We're desperate. Raw. Primal in our attempts.

Warm hands curve over my ass, pulling me closer. My thighs tighten around him as he deepens the kiss, nipping at my bottom lip. The growl he releases crawls up my spine.

One of his hands lifts and slides down the corner of my shirt. With a wicked look he abandons my mouth and moves his lips toward my exposed shoulder. At the same time, his fingers curl under the strap of my bra, sliding it down, leaving my skin uncovered.

His warm breath becomes hotter as his lips get closer. With a small whimper, my hand grabs the back of his head, guiding him forward as he bites and sucks the spot where my neck and shoulder meet. My eyelids flutter at the sensation of him biting down just enough to inflict a small amount of pain, which sends pleasure straight through me.

After several seconds, I lean back into his strong hands, which push against my back as he moves forward. When he does, the obsidian box falls onto the hardwood floor, opening with a thud. The sound causes us to pull away from one another and look down.

My lips part in surprise when I see the box is empty.

The knife is gone.

With my brows pulled together, I meet his eyes in question.

And that is when I see and smell it. The bloodlust heightens in me and the back of my throat becomes dry with thirst. In my peripheral vision, a fresh pool of crimson liquid seeps out from under the bedroom door. It's staining the wood as it crawls slowly toward the living room area.

When my eyes snap back to his, my entire body goes rigid, so much so that I cannot move my mouth to ask him what is happening. Vassago leans into me, gently pushing away the long strands of hair from my shoulders, lowering his voice.

"It is done. Your existence continues."

19

DIVINITY RELEASED

STOLAS

A deep rumble filled with rage bursts out of me. My arms snap out and in short, angry motions, I pick up and toss everything in my art studio. Wood easels snap like nothing and my charcoal lands everywhere, breaking and covering everything in a light coat of black dust. Hundreds of candles fall to the floor; pieces of wax snap off and hit the ground.

Enraged, I pick up the unfinished pieces of art on my canvases and, with a roar, hurl them at the walls, watching as they rip, bend and twist, mirroring my internal struggle and feelings, before they fall to the ground loudly. Panting, I seethe. I'm out of control.

After sufficiently destroying my studio, I meet my own eyes in a mirror. They're wild and fierce, like I'm ready to rip everything and everyone apart. My hands shake as I rub them over my face, trying to push away the frustration that always seems to be just under the surface lately. Stillness lingers around the vacant room. It gnaws at my nerves.

In a split second my body goes from being sedate back to outraged and wound up again as my mind drifts to Hope. It feels like a lifetime since I turned my back on her.

Hendrix and I are no closer to figuring out how to unmark her and prevent her from having to return to the Circles. If we don't figure it out soon, everything I have done over the past few weeks to protect her will be for nothing. I can't fucking believe how careless I was. Then, like an asshole, I gave her back her memories and walked away, again.

I let out a heavy sigh as the fury continues to build. I came into my studio because I thought I wanted a peaceful, quiet moment to myself, but now, the reality of what I've done is setting in. Taking in the destruction I've created, I hear the lock release on my door.

As it swings open, Lev lazily strolls in before he stops, taken aback at the state of my studio. His gaze runs over the room before landing on me. With a low whistle, he walks further into the room, staring at the mess with an amused expression.

"What do you want, Leviathan?"

"Not a fan of the arts anymore?"

I give him my best blank expression.

"They say that the more talented the artist, the more

temperamental." He pushes aside a broken canvas with the toe of his shoe. "If that's true, you must be the most talented artist in existence," he mumbles under his breath.

"Was there something you needed?" I growl out.

With his hand, he motions around the room. "Is this still about the human?" he asks, already knowing it is. With a knowing grin, my best friend walks around, picking up damaged chunks of my easels. "I'll take your silence as a yes." After he stares at the broken pieces for a moment, he throws me a disappointed look and tosses them to the side. "There are other ways to relieve your hard-on for her. I mean, other than throwing temper tantrums."

"Fuck off."

"Have you stopped meditating?" he questions. "Taking in a few soothing breaths every now and again might help you control your demon, instead of allowing him to demolish your hard work," he says. "These were good, too."

"Kagami was with Hope," I reply, trying to explain why I haven't meditated.

"Kagami was with Hope," he repeats.

Lev falls silent for a moment before sighing heavily.

"What?"

"Hendrix was with Hope. Vassago was with Hope. Lore was with Hope—" he drones.

"Your point?"

"My point is that everyone was with Hope. Except the one being who should've been."

I shoot daggers in his direction. "You know I can't be with her."

"Do I?" He steps over a pile of broken candles toward me. "You blood linked with her. You vowed a protection bond to her. Now, you've marked her. Do you need more proof?"

"Proof of what?"

"Maybe she is your fate. She survived the Circles once."

"She barely survived. You know I can't bring her back here."

"No. I fucking don't know that, Stolas. And truth be told, neither do you."

"She is mortal."

"Not for long. The mark will turn her, if it hasn't already."

A twinge of fear settles in my chest, that her soul has already turned dark.

"She's practically living in a form of the Circles in the mortal realm in that mental health facility they're pawning off as a retreat. They have her medicated and thinking she's insane. If she can survive that shit, she can endure the Circles," he argues.

"What if it's me who doesn't endure?" I say, in a detached and hollow voice.

"That what this is about? You? You're scared?"

"This place and her being here . . . what if it changes her?"

Lev meets my hard gaze, holding it.

"Or worse, changes me?"

With a tilt of his head, he inhales. "If you can find a small piece of light in all the darkness that surrounds us, then you've already endured. All you have to do is let it in."

"Like you've done with Avi?"

"Don't deflect. Avi and I are a love story in progress."

"Love stories aren't meant for dark souls like us."

"I know you only mean to protect her—" He hesitates. "But what if she doesn't need your protection? What if the mortal is ready to stand by your side? Don't you think it'd be good to give her a chance to prove herself? To let her in. Show you she's capable?"

I look away.

All this worry and guilt about Hope—maybe he's right.

"Vassago said the same thing. You sound just like him now."

He scoffs. "That is the meanest thing you've ever said to me."

"It can't be."

Lev falls silent watching me.

He is the only one who knows me.

He knows that I'm full of shit when I get like this.

Maybe he's right, and there's a possibility Hope could survive.

"If I bring her back, you need to promise you'll protect her."

"Without question." He doesn't hesitate.

"As if she were yours."

Leviathan fixes his gaze on me for a long time before answering. "As if she were mine."

I rub the back of my neck. "And the doctor?"

"His mind can be altered, erasing her existence. The same with her parents and anyone else who needs it."

"We'll need an entrance plan, as well as a protection detail while she transitions. I refuse to drag her down here blindly. My father can't sense her soul's presence," I hiss.

"What if we hide her in The City of Weeping? Lucifer isn't allowed to interfere with the Crystal Vault. Hendrix can mask her aura until we find a more permanent solution."

"That's not a bad idea. Limbo means that my father won't sense her soul."

I close my eyes, finally releasing the part of me that was clinging to my anger. "I fucked up. She's marked. No matter how hard I try to find a way, I can't reverse it. I'm left with no choice but to bring her back to the Circles. Gabriel can't protect her anymore, and I'm certainly not going to let her walk around unguarded."

Lev's expression turns entertained before he claps his

hands together. "About fucking time you came to your demon senses. Let's go claim your chosen, my Lord."

"Wait!" Avi suddenly appears next to Lev, looking between us, before her stare settles on me. She eyes me warily, which can only mean one thing—whatever she's about to say is bad.

Her chest heaves with each breath she takes as she stands before me, frozen.

"What's wrong?" I ask.

"It's Hope," she whispers.

———

The sinking feeling in my stomach intensifies with each step I take toward the closed door. My demon feels aggressive, like he'll lash out at any moment. The sight in front of me has my runes turning deep maroon. I focus on the fresh blood seeping under the doorframe. I stare at it for a moment, taken aback by the sheer amount. A low growl falls out of me and, panicked, I storm over and in one motion, kick the door in half. Once I step into her bedroom, everything around me comes to a complete stop, including my heart.

I stop breathing.

I stop moving.

I stop existing.

Dread creeps into my consciousness when I begin to understand what I'm seeing as I take in every inch of

Hope's limp body. My stomach roils. Her skin is a grayish color. The pulse at the base of her neck is barely detectable. I lock my focus onto her wrists, which are bleeding ceaselessly.

I take a step toward her and everything around me tilts and blurs.

"Hope." I whisper her name like a prayer.

"Oh shit," Lev breathes out, appearing next to me.

"She's in hypovolemic shock," Avi manages.

Within seconds, I reach her, kneeling next to her body. I pull her close, trying to feel her heartbeat. My hands shake fiercely as I assess her condition with a crazed desperation.

"We need to stop the bleeding!" Lev says to Avi.

When Avi doesn't reply, Lev shouts her name, causing her to snap into action and disappear.

Heavy breathing registers in my mind first. It sounds like whoever is trying to breathe can't get enough air in their chest because of the pain they're experiencing. Then I realize that it's my breathing. It's my reaction. I look at Lev frantically. The agony I see on his face nearly breaks me as I tremble, pulling Hope to me, crushing her unmoving body in a vise-like grip. I bury my face in her neck as I rock her, trying to erase the images of what I'm seeing from my mind, but I can't get rid of them. Fuck. This is my fault.

"The good news is, the cuts are across the wrists. Not

down the arm. I don't think she wasn't trying to kill herself," Lev points out.

"No?" I snarl at him. "It sure fucking looks like she was."

"Easy, my Lord." His voice is soothing.

"Let me see her wrists," Avi demands, reappearing.

Kneeling next to us, she fiddles with a first aid kit. My eyes snap to her, watching as she randomly pulls shit out of it. She looks wrecked as she hands Lev medical items. He moves toward her but I shake my head no and look into Hope's ashen face.

"NO. No one touches her but me," I growl.

"Stolas." My name comes out as a plea in Avi's broken tone.

I don't look at her, though; I look at Hope.

"Come back to me," I plead.

Lev is crouched down next to me. "Let us help her."

I narrow my eyes into slits at him and my body tenses, afraid he'll take her away.

"Hey," he says quietly. "We need to wrap her wrists and get her to Hendrix."

I look into his steely gray gaze as I continue to hold Hope firmly to me.

"She's lost a lot of blood," Lev continues gently. "So much that she's unconscious."

"Hope's on the brink of death. I can feel her soul releasing," Avi adds.

"She can't leave me. I still want her. I still—" My voice is rough. "I n-need her."

Lev leans toward me. "Then let's get her to Hendrix."

"How?"

"We can transfuse her." Lev's tone is even. "Your blood will begin to heal her and give us time to get her to the City of Weeping. But first, we need to stop the bleeding."

"She's marked. If you give her my blood, it will finalize our bond," I point out to Lev.

"This is where you choose. Her existence with you. Or your existence without her," he states matter-of-factly.

"Her blood is divine; it will reject mine. She'll be in pain."

"A little pain is better than death," Avi counters.

I nod and Lev hands Avi the gauze. She makes quick work of bandaging Hope's wrists, while I cling to her, afraid that at any moment, she'll disappear forever.

Once her wrists are wrapped, Lev produces two butterfly needles, each attached to a thin tube. "Stolas, you're going to have to release her so we can transfuse her."

I inhale. I know she needs my blood to survive.

At the same time, I've marked her.

This time, a blood link will be forever.

She'll be my mate. My chosen.

Avi leans forward, catching my eyes with hers. "She loves you. Hope would want this."

"I'm not sure," I murmur.

"We are. Trust us," Lev says, deepening his tone.

"That's a blind leap of faith," I mutter.

"As if she were my own," he reminds me.

I squeeze my eyes, praying she will forgive me and bend to Hope's ear.

"I swear to love you all my life," I whisper to her.

As I present Lev with one of my arms, I watch his every movement and press my lips to Hope's temple. He makes quick work of inserting the needle into the center of my runes and slides the other needle under Hope's skin on the teardrop.

Within seconds, the liquid from my hieroglyphs begins to light up like a fucking Christmas tree, flowing freely into the tube and then into Hope. After a moment, her tattoo ignites with the scarlet liquid. It swirls through the design and like a spider's web, crawls into her veins. Every vein beams under her skin as my blood makes its way through her body, healing her wounds.

Bringing her back to life.

Turning her soul dark.

And making her mine all over again as she breathes me in.

"Keep the tube in until we get her to Hendrix," Lev says.

"Can you carry her?" Avi asks me.

I nod my response, unable to speak.

"Lev and I will clean up the mess here."

"Okay."

"Then, we'll meet you at the palace," she adds.

I don't move. I just stare at Hope, wondering if I can do this.

"Stolas," Avi says my name with genuine concern in her tone.

Lev moves into my sightline. "Are you okay?"

With Hope's body crushed to mine, I lift her in my arms and stand.

"I'm fine," I reply harshly.

Before I dematerialize, I see Avi whisper something in Lev's ear. He's frowning at whatever she's saying.

My gaze follows his, landing on a spot next to where Hope's body was, near the bloodstained floor.

And that is when I see it.

The knife she used.

The Weapon of the Smoking Mirror.

20

BREATHE ME

HOPE

The darkness of the woods doesn't deter me. Merciless rain pelts my face, dripping in streams over my skin, and pools at the base of my neck. The spongy ground sinks beneath each of my steps as I continue to make my way up the hilltop. Once I'm close enough to the gates, my excitement grows. I did it. Just like Vassago said I would. I found my way.

I close my eyes and whisper, "Lasciate ogne speranza."

Seconds later, Stone appears out of thin air, wearing a predatory look. On pure impulse, I rush to him. He grabs my hands, placing them around the back of his neck as he brings me close, pressing his forehead to mine. I savor this moment, pushing away the sensation of déjà vu that I'm experiencing. Instead, I focus on the feel of being in his arms.

The smell of him enveloping me.

The devilish grin he flashes.

"You came." I smile, elated at the sight of him.

Stone studies my face, as if he's memorizing it. With this one look, I feel loved and rejected all at once. Needing to be closer, I curl into him, lift my face, and lean in toward his mouth. Just before I brush his lips with my own, he tilts his head and studies me.

"I'm waiting for you to open your eyes," he says.

My brows pull together, confused. "My eyes are open."

He breathes me in. "You don't have to fear anything."

"I don't," I assure him.

"I'll protect you."

"I know," I answer.

"Come back to me."

"I'm here. I'm yours."

"Then wake up, Hope," he pleads, before his form dissolves.

My eyelids feel heavy as I fight to open them. Actually, my entire body feels heavy and weak. After a few attempts my lids finally lift and I blink several times before focusing on the glow from the fire. I allow my gaze time to adjust before turning my head slowly toward the ceiling. The movement causes me some discomfort and a moan falls out of me. Everything aches. I'm sore and feel drained.

My eyelids squeeze shut. With my deep inhale, they flutter open again, and I take in the softly lit room doused in candlelight, before an unfamiliar woman unexpectedly appears above me. She's perched on the bed, wearing a flowing red-and-gold gown. It has golden spikes around the collar and sleeve edges. Her long reddish hair falls loosely with a single braid going across the top, almost appearing to be a headband. Two horn-like structures are twisted in the braid out of her hair. She looks to maybe be in her mid-twenties, with porcelain skin and kind brown eyes.

The woman leans over me. Her pink lips pull into a delicate smile. "Welcome back, my Lady. I'm pleased that you've decided to join us again," she says with a slight accent.

"Where am I?" My voice is rough.

I try to swallow, but my mouth is too dry.

"Somewhere safe," she replies, and helps me sit up before offering me a chalice filled with water. With a gentle expression she nods to the cup, encouraging me to drink it.

I take a small sip, the cool liquid soothing my parched throat. After another sip, she takes the cup away and helps me sit up a little more. At the motion, my head spins and a wave of nausea runs through me, causing me to take in a sharp breath and shut my eyes.

"Easy. You still need to regain your strength," she explains in a thoughtful tone.

Once the nausea subsides, I open my eyes, taking her in.

"Are you Italian? I hear a slight accent," I mutter, a bit dazed.

"How observant." She smiles brightly. "I was born in Florence, Italy."

"Is that where we are now?" I ask, trying to get her to give me information.

"You are clever." Her smile falls a bit. "And no."

"Who are you?" I glance around the large room.

It smells of lavender and antiseptic.

"My name is Beatrice."

"I'm Hope."

"The oracle of lost souls." She bows her head and I frown.

"How long have I been here?"

"A few days." She motions to my wrists. "May I?"

When I look down, dread crawls up my throat. Dots of pale blood stain the bandages wrapped around each of my wrists. My brows pull together at the unnerving sight.

"Oh shit." I exhale and try to sit up, but regret the decision when my stomach roils.

Soft hands land on my shoulders, easing me back.

"Take in an easy breath, my Lady," Beatrice coos.

"What happened?" I begin breathing heavily and panic as the memories of what I did come back to me.

"Shh. It's okay," she lulls. Her warm fingers run over

my forehead in a soothing motion, which immediately calms me. "The guardian will explain everything in a bit when he returns. In the meantime, remain calm. You're safe. You're alive. You're okay."

"Where is here? What is going on?" I mumble.

The room spins a bit and I become woozy.

"I've been tending to your injuries while you heal." Beatrice points to my wrists. "Your wounds were deep and you were in quite a bit of distress and shock from the loss of blood."

I inhale again and stare at her, but she becomes fuzzy around the edges. My head feels light and all of a sudden, I'm exhausted. Too tired to hold up my head and stay awake.

"W-wait. The w-water . . ." I slur, as realization hits me that she drugged it.

Her fingers brush over my hair with gentle, calming strokes. "Forgive me, but I didn't want you to become distressed when I changed the gauze. Rest now, you're in good hands." At her words, my eyelids flutter closed and I drift off into the darkness once again.

————

A FAMILIAR SCENT washes over me, a mixture of warm citrus, cinnamon, and smokiness. It triggers a comfortable calm to settle around me, as if I'm wrapped in a secure blanket. The heaviness in my body is gone. In its place is a dull, subtle ache. My eyelids flutter open and I turn my head to the side, meeting Stone's grassy gaze.

Shadows from a fire dance across his face as he stares down at me. He's shirtless, wearing only pajama bottoms.

With each second, his expression becomes more intense as he sits on the bed next to me. I lift my hand to his face, cupping my palm on his cheek before running my thumb over a dark circle under his eyes. It's so dark and deep, it looks as if he's bruised.

"You're here," I exhale.

Silence.

"You look tired," I rasp.

More silence.

Narrowing my eyes at him, I remove my hand.

"Where is Beatrice?" I attempt to start a conversation.

Stone doesn't speak. He simply watches me with a mixed expression. One minute, he looks like he wants to kiss me. The next, his expression is lethal, as if he wants to kill me.

This goes on for what feels like an eternity before I become frustrated and ticked off.

"Are you going to say something?" I challenge.

Stone's jaw tightens before he leans over me, placing his palms on either side of my pillow, trapping me. "You want me to say something?" he hisses. "You want to talk?"

I swallow, pressing my head into the pillow, trying to put some space between us. "No. Let's keep sitting in silence while you torture me." My tone drips with sarcasm.

"Torture you?" Stone moves closer; anger heating his gaze.

I hold my breath a bit.

"Let's talk, Hope."

"Okay." The word barely comes out.

"Let's talk about how you locked yourself in your bedroom. Let's talk about how I had to break down your door to find your lifeless body on the ground, bleeding out. Let's talk about how I panicked and pulled you close so that I could hear, and feel, your heartbeat," his voice cracks with emotion.

My lips part, but he continues, preventing me from speaking.

"Let's talk about the nightmare I just lived through. How fucking helpless I was. Hoping to fuck that your light didn't fade out before I got you help and medical attention."

"Sto—" I try again, but he just keeps ranting.

"Let's talk about the chill and shock that settled in my soul when I watched you being taken away on a table, lying still, almost dead, while I paced and my heart broke in two pieces. Let's talk about how I begged you to come back to me because I need you."

I watch his chest rise and fall in a fast, repetitive

motion, his fists clenched in the pillow on either side of my head. My eyes stay on his, which are watery as he looks at me.

"Let's talk about the knife Lore and Vassago gave you to do this to yourself."

"It was the only way to save you."

"I can't believe you would do this!" he growls, his jaw tense.

"I'm—"

"If you tell me you're sorry, I promise I will walk out of this room," he lies.

His forehead drops to mine, his breath caressing my lips with each angry pant.

"Were you punishing me?" The way he asks is haunting.

"What?"

"Was it revenge?"

"Revenge?"

"For walking away and letting you think you were alone? Because you weren't. I was always fucking there, Hope. Every goddamn night. Fighting for you and protecting you."

"No." I shake my head.

"Then why?" His voice is hoarse. "Why would you do this to me?"

"Ston—" He climbs onto the bed, straddling me.

"I told you never to cut yourself again."

"I know." I'm able to get out.

"That I didn't care what the reason was," he keeps going.

My gaze lifts under my lashes. The pain in his eyes is raw, and it makes my heart and soul ache. His hand lifts and smooths my hair away from my face as his expression softens.

"Why?" he asks.

"I was so lost without you," I reply in a raw voice.

"I was always there with you."

"I didn't feel you." I swallow, trying hard not to cry.

"That isn't a reason." Anger rises off his skin.

"I needed to find my way back to you." An ache builds in my throat from trying not to sob. "I was already marked. Vassago told me about the curse and Lore—he loves her."

His eyes are full of fury as he fixes them on me for a long time before he speaks. "His love for her could have taken you away from me. And then where the fuck would I be?"

"You walked away from me. Remember?"

"To protect you."

My body feels hot and out of control. I reach for his face, taking it between my palms. He tenses as my fingers run along his jawline and cup his cheeks. I need to center him.

"Look at me," I whisper, and his eyes meet mine again, full of hurt. "Vassago's love for Lore didn't take me away. It brought me back to you. I'm here." I lean forward, pressing my lips to his.

He doesn't kiss me back, but he doesn't move or push me away either. For a moment, all I do is my press my lips to his before I speak against his mouth. "There isn't anything I can say that will change the past, the future, or the fact that I am mortal. We're here now, and that's all that matters."

"You've fucked up everything in my world," he says hoarsely against my mouth.

"You've fucked up everything in my world too," I reply. "Guess we're even."

"You could have died," he whispers.

Tears I can no longer hold back fall, crawling over my cheeks.

"I knew you would come."

With the backs of his knuckles, he wipes each tear away.

"I should never have left."

Air catches in my throat at his words. I shift under him, and when I do, my bare skin rubs against him, sending a jolt of pleasure through me. That's when I realize that someone put me in a sleeveless nightgown. Nothing else. Just a nightgown.

His breath tickles my lips and I shudder.

Stone's gaze searches mine.

My breathing becomes shallow as I draw my bottom lip into my mouth and my hands reach between us, giving him his answer. Need consumes me as I slip my fingers past the elastic on his pajama bottoms, finding the length of him. At my touch, his breath tightens.

He swallows but doesn't speak as I release him and guide him to me. In one slow perfect move, he pushes into me. My eyelids flutter at the feel of him filling me. Heat travels down my spine and between my legs. Stone's eyes hungrily consume my face, his focus locking onto my parted lips. I feel lightheaded, the room swirls around me.

It's an odd and unfamiliar sensation.

Everything is so intense, as if I can feel his emotions and heightened pleasure seeping into my skin and crawling in my veins.

It's like I can hear his thoughts in my mind.

He throbs and twitches inside of me, and I release an animalistic sound I've never made before. Something flashes in his eyes. He places his elbows on either side of my head, keeping some of his weight off me, before he rocks forward and my breath hitches.

My body trembles underneath him with every slight movement and touch. I've never experienced pleasure this intense in my entire life. Even with him. Our runes glow between us and my body shakes with both need and an overwhelmingly powerful desire.

Stone's open mouth presses against mine, but he doesn't take my lips in a kiss. Instead, he breathes in each of my exhales. Our strained breaths mingle with each movement and pleasurable sound we make. With each aching motion, he slides deeper inside me without ever pulling out of my body. The entire time his eyes bore into me, trying to convey something as our bodies move together in a slow, smooth manner—as one. Neither one of us can seem to get close enough, or have enough of each other.

It's all-consuming.

Stone pushes deeper and harder and I grab at him, holding on, trying to keep from floating away. Friction builds and I can't swallow. With my mouth on his, I grunt while he pushes deeper into me.

Desperate, I grab the back of his head and my forehead meets his again. He pushes into me hard one last time before everything explodes inside of me.

Both of us release deep, strangled sounds of pleasure. My body shatters with my orgasm as Stone rocks into me one final time and releases inside me. A deep roar vibrates through him as he slows his pace but remains inside of me, sending small orgasms rippling through both of us.

With his forehead still on mine, we both breathe in deeply. "It was a bit presumptuous of you to assume I needed protection, or saving," he pants, throwing my words back at me.

"I'm really confident in my damsel-in-distress-saving abilities."

He bursts out laughing before shifting a little, still inside of me. "I'm your damsel-in-distress now?"

"Damsel. Demon prince. It's a fine line."

He looks into my eyes deeply and exhales. "I never meant make you mine," he whispers. "And I never meant to make you bleed."

"Neither were your choice."

"No?"

"They were mine. I chose to become yours."

His expression softens. "I had to transfuse you."

"So?"

"It completed the bond."

"Then I guess the only thing you breathe in now is me."

21

DEVIL ON YOUR SHOULDER

VASSAGO

G race is weakness. My father instilled that in me. Looking at my reflection in the mirror this morning, all I see is the devil on my shoulder reminding me of that fact. My past has tasted bitter for centuries, so I've become cold. Merciless. It's how I've survived. But for the first time in my existence, the blood on my hands has triggered culpability.

Maybe I'm waking up. Perhaps the ache of guilt is my penance for all the innocence I've destroyed, the bruises I've caused. It was cruel of me to use Hope's fears against her, and yet I did, in order to save the one I love more than anything. And I would do it again.

I splash cold water on my face and lean over the sink for a moment. Streams of the cool liquid run down my face, traveling over my cheeks and across my neck and bare shoulders. My palms flatten on the stone counter on either side of the sink as I inhale.

My body comes alive with awareness and my blood surges, igniting my runes as she enters. Without standing to my full height, I lift my gaze and stare at Lore in the mirror.

"I spoke to Beatrice. Hope's pain is minimal. The divinity is fading," she says. "Stolas is with her."

Beatrice used to be my father's favorite consort, before my mother, Lilith. When Lucifer became bored with Beatrice, Hendrix took her in to help him calm souls who are waiting in limbo, in the City of Weeping. Beatrice doesn't belong in the Circles, any more than Hope does, but she too followed her heart and is now paying the price—for eternity.

I drop my gaze, not saying anything as Lore walks to me.

The fallout and repercussions of what I've done will no doubt be knocking on my door soon. Lore's warm hand runs over the corded muscles on my back as I close my eyes, basking in her touch. My chest heaves with each breath I take in, my entire body rigid as I stand bent over the sink. She presses her lips to my shoulder and I try not to remember how addictive being inside her is. Opening my eyes, I lock gazes with her in the mirror.

And just like that, I'm lost.

Everything happening around us ceases to exist.

Nothing else matters but Lore.

I've been so engrossed in my need to protect her, I've ignored every carnal thought and desire I've had for her as of late. With each look and touch, Lore brings me closer and closer to the edge, until I break. I no longer want to fully deny myself or push her away.

A small, shaky breath escapes her. To most, it would barely register. But I notice it. I'm hyperaware of every breath she takes.

I can taste her arousal in the air. Smell it. It makes me hard even before she touches me. Her eyes hold mine, as all the things we can't say out loud pass between us.

Her silky hair brushes my skin, and that's it.

Game. Over.

With a deep groan, I push off the sink. At the same time, I wrap her long hair around my fist, pulling her in front of me. With my other hand I drape my fingers lightly around the front of her throat, walking her toward the wall, and push her up against it.

Immediately, her palms flatten on the stone tiles. She twists her head to the right so her cheek is gently pressed against the marble and my lips find her ear.

"Take off your panties," I order in a deep voice.

Under my fingers, I feel her throat as she tries to swallow.

"I'm not wearing any."

Fuck. My blood surges at her admission. Releasing

her hair, I undo the knot on my towel and lift up her short dress, positioning myself behind her. With one quick thrust, I'm inside of her.

She grunts at the suddenness. My fingers tighten a bit on her throat and my arm wraps around her waist as I plunge in and out of her at a merciless pace.

Lore's fingers spread wider against the wall as I take her, growling in her ear. Her curves meet me each time as I lose complete control of myself, getting lost in the feel of her. With each thrust, all I can think about is wanting to brand her.

I move behind her, faster and faster until she screams out my name in a growl. I close my eyes, my own tension building from my center, rendering me powerless. As I release inside of her, I finally relinquish of the last part of me that was clinging to the idea of letting her go.

Lore whimpers and a shudder runs through me as I slump against her. Breathless, she rolls her head so her forehead is on the tile as she tries to pull air into her lungs. Instead of releasing the hold I have, I push into her, leaning my full weight against her back.

My lips kiss the top of her head as I cover her body, pressing it against the wall completely. My hand never leaves her throat as the other splays across her stomach, keeping her pressed against me fully as I remain inside of her, not wanting to separate.

Lore jerks against me, making my world explode, and in response I groan. Needing to just feel her, I hold her firmly to me, with possession. Her body shivers in my arms.

My lips move until they brush against the shell of her ear. "You're mine, goddess."

Lore remains silent, but her fingers curl into fists and her body sags against me.

"I'm done pretending that we don't exist," I rumble quietly. "Or—"

"Or what?" she challenges.

Her voice vibrates in her throat under my fingers.

I release her, sliding out of her and taking a step back. Her skirt drops, falling back into place as I grab the towel from the floor and cover myself up. Lore turns, but keeps her back pressed against the wall as she crosses her arms and intensely stares at me.

Looking at her, my heartbeat accelerates in fear of what I know I have to say.

At my hesitation, some of the fight leaves her expression. Lore is brave. Fearless. But the sad truth is, I know the power I have over her. I can bring her down. Destroy her.

I rub my hands over my head, interlacing them on the serpent tattoo on the back of my neck. When I look up at her under my lashes, her head tilts, waiting for me to speak.

"I don't know how to do this," I confess in a soft voice, holding her gaze. "Protecting myself is instinct. Hiding my weaknesses, necessary. And you, goddess, are a vulnerability that I can't chance having in the Circles. You make the world under my feet unstable."

Lore scoffs, shaking her head as she pushes off the wall and steps toward the door. Frustrated I can't say what I need to, I grab her elbow, twisting her to face me before she walks away. Her eyes snap up to mine and narrow in a menacing and challenging way.

"Wait a fucking minute," I growl.

"For what? The rejection?" she snaps.

"I love you."

All the fight leaves her body as her limbs fall limp.

Motionless, she just stares at me.

"What?" she barely says, taken aback.

"I said . . ." I pause and swallow. "I love you."

"You've . . ." She hesitates, searching for words.

"What?"

"You've never said that to me before."

My jaw clenches. "Maybe not with words. My actions, though . . . I've turned my back on the Circles. My father. My brother. His chosen. Everything I believe in and fight for, for you. If that doesn't prove how I feel about you, then I don't know what does."

EVERYTHING I WANT

LORE

My body tenses with nervousness and maybe a bit of dread of the unknown. Vassago's words are terrifying. He's never, not once in my entire existence, said out loud that he loves me. This is what it must be like when mortals go into shock. As I stare at him, his expression turns into one of deep concentration.

Like he's trying to read my thoughts.

Not having the right words, I lift my hand and cup his cheek. His eyes slide closed and he exhales roughly, burying his head into my hand. I step forward, my mouth meeting his in a long languid kiss. The kind that makes you dizzy with sensations.

Vassago deepens the kiss, moaning as I step closer, pressing my body against his. Within seconds, his towel is gone and my skirt lifted again. Vassago grips my hips, walking us backwards until my back hits the closed bathroom door. His hands grab my ass, lifting me. I wrap my legs around his waist as he positions himself at my entrance.

When his gaze meets mine, I'm overcome with my emotions, mixing in with my heightened sensations. For a moment, we hold one another's gaze. As he stands before me with his powerful godlike body between my legs, I realize he is both demon and god.

Everything I want.

"I love you too," I whisper.

His head drops to my shoulder.

"Fuck." He breathes against my neck.

With one of my hands on his shoulders for support, I place the other on the back of his neck, over the serpent. The touch causes him to lift his head and stare into my eyes.

He's darkly breathtaking. The scars of his battles are worn with pride, his strong jaw clenched as he slowly teases my still oversensitive entrance. I let out a gasp when he unhurriedly eases into me. Pressure builds inside of me again, an intense wanton need.

His lips graze my mouth and then he's kissing me. Gently. Steadily. This kiss isn't like any other we've shared. It's meant to be all-consuming as we breathe as one being.

A pathetic whimper falls out of me. His body moves in and out of me, building up a gradual cadence and then slowing his pace to a tender, gentle motion. Both create a slow, maddening burn, swirling through my veins and runes, until I'm ready to explode.

I cling to him as he shows me that this is more.

That we're more.

He wanted us to be simple.

And then, he wanted us to be nothing.

When in reality, we're everything.

A pained expression crosses his features as he slides in one last time, his body pressing into mine as our lips dance across one another. Vassago swallows my gasps as my orgasm hits me hard. The trembles are merciless as he finds his own release, collapsing against my body. With our chests heaving, something shifts between us.

Something epic.

"I know the consequences of being with you," I whisper.

"Lucifer will use you against me."

"I am a dark-souled goddess. I am worthy of you."

"I think the real question is, am I worthy of you?"

"We are worthy of one another."

"Then, no more hiding or denying this," he adds in a calm voice.

Behind my head, a fist pounding hard on the door forces Vassago's gaze to shift.

"What?" he barks out.

"Stolas wants to see you. And Lore. Now," Lev states, coolly.

Vassago's eyes meet mine with resolve and I dip my chin.

———

THE THREE OF us step into the large foyer before making our way down the elongated hallway. Indigo light glints off the enormous crystal chandelier as we walk under it and past the floor-to-ceiling cylindrical tube filled with glowing cerulean liquid.

I've been to the Crystal Palace, in the City of Weeping, thousands of times, and with each visit, it never fails —goose bumps appear along my skin as we walk down the long, cold corridor known as the Hall of Judgment.

The dangling strands of lit crystals sway in the cool breeze. Their chimes echo off the precious crystal surrounding us, heightening the sense of dread I feel as we pass by the Albino monks seated in archways, concealed by their hooded cloaks. None of them move or speak. Their blank, sallow eyes follow our movements, judging. It's unnerving.

Shaking off my trepidation, we climb the great staircase and at the top, I follow behind Lev and Vassago as we walk through the draped archway. After we round the corner and step into the oval-shaped assembly room, Vassago immediately stops about a foot away from Stolas. I try not to slam into his back as his arms dart out protectively behind him, blocking me from his brother's wrath. Leviathan walks around us and stands in between the two brothers, waiting to intervene if needed. Hendrix and Avi are seated on one of the hunter-green-and-gold medieval sofas, watching us all carefully.

"It's nice to have the team back together again," Hendrix states.

Silence falls around us.

I'd be lying if I said I knew Vassago was okay. The entire way here, his gaze was heavy, pain and worry etched onto his face. I know he's struggling to remain in control.

"What the FUCK did you do?" Stolas shouts, lunging for Vassago. "You had no right."

I go to step in front of Vassago to protect him from Stolas, but Lev produces a wall of water keeping me back. I growl at the barrier and throw an annoyed look at Leviathan. He just laughs at me and rolls his eyes. Sensing my anger rising, Avi appears at my side, gently placing her hand on my shoulder and shaking her head at me.

"Let them work it out," she says.

Stolas approaches Vassago, getting in his face.

"I warned you what would happen if you betrayed me."

Placing his hands in the front pockets of his dress slacks, Vassago tilts his head. The vibe coming off his body screams that he's bored and unfazed by his brother's tantrum.

"I didn't betray you. I told you that I would handle it," he replies. "It's handled."

The minute Vassago stops speaking, he receives a punch in the jaw. Then another. And another, until blood dots his shirt. I watch helplessly behind the barrier of water as Stolas uses his brother's face as his own personal punching bag.

"Enough!" Hendrix steps between them, pushing Stolas back.

Vassago spits blood from his mouth onto the floor before he stands taller. "You'd have me give up Lore's existence, for your mortal?" I can hear the grin in his voice as he taunts his brother. "That would never happen."

The prince turns his rage-filled eyes back onto Vassago and takes a furious step toward him again, pushing against Hendrix's hold. "SHE IS MY CHOSEN!" he shouts.

"EXACTLY!" Vassago roars back. "You bonded with her. Twice. You marked her. And then," he deepens his voice, "you left the mortal to turn while you came here to sulk like a spoiled child instead of a demon prince—the great heir to the Circles."

"You're one to talk. You walked away from Lore centuries ago," Stolas snarls.

"Father was right. Loving Hope made you weak. Like a coward, you ran back to the safety of the Circles and left the mortal to fend for herself," Vassago spits out.

"I was trying to find a way to reverse what I had done."

"She didn't want you to," Vassago yells back.

"You have no idea what she wanted, or didn't want," Stolas counters. "Don't pretend to know anything about her. In fact, stay the fuck away from her!"

"With pleasure," Vassago replies.

Having had enough of this, I produce a blast of heat that steams away the water Lev threw at me. It turns to mist and disappears. Once it's gone, I shimmy away from Avi's hand and move to stand in front of Vassago, shielding him.

"He's telling the truth, my Lord," I bite out.

"Lore . . ." Stolas flexes his jaw, his teeth grinding together. "Stay the hell out of it."

"I will not." I cross my arms. "Not until you both calm down."

His icy stare narrows at me before he looks around the room.

"Lore's right. Let's all take a breather," Lev interjects.

"The truth." Stolas paces in front of us. "All of it. Now."

The room falls into a tense silence before Vassago steps around me and approaches Stolas slowly. "Hope was already damned. The moment you vowed to protect her, you sealed her fate. The pantheon wants Lucifer out. In case you've forgotten, so do we."

"No shit," Stolas replies.

"It's what we've been working toward for centuries, Stolas," Lev adds.

"And a war between the Circles and the divine, over one mortal soul, hinders us from accomplishing that," Vassago argues. "We can't afford to have a war against the divine pull our focus and resources away from our fight to control the Circles."

Stolas clenches his jaw, knowing Vassago is right.

"Hope was innocent in all this," he exhales.

"Don't be naïve, my Lord. How many innocents have we destroyed in order to secure your reign?" Vassago challenges with a harsh tone.

Lev groans and steps toward the safety of Avi, away from the brothers.

"Hope is different."

"Why, Stolas? Because you love her?"

Stolas keeps his face impassive.

"Sacrifices must be made for the greater good," Vassago says.

"I should just end your existence now."

"Then do it," Vassago challenges. "Instead of making empty threats. You know I am right. You know it had to be done."

"It's not what we"—Stolas motions to himself, Vassago and Leviathan—"do. We don't coerce or trick free will. Regardless of what our piece of shit father does during his reign, we don't promise mortal souls anything for their alliance. They must come to the Circles cleanly. Because of their own selfishness and greed. That is the price mortals pay for being gifted the ability to decide their fates for themselves. It's what we built the Circles on. Free. Fucking. Will. It's why we've been working to remove Lucifer from power. It is the principle the three of us agreed to stand on when we rule together."

"How do you know Hope wasn't exerting her free will?" I ask.

"And you do, Lore?" he retorts.

"You weren't there," I point out.

Stolas glares at me, his nostrils flaring. "Are you staying it was her choice?"

"I am saying that Vassago didn't do anything wrong." I soften my tone. "Or break his oaths to you."

"No?"

"All he did was give Hope what she asked for."

"Of course you would say that," Stolas spits out.

"What the hell does that mean," Vassago growls.

"She'll always protect you."

"Watch it." Vassago steps in front of me slightly.

"And I always will," I add. "The way you protect Hope—our weaknesses."

At my words, Stolas looks between us. The anger fades from his face and voice.

"Tell me what happened, exactly," he orders.

"Despite what you think or say, Hope had already made her mind up. Even before you walked into her life.

She was chosen to be the oracle, by the divine, for a reason."

"Which is?" Stolas inquires.

"As a mortal, she has seen the deepest, darkest corners of her mind, and survived. You brought her here to the Circles, into the depths of pure Hell, and she survived. Even after you walked away from her, leaving her vulnerable, she survived. Have you ever considered that perhaps everything that has happened to her over the past few years was so that she could find her way to you? In spite of the fact that you believe she is an innocent, she is not. She is a strong, skilled fighter," I point out. "She is one of us."

"Because she had to be," Stolas argues.

"Because she chose to be. For you, my Lord."

"I agree." Avi moves closer to us, her voice quiet as she speaks. "Even though you vowed her protection, Stolas, under false pretenses, the moment she saw you, she became yours. Hope came to you of her own free will. She chose to align with the Circles without coercion. Of her own doing, she blood linked with you. And even when you cast her aside, she still felt you. She knew and wanted to fight for you. Maybe, just maybe, what she did, what she lived with on a daily basis, was so that she could trace her steps back to you."

23

MARK OF THE DAMNED

STOLAS

Damn her. I hate that of all the weaknesses in the world, Hope is the one I can't shake. The one I will never conquer. I look between Vassago and Lore and pinch my brows together as realization dawns.

What did I truly expect of him? I knew how he felt about Lore. Vassago coming to me with information about the Weapon of the Smoking Mirror was his way of letting me know that, no matter what, he was always going to save her existence. As he should.

As I should have with Hope.

And now, I'm not so sure I can live with the fact that she's suffering while her soul turns dark, because of me. For a moment I allow my mind to drift. How bad would it be to have a chosen, a mate, someone I love with so much of my soul it hurts to breathe.

Then again, what if Hope sees her choice as a prison sentence? Or maybe she realizes I'm not even a choice in the first place. Just a happy accident that occurred because of Vassago's love for Lore. Either way, Vassago did for Lore what I should have done for Hope.

Secure her continued existence because I love her.

I frown. "If that's true, Avi, Hope has sentenced herself to a very dark existence."

Avi examines my face. "I thought you loved her?"

"I do," I state with confidence.

"Then why are you fighting this?" Avi asks.

"What if she realizes she doesn't feel the same?"

"Then she should have thought about that before she chose to release her divinity," Vassago replies flatly.

"I thought I was protecting her," I admit.

"I know," Avi replies.

"I thought I was doing the right thing," I say under my breath.

"Hope is capable of making her own decisions about what is right," Avi answers.

"Avi has a point, Stolas. Hope is a grown ass woman with her own mind," Lev interjects. "In the meantime"—he steps in front of me—"we need to figure out what our next steps are going to be."

I nod.

"She's still recovering. It's going to be a few more days before her blood turns immortal and the divinity is fully released from her soul," Hendrix speaks up.

"And after? Will she be okay to fully enter the Circles?" I ask.

"She won't burst into flames crossing the gates, if that is what you are worried about," Hendrix replies. "Your mark and blood will protect her this time."

"The mortal is no longer seen as a threat to the dimension?" Lore asks.

The last time we brought Hope into the Circles, we had to walk her through the gates in a triangle formation, representing fire, in order for the dimension not to reject her divinity, or see her as a threat for crossing over without permission.

Avi smirks. "Pretty sure you can't call her mortal anymore."

Lore sneers at the comment and I narrow my gaze at her.

She simply rolls her eyes, waiting for someone to answer.

Hendrix drops his shoulders. "The Circles will sense Hope's transition. So no, the dimension will not view her as a threat anymore." Hendrix meets my cool glare. "Since she will no longer be mortal, she will also need to wear the mark of the damned."

"No," I snap. "She isn't damned."

"Sto—"

I step up to Hendrix and narrow my gaze. "She. Isn't. Damned."

At my anger, the tattoo across my chest tingles. Every

soul in the Circles, including me, is branded with the same words: Lasciate Ogne Speranza. It's the script from the gates. It marks you, chaining your soul to the under-world. My fingers run over mine, sitting under my shirt.

Lev rolls his neck and grabs my elbow, pulling me away from the guardian. "Until then, how are we keeping Hope safe?" he asks Hendrix.

"Beatrice and I will keep her comfortable while she finishes her transition." Hendrix responds without taking his eyes off me. "Now that her divinity is almost gone, Hope will have to remain here in limbo, where Lucifer can't detect her."

"And Kagami?" I inquire.

"She will continue to help Hope with her oracular gifts. They'll be stronger now that your demonic magic runs through her runes and veins. I'm surprised that when you transfused her, she didn't writhe in pain. Hope's divine blood should have rejected yours."

"Maybe it's because we already shared a blood link?" I surmise.

"Possibly. Since she now carries the mark of the Eighth Circle, when Hope is ready to go home with you, Stolas, she'll be protected," he assures me.

"You mean, as much as one can be protected in the Circles." My voice is rough.

"Will her soul be fully dark?" Avi asks.

"Hope will be like Stolas. She will always have a hint

of divine fire in her, but should take on much of the prince's gifts and demonic abilities," Hendrix explains.

"What happens after she turns and Lucifer discovers she is not only alive, but now your chosen and living amongst us?" Lev asks, meeting my gaze.

"We need to remove him before that happens," I growl.

"That would take a fucking miracle," Vassago says.

At the remark I spin and face him. "Perhaps timetables are something you should have thought about before you handed her the weapon to use."

"I gave her a choice," he bites out. "I explained the consequences. I explained why I was chosen to give her the weapon. And I explained the need for Lore's protection. She made an informed decision, my Lord." He spits out my title with disgust.

My gaze falls to his chest and I wish that I could peer into his soul and then rip it out. Anger curls in my throat as I stare at him.

Even though he's right, I fucking hate him.

"Maybe we should focus on the future. Less on the past," Lev suggests, trying to keep things calm. "What's done is done. Say what you will, but Vas came through. And with a pretty fucking bow no less. Hope gets you. You get Hope. Vassago and Lore have pleased the pantheon. The divine are no longer breathing down our necks. Now, all we need to do is place the new king of the Nine Circles into power and take what is rightfully yours: the throne and Circles."

"You're welcome, asshole," Vassago snarls, taunting me.

I step toward him, but Lev steps between us again.

"All right, enough," Lev sighs. "Next steps, Stolas," he implores.

My expression turns stern. "Hope and I will remain here in in the Crystal Palace. Hendrix, Beatrice, Kagami, and I will be the only ones that have access to her until she's finished transitioning," I state coolly, ignoring Avi's frown.

"And the rest of us?" Lev asks.

"Lev, you and Avi clean up the mortal realm. Leave no trace of Hope's existence. Especially with Tazia," I exhale.

Avi meets my gaze. I can see the idea of altering Tazia's mind confuses her.

Lev nods in agreement. "Consider it done, my Lord."

I soften my features. "Remembering Hope will put Tazia in grave danger. Especially if Lucifer finds out she was involved," I explain, hoping to curb Avi's hesitation.

Avi dips her chin. "I understand."

"After you clean up the mortal realm, the two of you need to step up things with the legionnaires. Thanks to Vassago, we no longer have the luxury of time on our side if we are to overthrow my father and end his reign," I continue.

"Will do," Lev replies cheerfully. He loves this shit.

I turn to Vassago, our gazes finding each other once more. "Since you and Lore have the pantheon's favor now, the two of you meet with them. I want a binding contract outlining their agreement to align with us. No loopholes. They need to agree to be by our side in the event of war. Do not leave the council until that is done. Do whatever it takes."

Vassago scoffs and crosses his arms.

Lore steps in front of him. "It would be our honor to request the allegiance of and align with the pantheon, my Lord," she replies formally, on behalf of Vassago.

I step closer to Vassago, lifting my chin. "Our trust has always been weak. And my forgiveness will not be easily earned back after this last stunt you've pulled. For now, until I speak with Hope more, Lore is not in danger of my wrath. You, however, brother, should watch your fucking back."

Vassago's mouth quirks up with amused malice. "Threaten me all you want, Stolas."

I lean in, closer to his face. "I plan to. For eternity."

His gaze is serious. "Then, long may you reign, my Lord."

24

ESCAPING MY DREAMS

HOPE

I stare at the fire as it dances behind the glass. The expansive room around me is drenched in tension. It drips from every corner. I squeeze my lids together as the sound of shouting floats in and swirls around me. Loud voices bounce off the crystal chandeliers and lamps. Vassago warned me that he would be on the receiving end of Stone's wrath when Stone found out. Even so, it's hard to listen to.

I'm unsure how long I've been sitting here as he releases his anger onto his brother. My eyes slide over to the massive bed. It sits on a raised platform. The two stairs on either side of it are covered in a white fur rug, which matches the blankets. The silver silk sheets complement the heavy drapery hanging from all four corners, attached at the top by a large mirrored-box canopy frame.

I should be lying down and resting, but I'm restless.

Suddenly, the shouting ceases and silence falls across the room.

Standing, I make my way over to the modern seating area and curl up on the couch that sits across from two matching gray seats. A round mirrored table sits in the middle, adorned with books and magazines to keep my mind off things.

Oddly, there are no windows in the room. I'm guessing all the mirrors and shiny silver is meant to keep it light and airy in here, to feel open. The décor reminds me so much of Shadowbrook, even the silver-wallpaper, it's unnerving.

Beatrice knocks and enters without an invitation, rushing over to me with a leather bag that I know is filled with herbs, lotions, and bandages. And while I didn't appreciate her drugging me before, I understand why she did it.

"My Lady." She curtsies upon reaching me.

Kneeling down, she motions to my wrists with her hands and without argument I present them to her so that she can change the bandages. It's only been a few days, and already the wounds are almost healed. Quietly, she begins to remove the old dressings, and clean and medicate the skin before she rebandages them.

"Almost as good as new, my Lady." She smiles up at me.

"You don't have to do that," I state.

"Taking care of your wounds is my job."

"I meant curtsy and call me my Lady every time you see me."

"You are the prince's chosen. It is proper etiquette."

"I, um, I don't really like it," I mumble.

"Why not?"

"It makes me uncomfortable."

She doesn't answer, ignoring my protest.

I study her. She's striking.

So much so, it's as if she isn't real.

"May I ask you something?" I ask her quietly.

"Of course."

"Why are you here?"

"I've been appointed as your nursemaid."

"No." I pull my wrists back. "I mean, in the Circles."

"The Circles?" she repeats.

I nod.

Her gaze darts around nervously. "I loved someone once." Her voice is small. "We met for the first time at a May Day party. He was nine and I was eight. He was smitten and I was—well, I thought he was the cutest boy I'd ever seen." We smile at one another and her retelling of the memory. "Nine years later, we unexpectedly saw one another again on a street in Florence, along the Arno River. I was wearing a white dress . . ." Her voice trails off. "Anyway, he bestowed me with a collection of love poems he'd written over the years. Each explaining the true nature of his feelings for me."

"That sounds romantic." And oddly familiar.

"It was." Her sad eyes lift to mine. "At that time, well, things were less modern. I gave myself to him, believing completely in his commitment to our love. After, he was summoned to join the Crusades. I was heartbroken and desperate to make sure he returned home safely. In my desperation, I made a deal with the Devil." Her voice is full of regret.

My lips part and my brows pinch together. "What kind of deal?"

"Lucifer ensured me that my love would return home safely."

"I see. And at what price?" I drop my tone.

With a small exhale, she sits back on her heels. "I loved him. I believed in him. In us."

"Of course you did." I whisper, sensing her heartache.

"Lucifer told me that if my love stayed faithful to me while away, then he would return him to me, unharmed. However, if he failed at being faithful, I would have to agree to give Lucifer my soul, and become his consort." She swallows, watching me. "I had no reason to doubt my love or his faithfulness, so I foolishly agreed and made the deal."

As I listen to her, a conversation I once had with Kagami comes back to me. She once told me that I was naïve in my thinking, because in this world, you don't make deals with the Devil. The reason? Evil never holds up its end of the bargain.

"He was unfaithful?" I surmise.

"Yes. While guarding hostages, he slept with a slave girl who offered him 'comfort' in exchange for her freedom and that of her brother. It turned out her brother was actually her husband. Like most women, she did whatever she felt necessary to protect the man she loved. Even laying with another's love. The infidelity caused me to lose my end of the deal. And my love's life, because the slave girl's husband killed him," she recounts.

"That's awful. I'm so sorry, Beatrice."

She stands, fixing her skirt with the palms of her hands.

"What is done is done." She rights herself.

My eyes roam over her face. I understand her fear and sorrow, more than anyone. It takes everything in me to remain calm. I can't believe that she is stuck here. I want to lash out, storm into the Ninth Circle and demand that Lucifer release her from her sentence. He tricked her. Coerced her, knowing that her love would not be faithful.

Something Stone assured me the Circles doesn't do.

I stand and take her upper arms in my hands. "It's not your fault that you loved him. You thought you were protecting him by agreeing to Lucifer's deal. There is no shame in that. Nor should you be punished for all eternity for loving and trusting one man."

Beatrice falls silent for a moment before she steps away. "The same could be said of you, my Lady. When one has blind faith in love, one's soul never emerges unscathed."

I contemplate her words as she walks toward the door.

Before she leaves, I clear my throat. "What was his name?"

"Who? She opens the door, looking back at me.

"Your love?"

"Dante."

Dante and Beatrice? Dante's Inferno? I frown. Dr. Foster referenced the well-known fourteenth-century poem when he said I tried to commit suicide in the library at Shadowbrook. He cited the book's absence as the reason I became agitated and upset.

I look around the empty room before staring at my bandaged wrists. Once again the lines between reality and fiction become blurred in my mind. They grow thinner with each passing moment.

Is all this real, or am I just twisting reality again?

Why does it feel like I'm teetering on the edge?

Just about to lose my sanity?

———

WITH A STRANGLED GROAN, I curl into myself on the bed. My eyelids flutter as they try to open. It takes several attempts, but finally I manage to open them and gaze into the dark room, confused about where I am. My whole body aches and feels heavy.

And hot. So. Friggin. Hot.

A deep moan rumbles around my chest as I slide my hand over the damp sheets underneath my body. They're soaked. As am I. I'm covered in sweat. My T-shirt and hair are drenched. My fingers run over my forehead and rub away beads of sweat that are trickling down my face and the back of my neck. My skin feels like it's on fire.

There is a foreign sensation running through my veins, burning me from the inside out. It feels like my insides are being ripped away from my body. My fingers curl into the sheet with each wave of aching that runs through me. I begin panting, my breathing becoming erratic, along with my heart rate.

A dark figure moves near me, and the bed sinks.

"Stone?" I whisper, barely managing to say his name.

"I'm here," he murmurs.

My gaze slowly traces his face. Even in the dark, he's beautiful. I can see why everyone is drawn to him, and at the same time, fears him. Power and confidence leaks off him.

Even now, with worry marring his features.

"It's uncomfortable," I whimper.

A large hand lifts and runs over my damp hair, pushing it off my face. His cool touch soothes me. "I'm sorry, Hope. It's going to be like this for a little while. I can't give you any medicine to take away the pain, given your addiction history."

My gaze focuses on his dark hair and green eyes, glinting in the darkness. "That's never stopped you before," I tease. "You did drug and kidnap me."

His jaw clenches. "One time."

"One time too many," I huff out.

Stone sits up, gently helping me curl into his side, tucking an arm around me. "Better?" he asks.

Melting into him, I nod because for some reason, with his touch, the soreness subsides. Stone always used to feel hot under my touch, but now he feels cool. He soothes the scorching heat of my skin, like a cold ice cube running over me.

"The transition is going to be painful at times. You have to keep fighting through it."

"I know." My fingers grip his T-shirt, pulling him closer.

"The heat you feel in your veins is the divine blood releasing. My demonic blood is taking it over and it's trying to fight to stay alive. Your blood is literally boiling; the darkness is attacking what it perceives to be an enemy, the divine light."

"Sounds fun."

He draws me closer, falling quiet as I grip him

tighter.

"I'm planning to claim my right to the throne," he replies.

At his announcement, emotions flicker through me, threating to rush to the surface. While I'm the one whose mind stumbles through the dark, I can't imagine what it was like for Stone growing up here in the Circles. Truth be told, I don't care for this place.

It's a living nightmare. Stone's time here has been nothing but horrendous. The pain and suffering he's survived—well, let's just say that I know the scars are darker and run deeper than even I probably know. But to rule over it, for the rest of his existence . . .

The heat pulses under my skin again. I grit my teeth and push through it. Sensing my discomfort, Stolas leans over me, sliding his hand roughly through my hair, tugging it back as his lips take mine in a hot and frantic kiss. A growl vibrates in his chest as our tongues dance across each other and my nerves come to life.

Without thinking, I twist and throw one of my bare legs over him, straddling his lap. His other hand finds its way into my hair, yanking on the clammy strands. The sweet agony of lust is a welcome sensation against the tenderness vibrating under my skin.

After a long languid kiss, Stone pulls back but keeps his hands in my hair, holding me. "Did you hear what I said?" he asks. "I am going to claim the throne."

"I heard," I reply, staring into his gaze.

"And that doesn't scare you? Me being the king of the Nine Circles of Hell?"

"Beatrice told me today how she came to be your father's consort," I say quietly. "Your father's reign scares me, Stone. Not yours. He has no hard limits. You once told me that souls aren't coerced or tricked into aligning with the Circles. But your father, he does that. Innocent souls are chained to the Circles because of his power and cruelty."

"And how do you know I don't share his thirst for power, or cruelty?"

"If you could, would you release Beatrice?"

"I can't."

"That wasn't my question."

"She made an agreement with Lucifer. Even I can't break that bargain."

"But if you could, would you?"

"In a heartbeat. Just like I would release you."

"I don't want to be released. I choose to be with you."

Stone's fingers curl, holding me tighter. "Isn't that what my brother and Lore did to you? Trick and coerce you into believing that it was your choice?"

"Whatever you think Vassago and Lore did, you're wrong. I asked him to show me how to survive the Circles. And after, I asked him to show me a way to love and protect you, without losing who I am. Give me some credit. Do you honestly think I care if Lore continues to exist? She's mean and threatens to kill me on a daily basis. And Vassago scares the shit out of me. There was no coercion. I used the weapon so that Lore may continue to exist, but that was a sacrifice I was willing to make, for you. Not them. Only you. You are the reason I am here, Stone. You," I repeat, so he hears me.

"The Circles . . . this is not the mortal realm."

"I know."

"You can't protect me down here, Hope."

"I can. And I will."

At my vow, my runes begin to glow as they reach out to Stone's.

His illuminate, brightening the darkness that surrounds us.

"You're going to get yourself killed. Be careful what you vow in the Circles, and to whom. Your word is binding here," he scolds.

"Hendrix said once I fully turn, I'll be immortal."

"And?"

"Death doesn't scare me."

He lifts an eyebrow before leaning over and kissing me again.

"No one has ever sacrificed for me before," he mutters across my lips.

"You're just going to have to get used to it. Unless there is a bagel and cream cheese involved. Then I'm afraid that you're on your own, my Lord," I tease, using his title.

A small smile crosses his lips as he falls quiet.

His gaze roams over my features.

"Where's Avi?" I break the tense silence, hoping to her.

"She and Lev are on assignment."

"Assignment?"

"Circles business."

"If this is going to work between us, you are going to have to be more forthcoming with information. Less vague." I shift a bit as another round of heat scorches my skin.

"I sent them to the mortal realm to wipe the memories of all humans you've ever come in contact with," he states. "Including your parents, Dr. Foster, and Tazia."

My heart slams against my chest at his words, sadness suffocating me. When I made my decision, I hadn't given any thought to my parents, friends, or those I'd leave behind.

Stone cups my face, forcing my attention to his. Anger tightens his features, his demonic magic curling off him.

"You've sacrificed everything."

"I've gained everything."

"What you've gained is a living nightmare."

"I was never going to escape my dreams."

"The cost to you, it's too much."

"I love you. No matter the price."

CHILL IN MY BONES

VASSAGO

I take in the city streets of the Eighth Circle. Soon, they will run with the blood of everything I hold dear. Stolas and I used to hide within these city walls as children. Back then, we never expected that we'd make it this far. For as long as I can recall, all I wanted was to rule this Circle. And yet, when it came time to appoint leaders, Stolas was chosen.

My brother never wanted the Eighth Circle. His heart was always somewhere else, his soul constantly unsettled and restless as it searched for something he could never find. Ironic, given that out of the two of us, I'm the Seeker. And yet, all I wanted was to settle here and reign over the city that used to protect us as children.

The realm I love.

I thrive in the mental anguish here.

Perhaps it's because I suffer from my own form of the Black Mercy. Regardless, our desires didn't matter to our father. In his cruelty, he gifted me with Seeker abilities, so that I was always drifting, searching for souls. And Stolas, the pureblood heir, was appointed leader of this city.

Trapped in his own restlessness.

Lore steps out of the high-rise with a weapon that Stolas had been safeguarding. When her eyes meet mine, I realize it's beginning—the war that Leviathan, Stolas, and I have been planning for since we first discussed overthrowing Lucifer.

I knew this day was coming the moment the oracle of lost souls walked into our lives. I felt it in my soul. Even so, I can't shake the chill in my bones telling me that this is going to end badly.

My gaze goes dark and my nerves twitch along my jaw as Lore slides into the passenger seat of my Maybach Exelero. She doesn't move or speak, her goddess filling the space, taking up all the air around us. This is how Lore handles fear; she shuts down emotionally, allowing her goddess to be in control.

"What I have always warned you about is finally coming to fruition," I say, almost inaudibly.

"I know."

"There is nowhere to hide. The darkness will always find us. The more we resist, the more it goes after those we love," I point out.

"We are powerful enough to claim the throne," she assures me.

"Then we claim it. Together." I take her face in my hands and stare into her eyes. "It's you and me, goddess. We survive this, at all costs. I would destroy a thousand realms to ensure your existence."

———

With our shoulders squared Lore and I walk toward the temple pyramid that houses the Aztec pantheon. The stone ziggurat structure is built on four platforms, with a grand staircase running up one side. Nothing but endless desert surrounds the edifice as it stands tall in the hidden dimension's unforgiving sun and heat.

Since our demonic magic doesn't work in this realm, we can't teleport. Instead, we climb the stone steps that rise sharply to the entryway of the enormous structure. Once at the top, we step into the open doorway and look down into the massive, empty chamber.

The entire interior is hollow except for a giant circular table sitting in the middle of the assembly room. It has the Aztec sun stone calendar carved into the top of it. A single beam of sunlight shines in through an opening in the roof. The stream of light hits the middle of the table's design, like a spotlight. Particles of dust dance in the yellow ray.

Ten chairs built out of the same stone have been

strategically placed around the table. Each is adorned with a detailed carving representing the deity who sits in the seat.

Lore motions with her chin to the staircase.

"Someone should have considered putting the door on the ground floor," I grumble.

Within seconds, nine deities step out of darkened porticos. Each approaches their designated seat, standing behind it, but not sitting. All eyes follow us as the goddess and I make our way down the hundreds of stairs and walk into the center of the chamber.

We wait for the deities to speak or direct us. Their eyes bore into ours and we stare back, not showing weakness or fear. After a long moment, Tlaltecuhtli's massive form fills an entryway, his eyes hard with tension as he scours the chamber, settling first on Lore and then me. With a respectful dip of the chin toward us, he approaches his seat. Once he's there, all the deities take a seat.

"Your visit is unannounced, daughter," Tlaltecuhtli greets.

"Apologies. There is an urgent reason for our presence," Lore replies respectfully.

"The oracle?" he inquires. "So soon?"

"The oracle is no longer divine."

"At your hands, red serpent?" Huitzilopochtli, the god of war and sacrifice, asks me.

"At my hands." My answer is curt.

Huitzilopochtli glares at me for a moment before promptly ignoring me while Lore steps forward, presenting the Weapon of the Smoking Mirror to the pantheon. With their permission, she places the black obsidian box in the middle of the table, opening it.

One of the seated goddesses places her hand on the knife, closing her eyes as she meditates. Seconds later, her gaze opens and snaps to Lore's with curiosity. "The vision tells me the oracle of lost souls still exists. However, her divinity is no longer a threat to the Circles. As Lore has said, it has been released," she announces.

"Why does the oracle continue to exist at all?" Huitzilopochtli questions.

"Stolas marked her as his chosen," Lore states.

"Then her soul will darken?" he prods.

"She is in the process of transformation," I answer for her.

"You both have pleased the pantheon," Tlaltecuhtli praises.

"It was our honor to do so," Lore replies.

Lore shifts a bit and tries not to fidget under the weight of her father's admiration. I know it makes her uncomfortable. The goddess dislikes being complimented.

"Both of you have fulfilled your calling," Tlaltecuhtli announces.

"We have," Lore confirms.

"The pantheon thanks you for your loyalty and efforts," he dismisses us.

"Your gratitude isn't why we are here." I step closer.

Tlaltecuhtli narrows his eyes at me. "What is it you seek from us, then?"

"Your allegiance."

All ten deities lift their surprised and confused gazes to us at the same time. Each registers shock and curiosity as their gazes slide between Lore and myself.

A grim smile appears on Tezcatlipoca, the deity of light and shadows. This asshole is the god who assigned Lore the curse of protecting the Weapon of the Smoking Mirror. I meet his cold, dark stare, wanting to rip him limb from limb for placing both her and me in the positions he did, and for threatening her continued existence.

"Is this a test?" Tezcatlipoca asks.

"No."

"Are you being facetious, Vassago?"

"I am not."

"What you have come in search of already exists." Lore's father says in a tone that suggests he is warning me not to push the pantheon's boundaries or patience.

"The Circles will no longer honor your allegiance under the current regime."

Lore's father sits forward. "Are you asking us to align with a new regime?"

"We are."

A stir of whispering circles around the chamber, echoing off the stone. The deities catch one another with side glances, but Tezcatlipoca holds my gaze, assessing me.

"And just who plans to dethrone Lucifer?" Tezcatlipoca asks, half amused and half intrigued.

"Prince Stolas will claim the throne," Lore replies.

The deities' faces become deadly serious as they fall silent.

"It is this pantheon who legitimized Lucifer's right to rule when he fell," Tezcatlipoca points out. "It took many years for me to convince the deities on this council to pledge our allegiance to the shunned archangel. What makes you think we will give Prince Stolas the same courtesy within a few moments of your request?" he asks haughtily.

"We understand it is also you who is displeased with Lucifer's vengefulness," Lore points out. "You yourself, Tezcatlipoca, have said Lucifer has lost sight of his cause," she continues. "Isn't that why you charged me with protecting the ancient curse, and asking Vassago to wield it? To prove our loyalty in the event the pantheon declared war between the Aztec deities and the Circles?"

"Tlaltecuhtli's child does speak the truth," one of the younger goddesses says.

Tezcatlipoca sighs. "We charged you, Lore, with the ancient curse because the oracle was a divine threat to our vested interests in the land of the dead. Vassago is your chosen. Therefore, this council agreed that he must prove his worth to the pantheon. He has done so by wielding the weapon," he explains. "As for war within the Circles, it is true that I and the council are displeased with how Lucifer has handled himself over the centuries."

"War can be prevented between the Circles and pantheon," I declare. "With Prince Stolas on the throne, the Circles will no longer suffer upheaval or threats of divine war."

"How does Stolas plan to claim the throne?" Tezcatlipoca asks.

"By ending Lucifer's existence," I reply plainly.

"Impossible," Tezcatlipoca states.

Clenching my jaw, I run my gaze over the deities.

"Nothing is impossible."

Huitzilopochtli's gaze meets mine. "We created the land of the dead side by side with your father, Vassago. The Circles' energy is tied to the fallen archangel. If Lucifer fails to exist, so do the Circles. It was our contingency in order to ensure that the balance between light and dark was maintained on the mortal realm, so humans have free will."

His admission is like a kick in the gut. By the expression on the deity's face, I can see his words are truth. None of us in the Circles knew this. This key piece of information means we can never truly reign or overthrow my father, because without Lucifer, there are no Circles.

"There is another way." Quetzalcoatl, the deity of knowledge and learning says, bored.

"Which is?" I ask through gritted teeth.

"The Eternal Sealing Chamber," he replies.

"What is that?" Lore inquires.

"It is a spelled chamber we created here in the pantheon. When we helped design the Circles, the deities fashioned the chamber," Quetzalcoatl explains. "It is our loophole in the event Lucifer ever became . . . uncontainable in his thirst for power."

"Which he has," Lore's father interjects.

"The moment I'd first met the fallen archangel, my Seer gifts showed me that his thirst for power, hunger for greed, and his own darkness would overtake his quest for free will," the goddess who read the weapon says. "We knew this day would come."

My brows pinch at her confession. "What happens once he's in the chamber?"

"Once imprisoned, it is spelled to hold him for all eternity. The chamber's energy drains his powers and transfers them to the new ruler. He will be unable to use demonic or divine magic," Quetzalcoatl enlightens us. "It will be as if he ceases to exist."

"How do you know the chamber will hold him?"

"It will hold him," Lore's father says.

My gaze darts around the room as I contemplate

everything that has been revealed to Lore and myself. The deities have always known Lucifer would one day need to be removed from power, even when they placed him there themselves.

They've been prepared all along. When my gaze meets Lore's, it hits me. This entire time, she and I have been played liked fools. The Aztec gods never do anything by coincidence. My expression hardens as I face the pantheon and speak.

"How could you let him remain in power for so long, when you knew his thirst for revenge would overtake his devotion to free will? Something you've known would happen, by your own admission, even as the Circles were conceived. You've even prepared for it with a spelled chamber," I state, my tone hard. "To hold him in when it was time."

"Are you accusing the pantheon of something, Vassago?" Tezcatlipoca snarls.

"You allowed Lucifer to rule the Circles for centuries while his wrath grew," I emphasize. "All that suffering and pain could have been prevented by this council."

"The dark soul's consequences were unescapable. It was fated," he stresses.

"Fated," I repeat. "If that is true, then Lore wasn't created to protect an ancient curse. And I wasn't created to wield your weapon."

Tezcatlipoca's jaw clenches at my allegation.

"We were created as another of your contingencies," I finish.

Lore steps in front of me, narrowing her eyes. "Whatever you are doing, or whatever you are alluding to, end these accusations before the pantheon takes action."

"Step aside, goddess," I order.

After a brief standoff, she does, but remains facing me, angrily holding my gaze.

"The pantheon's seer must have seen both Stolas's and my creation," I speak to Lore.

"What does that mean?" She frowns, studying me.

"They've been waiting for Stolas to reign over the Circles. Since he was created."

Lore shifts, considering what I'm saying. "If that is true," she struggles, "they must have also known that the oracle would be created for Stolas's protection."

"What the deities didn't foresee is that Hope had free will, which meant her future and purpose could change at any moment. She was a wild card in their plans for the Circles."

Lore's shoulders fall at my words as realization settles in. "Because she is human."

I nod. "They never expected Stolas to fall in love with Hope. Or that she would sacrifice what she was created for in order to love him back," I continue. "While pleased that Stolas accepted his birthright to the Circles and declared his loyalty to my father, they knew one day, he would give it all up to protect Hope. And they couldn't have that."

"They need him in power to control the Circles," Lore whispers. "She threatens that."

I meet her father's eyes once more. "And so, as a contingency, you created Lore for me? For me to love. For me to bond with. I was your fallback in the event Stolas couldn't be used as a pawn in your desire to regain control of the Circles from Lucifer."

Lore frowns, turning to the table of deities. "When we last met, you said Vassago's and my fates were connected for the purpose of destroying the oracle's divinity," Lore recounts. "It was never about the divinity in her blood causing upheaval or unrest in the Circles; it was about Stolas remaining in power. So that you could control him. And when you learned that he was in love with Hope, you used her as a weapon against him. As you've done with me against Vassago," Lore surmises.

"Vassago proved to the pantheon early on he would do anything to protect you from Lucifer's wrath, Lore. He walked away from you, so that you may exist without suffering or torture," Tezcatlipoca points out. "We knew he'd be worthy of your affections."

Lore's lips part. "And knowing he would do anything to keep me safe, you leveraged my love for him against us. Gifting me the weapon to protect, under false pretenses, because no matter what, Vassago would not allow me to cease to exist."

At this, the room erupts again in hushed murmurs.

Lore's father lifts his chin, watching the two of us as he waits for everyone to finish whatever discussions they're having amongst themselves before he speaks.

"Only some of your assumptions are accurate," he says.

"Which ones?" I growl.

"This council failed to recall that you too, Vassago, have humanity in your mixed bloodline. Gifted to you by your human mother, Lilith," he replies.

"What does that have to do with anything?" I ask.

"The oracle's death was supposed to trigger vengeance and absolution in Stolas. He was supposed to hand over Lucifer to us," Tezcatlipoca states, "and in his maddened state, step away from the Circles. Instead of wielding the weapon to end the oracle, your free will changed the outcome. You ended her divinity, yet she still exists, now as a dark soul. The prince's chosen. And while we all have a common end result—Lucifer out of power—your misstep with the oracle has caused a change of outcome for which we had hoped."

"And what outcome is that?" Lore inquires.

A cruel smile crosses Tezcatlipoca lips. "Once the pantheon removed Lucifer from power, it wasn't Stolas who was to rule.

"Then who?" I question.

"You. Vassago."

WHATEVER IT TAKES

LORE

I study the faces of the council while they wait for Vassago and me to respond. I'd always been taught to never trust another soul, and yet, my breath escapes me at the treachery my father and the pantheon have been orchestrating all this time. Plotting and planning against the Circles and their leadership since conception.

A part of me hurts for Vassago; his entire life everyone has always used him as a pawn against Stolas, even now.

Realization falls across me that we have to be careful how we respond; there is a fine line limiting what we need to say here. We still need the pantheon to remove Lucifer from power. I chance a look at Vassago. He's digesting all the information being thrown around. When he's finished, his eyes rake over me.

He looks fierce and wild as he takes in every inch of me.

Since no one says anything for a long time, I decide to take control of the situation. After all, I made a vow to do so.

"We accept the pantheon's terms of partnership."

"What?" Vassago snarls. "They haven't offered anything, goddess."

"In exchange for imprisoning Lucifer indefinitely, Vassago will agree to reign over the Circles," I rush out. "And he will do so side by side with the pantheon."

When I look back over at Vassago, he isn't looking at the council members; instead his eyes are focused on me, like he's stalking me with his mind—his expression is lethal.

The anger I see on his face nearly breaks my resolve, but this is for the best. I'll deal with the fallout later.

"Vassago?" my father prods. "Is this true?"

A cold, calculating stare replaces any warmth in Vassago's face as he turns away from me to face the deities. He doesn't speak; instead he just studies them, breathing heavily.

"What are the terms of the agreement?" Vassago asks angrily.

"You, son of Lucifer, and the goddess Lore have come here today on behalf of the Circles, seeking the allegiance of the pantheon, under a new regime. The pantheon grants our allegiance to you, and the Circles, with the following stipulations. First, we are to remove Lucifer from power by any means necessary and contain him in the chamber here in the temple, so that the pantheon may guard him. All his demonic and divine powers will be transferred to the new ruler. Our second condition is that you claim the throne. Not Stolas. It is our wish that the Circles continue to thrive under your steady hand. They must act as a form of balance between light and dark, so that mortals may continue to enjoy free will. If you agree to our terms, the pantheon will forever be an ally."

I step in front of him, afraid he won't agree.

"Stolas said to do whatever it takes," I remind him. "This is what it takes."

"What this is is treachery."

Exhaling, I plead with my eyes. If Vassago doesn't agree to these terms, Lucifer will remain in power, and he will never be free.

"Choose me," I order.

Vassago pinches his brows. "I already have," he replies.

I shake my head and he growls.

"We're bonded," he reminds.

My voice is stern. "Choose me, of your own free will."

"I am a dark soul, Lore. I do not have free will."

"You have humanity in your blood," I refute with authority. "Choose me. I have earned the right to love

267

you. I no longer want to put our fates or existences in someone else's hands."

"What you are asking me to do is betray Stolas."

"What I am asking you to do is choose me. I cannot exist without you. I've tried, and it was as if a piece of me was dying a little each day. Stolas will understand this," I breathe out. "Please," I whisper. "You vowed. Whatever it takes."

Vassago remains still and calm. My heart beats faster when I realize I can't read anything about him. I don't know what he's thinking or which way his decision will go.

Suddenly, the air is heavy, thick with the tension floating between us. Normally, when I become emotional, I take in a breath and let my demon goddess take over and gain control, but this time, I push her away. Deciding not to detach from the outside world.

A chill makes its way up my spine as Vassago's eyes run over me, taking in every inch of me, as if he's memorizing the way I look for the last time. My bottom lip begins to tremble with fear, and an unfamiliar emotion runs through me. Without realizing it, a single teardrop falls from my eye and runs down my cheek. Vassago watches it with astonishment.

His lips part as his hand lifts, and gently, he wipes it away.

"I will always choose you. Above all else."

"Then it has been decided," Lore's father states.

Vassago lifts his gaze to the council. "The Circles agree to the pantheon's alliance and your conditions with one addendum. I will be the one to tell Stolas he will not reign."

————

VASSAGO WALKS INTO HIS PENTHOUSE. He isn't speaking to me. The light has drained from his eyes, missing ever since we left the pantheon. It's in this moment my father's words come back to haunt me, the weight of darkness falls on his shoulders. From this moment on, it always will. And it was all my fault. What I did wasn't intentional; it was done to protect him. Even if it means ending us in the process, because I am owned by him.

And in the end, this will be our downfall.

Our love for one another.

"Are you upset with me?" I ask into the silence of the room.

He stands in front of one of the fires lit around his home, shoulders tense. "Am I upset?" he repeats, the muscles in his jaw flexing.

"Yes."

"Upset would mean that I care about Stolas. Upset would mean that I gave a fuck about the Circles, or my father. Upset would mean that I feel, or have a heart," he snaps.

I stare, taking in his larger-than-life presence.

Vassago radiates power. Everything about him is powerful—the way he talks, the way he looks at you, the way he commands respect and attention without using words. Cautiously, I take a step toward him.

"For what it's worth, I am sorry."

He laughs without humor. "I'm used to treachery. To lies and manipulation. I live in the Circles. I thrive on it, Lore. Deceit, conniving—it's all a part of my soul."

"Then why are you distraught?"

"My loyalty has always been to my father and the Circles."

"I know that."

"Not anymore."

"I don't understand."

"Today, that changed. You made me choose. I chose you."

My breath catches in my throat and my body freezes as the heaviness of his words hits me. I never thought about what I was doing. I simply thought about my love and protection of him.

I'd put him in an impossible position.

One that he would eventually resent me for.

GO OUT IN FLAMES

STOLAS

There is nothing poetic about death when you are a dark soul, no nobility in it. Being here in the City of Weeping is a constant reminder of that. I have no idea how Hendrix bears the weight of limbo on his shoulders, evaluating information from the monks and deciding which Circle each soul is sent to. It's a heavy burden to carry.

My fingers run over the wall of crystal, made from angel tears. Whenever a soul turns dark, an angel sheds a tear. It descends into the underworld to protect the soul from the tortures that await it. Lucifer ordered Hendrix to collect them before the tears entered his gates. It's why the water is so pure in the Crystal Vault. If you remove the tear from the pool, it crystalizes, losing its protection ability.

"Do you ever wonder why I listened to Lucifer and

disallowed the tears to fall and protect the dark souls?" Hendrix asks, appearing out of thin air behind me.

"I assumed it was because defying Lucifer meant death."

Hendrix steps to my side, placing his palms on the wall of crystal. "When blood and water mix, the liquid becomes diluted. The blood doesn't become unstained, or untainted," he explains quietly. "Pure water causes blood cells to swell as they dilute. Eventually, the cells stop taking in water when full and then, they burst. Ceasing to exist."

My brows pull together as I meet his gaze. "Are you saying the tears aren't meant to protect dark souls, but to destroy them? If absorbed, the souls would . . . burst into nonexistence?"

Hendrix meets my eyes with a sad smile. "As hard to believe as it is, there was a time when your father was created of divine fire, and believed that every soul had the right to exist freely and choose their own fate. Most of those who fell believed the same. Including myself." He sighs and runs his hands down the wall before removing them. "And there was also a time when the divine would stop at nothing to prevent Lucifer from spreading what they perceived to be jealous madness."

"Ever think they were right to want to stop him?"

"And why would that be, my Lord?"

"He's become the darkest kind of monster," I point out.

"Perhaps. Or perhaps, truth lies in the eye of the beholder."

"Are you implying that my father hasn't turned into something none of us recognize?"

"I am not. In some respects, Lucifer is no longer the friend I knew and loved before the fall," he replies. "Yet, there are fleeting moments . . ." he trails off.

"Is that why you followed him? Why you fell? Were you blinded by friendship?" I question with sincere curiousity.

"If I am blinded by anything, it would be redemption. I believe that even the darkest of souls deserves love and protection," he replies. "That is why I oversee limbo. And that is why I prevent the angel tears from falling and destroying the dark souls."

"Because if you allowed the tears to fall, the souls would cease to exist and therefore, never have a chance to be redeemed," I deduce. "You are misguided, Guardian, naïvely so."

"How so?"

"There is no redemption for the dark souls in the Circles."

His eyes meet mine. "Do you think every soul that passes through the Hall of Judgment is sent to the Circles?"

"Then why continue to allow the Circles to exist at all?"

"The underworld has its place in the world. As does free will."

"And yet, the convictions on which it was founded are no longer present in its ruler," I argue.

"Do you think you could do better?" he questions. "As the Circles' ruler?"

I pause, taking in a long breath. "No. Nor do I want to."

"Before we pass judgment on someone else, we need take a good look at ourselves."

Silence falls between us as I drift off into a daze. From one moment to the next it seems my world is constantly being turned upside down. I can never find peace. No matter how much I want to. I'm doomed to an existence of turmoil. Even with Hope by my side.

"I don't want her here." I whisper my admission so quietly, I barely even hear myself.

"It pains you that Hope has chosen you because you think she's damned herself?"

"Hasn't she?"

"Can anyone truly be damned if they've sacrificed in the name of love?"

I hold my gaze on him, not bowing to its intensity. "You tend to idealize things too simply." My voice empty of emotion. "A flaw of yours, Guardian."

"Just like a flaw of yours is trusting Vassago."

My head bows and my lips press together as tension grows between us.

"Trust is a strong word when used with Vassago."

"Promises and vows link your fates."

"Yeah. Well, we all know how promises go between us."

"And yet, whenever something is needed, it's him you turn to."

———

VICIOUS STROKES of black charcoal darken the pristine white canvas as my fingers move quickly across the blank backdrop. It's been weeks since I've created anything, which has caused a higher level of anger and frustration to build within me lately.

Shadows from the candles flicker around me, shimmering off the silver wallpaper. Careful not to wake Hope, I sit in the armchair placed in the corner of the room, drawing.

It's been weeks since I brought her here to the City of Weeping. Her wounds are fully healed now and the transformation of her soul from light to dark is complete. She's become immortal and all divinity in her has vanished. At the thought, my charcoal strokes become darker as I sketch.

Aside from some minor physical changes—her skin has a new sheen, her eyes are brighter and her hair thicker and more shiny—she's still Hope. Each day, she gets stronger as she learns to hone her oracular gifts, as well as a few new demonic ones she's picked up as my chosen. Our bond is also stronger. I can feel her anywhere now. Especially when she's around me. The pull and hold she has over me is something only she possesses.

"I'm not sleeping," she whispers.

Stormy blue eyes open and lock onto mine. Even in the darkness, I see something has changed in her eyes. They hold mine with authority. Without speaking, we stare at each other for the longest time before she slides out of the bed, steps down the two stairs, and makes her way over to me. I hold her gaze as she slides onto my lap, straddling me.

Taking in a deep breath, she studies my sketch.

"Do you ever think you'll draw something happy?"

"Happy?" I repeat, trying not to smile.

"Flowers? Butterflies?" she teases.

"You should be resting," I say, turning serious.

"Have you been watching me sleep every night?"

"Yes."

"Why?"

I lift my hand and pick up a piece of her hair. "It's my way of protecting you."

"I'm not weak," she argues.

"I agree. As a mortal, you've endured more than most dark souls," I speak quietly. "You are stronger than most are, Hope. I've never thought you weak."

"Then why do you feel the need to hover over me?"

I throw her a fierce look. "Because you are my reason for existing."

She gazes down at me. "And you are mine."

"Then let me hover and ensure you continue to exist."

"Is this how it's going to be? You're going to watch me all the time? Afraid that at any moment I'll disappear, or something bad will happen to me?" she asks.

Releasing her hair, I run my fingertip over the heart on her forearm. At my touch, it comes to life and produces a scarlet glow. My own runes ignite, reaching out to hers.

"I'm afraid at some point, something will make you leave."

Hope stares at me as if she has never seen me before. A smile lifts on the corner of her mouth. "I've missed you."

Her words confuse me. "I'm right here."

"Physically," she states. "But mentally, you've been elsewhere. Far away." Hope takes my face in her warm palms. "Talk to me."

"I'm afraid," I admit, unable to stop the words from tumbling from my lips. "For the first time in my existence, I am truly terrified of my father."

She strokes my cheeks in a soothing manner with her thumbs. "There is nothing for you to fear. I'm here. You are mine. And I am yours."

"As much as that pleases me, those are the two reasons that I am terrified."

Gently, I grab her wrists, pulling her hands away from my face.

When I shift, she slides off my lap, allowing me to stand as well. I toss my charcoal and drawing onto the chair before walking over to the fireplace. At my approach, the flames come alive, climbing higher the closer I get to the hearth. I place my hands on the mantel. Bending over slightly, I stare at the inferno as it blazes and combusts.

The crackling and snapping sounds echo around us.

"You have no idea how much pain and anguish I suffered when I left you at Shadowbrook. In Gabriel's protective care, no less." I pause, swallowing. "I wanted to stay. To keep you with me. Then again, the son of the Devil has always been selfish," I add.

"You never should have left me there," she says.

The pain in her voice hurts me.

"I know that now," I reply. "I thought I was doing what was best for everyone."

"You thought being without you was best for me?"

"I thought it would save you from a fate far worse than mental anguish," I explain.

She takes a step toward me.

My back becomes rigid as I feel her approach.

"The fact that you used my mental instability against

me . . . knowing how much it would hurt me if I found out, that was pretty shitty of you—"

"I know," I interrupt her.

Warm hands slide up and across my back. The muscles under her fingers jump at her touch and my skin tingles.

"I wasn't done," she scolds. "I've forgiven it."

"How many times will you forgive me? I keep hurting you."

"As many times as it takes. Forgiveness is something that you do when you love someone. You forgive stupid actions done out of love, even if misguided."

"I couldn't stay away from you. The pull was too great."

"I know."

"I was there. Every night that Vassago and Lore weren't."

"I felt you," she replies with tenderness in her voice.

"I'm sorry. For not being strong enough to exist without you."

Hope falls silent as she steps around me, ducks under my arm and stands to her full height between my arms. With her back to the fire, she looks up at me from under her lashes.

"Never be sorry for that. Ever. Loving me is not a weakness, it's a strength."

Swallowing, I hold her gaze.

Her fingertips lift and brush over the script on my

chest. At her touch, my eyes slide closed and I take in a deep inhale through my nose.

"I was wrong." Her voice is quiet and thoughtful.

"About?" I keep my eyes closed as her breath caresses my lips.

"This script. Lasciate Ogne Speranza," she reads.

My eyes open and I give her a questioning look. "You speak Italian now?"

Hope shrugs. "Lev said I needed to learn it. Beatrice has been teaching me."

"Impressive."

She smiles and with a light touch, her fingers trace the words.

"When you told me that Abandon All Hope was the mark of the damned, I wanted to erase it from your body. I hated that you wore it. That it chained you to the Circles. All I want to do is free you from this place." Tears fill her eyes. "To save you, Stolas."

A small sound of pleasure slips from my lips as she calls me by my demonic name. Her soul is now dark; therefore, she can no longer call me by my divine name, Stone.

She steps closer. "What I failed to realize is what you need more than saving is hope by your side. I'm here. And with me by your side, you will never be damned."

Her lips lightly brush across mine before I pull back a bit.

"We'll have to leave the City of Weeping soon and

return to the Eighth Circle," I change topics, using a soothing voice. "Vassago and Lore have met with the pantheon, they've agreed to align with us. Leviathan and Avi have taken care of everything in the mortal realm. And while we're nowhere near where we need to be with our legionnaires, many of them have agreed to go to war if necessary, now that we have the backing of the Aztec deities. Hopefully, that will be enough to keep us safe from Lucifer's wrath."

"It will."

"And if not?"

"Then we'll go out in flames."

28

BATTERED MIND

HOPE

Panic threatens to crush me. Last night, Stolas confirmed we'd be returning to the Eighth Circle tomorrow. At the thought, my lungs squeeze in my chest, making it impossible to breathe. It's as though someone has literally reached inside me, wrapped their hands around my lungs, and squeezed until every last ounce of oxygen has disappeared.

A sinking feeling makes its way into my stomach. It's been too long since I've last seen Lore and I'm starting to worry that she wasn't able to fulfill her end of our deal. I should never have placed my trust in her. I wanted so badly to believe everything she promised me before Vassago handed me the Weapon of the Smoking Mirror.

I can't afford to be wrong.

Being wrong means that Stolas will never be free from Lucifer.

"Focus," Kagami orders, startling me.

"I am."

Judgmental silence wraps around me and I exhale roughly, opening my eyes. When I do, she's watching me with a disapproving look. Her lips are in a permanent frown.

"Your mind is unfocused," she scolds. "Tell me why."

"I'm fine." I fake a smile and look her in the eyes.

"Your ability to lie is as poor as your ability to concentrate."

Kagami's eyes search mine, seeking out my soul. That is what she does. She reads souls. It's how she senses so much. I blink several times so she can't see into mine.

The doors to the dojo slide open, and Lore and Avi step in, saving me from another one of Kagami's many lectures. As soon as my eyes meet Avi's warm honey gaze, I can't help but smile.

Like the first time I saw in her the library at Shadow-brook, her hair is wild and untamed. Each curl stands at attention with a life of its own. She smiles brightly at me before running over, tackling me, and squeezing the life out of me with a hard hug.

"I've missed you," Avi squeals.

"Can't. Breathe." I manage, pinned on the floor.

She falls into a fit of giggles, releasing me and helping me stand. "Please, you're immortal now. One of us! Breathing is overrated."

"Dark-souled or not, she still needs to breathe," Lore snips.

Relief runs through me at Lore's presence, even if her cold eyes look me up and down with disgust and complete annoyance.

"Let me look at you," Avi demands, walking around me.

I've missed having her around.

"Well?" I inquire.

"You look like you."

"Gee, thanks."

"Maybe a little more healthy, and sparkly." She winks.

"Sparkly? Sounds just like me," I reply sarcastically.

"Powers?" Avi questions, her thoughts scattered as usual.

I hold out my hand and produce a small ball of fire. With a quick flick of my wrist, it flies across the room. Before it hits the wall, I wave my other hand and it snuffs out, disappearing into thin air.

"Killer!" Avi claps with delight in her voice.

"Avi, please try and remain calm. The dojo is a sacred space," Kagami admonishes.

Avi rolls her eyes. "One of your demonic gifts is fire?"

"Just like Stolas," I reply.

Kagami sighs at Avi's bright energy, taking her leave.

As soon as she slides the shoji closed, I meet Lore's

gaze. A look of confusion falls across her face, like she doesn't know quite how to deal with, or speak to, me.

"What's wrong?" I ask. "Did something happen?"

"The pantheon has ruled," she states.

"I know. Stolas mentioned it last night. Has something changed?"

I hold my breath.

"No." Lore's eyes shift between Avi's and mine.

"Then why does your face look all tight and angry?"

"That's how she normally looks," Avi giggles.

Lore's eyes fill with fury at Avi's insult.

"Nothing has changed. The pantheon has agreed to align with the Circles under a new regime. They declared that Vassago must be the one to claim the throne," she says slowly.

I exhale in relief. "Then it worked? Our plan worked?"

"The first part has," Lore confirms, not showing emotion.

After Vassago agreed to prepare me for the Circles, Lore was tasked with training me mentally through her gift of transference.

When I didn't break at seeing the visions she showed me, she was impressed. That is, until she showed me Stolas's history. Seeing what happened to him here, what happens to him on a daily basis—I couldn't stomach it.

To calm me, we started talking. We both realized that we love demon princes who will never break free of

Lucifer's or the Circles' hold over them. After a bit, we decided neither of us would continue to allow Vassago or Stolas to suffer at Lucifer's hands.

That night, we came up with a plan to free them both. When Lore returned to the Circles, she brought Avi in on it.

And now, the three of us have set it in motion.

We're going to free and save them.

No matter what it costs us.

"What about Vassago?" Avi questions. "Is he upset?"

"Upset doesn't even begin to address his state of mind. Regardless, I've managed to convince him to agree to the pantheon's terms," Lore states. "That said, he isn't happy about betraying Stolas. If we don't act fast, he will go to him. But for now, he's agreed."

"I can't believe the three of us pulled this off," I whisper in awe.

"I can't believe Avi agreed to our plan," Lore retorts.

"Kill or be killed, right?" Avi counters with a smile.

My eyes meet Lore's. "Love is their mercy."

Her chin dips, understanding the meaning of the words Hendrix whispered to me when we first met. Hendrix is a fallen archangel, one of the few who were allowed to keep their divine gifts, because he is a powerful and revered seer. That is how he knew who I was when Stolas first brought me to him. It's also why the monks could read my aura as I passed through the Hall of Judgment, revealing my true purpose to him and confirming the visions of me he had before he met me.

Hendrix's secondary ability is subconscious control—he can manipulate thoughts, hiding them in others' subconscious, allowing him to manipulate minds, which is how I knew that Stolas would send me back to the healing retreat, wiping my memories. Hendrix pulled me into one of my own dreams, my own vision of the future. My gifts were not fine-tuned then, so the visions were vague, allowing him to enter my conscious and plant memories for me to recall after Stolas would remove them.

Hendrix releases my hand and walks over to my sleeping form, placing his hand on my forehead and bowing his head slightly. I watch as my body relaxes onto the mattress.

"Be still, child of Eve. When the darkness settles and colors you with fear, be still. For when morning comes, he will come for you." She relaxes at his words.

Hendrix steps away from the bed and turns to me, pinning me with a hard expression.

"Remember these words I have said. The mortals will cloud your mind with medication and lies; you will forget that you two share one heartbeat. Do not abandon all hope, for your love will come. Simply call him by name, and Stolas will come to you. This is my vow."

My gaze slides to the sleeping form in the bed as his words sink in, matching the earlier message from this very same vision. Something strikes a chord, and I remember trying to remind myself of this very conversation.

"Listen to Hendrix," I whisper, and then suddenly Stone's voice floats into the room.

"Don't be scared, I'm on my way," his soft voice promises. "I'll take you home, I promise. Just hold on a little bit longer."

"The dark prince and you will be connected, child of Eve."

"How did I just hear him?"

"Ancient legend states you will make his heart your own. Stolas's birthright and the Circles will settle again in his soul, darkening it further. It will tear you two apart and he will fade into the night because he thinks there is a strange love in letting go. But love is mercy; it will save you both. When you call, he will come to you."

"It's not over yet," Lore replies. "There is a complication."

"What kind?" Avi asks, losing a bit of color in her cheeks.

Lore's jaw clenches. "Lucifer's power is tied to the Circles."

"What does that mean?" I question.

"If Lucifer ceases to exist, the Circles do as well."

"Shit!" Avi exhales.

"To prevent that, the pantheon has created a chamber to hold him in. It's spelled so that once he's captured, the chamber will pull his energy into the Circles and transfer his powers to the new ruler," she explains.

Avi frowns at Lore. "That's good, then, right?"

Lore nods. "Lucifer will need to be taken to the pantheon alive."

"How do we do that?" I ask in an even voice, proud that my voice doesn't break or crack at the idea of kidnapping the darkest demon in the world. "Sounds impossible."

"Only if we let it be," Lore replies. "I have an idea."

"Spill it," Avi encourages.

"Our ability to execute it is going to depend . . ." Lore starts.

"On what?"

"On you."

Avi's head snaps to mine. "Oh. No. That is going too far, Lore."

I look between them. "What? How is it too far?"

"She wants to use you to lure Lucifer."

"What?" I screech.

Lore's expression hardens at my freak-out. "You would be an enticing bait."

My lips part. "Stolas is terrified because he thinks his father wants to destroy me," I point out. "And you want to just what? Hand me over? Just like that?"

"Lucifer is too cunning to destroy you," Lore says quickly.

"Meaning?" I prod.

Lore points between Avi and herself. "We will convince Lucifer that your existence is necessary if he is to bait the divine into war. That is his ultimate desire; revenge against the divine. And he has never backed down when handed a weapon to destroy them."

"And just how the hell are we going to do that?" Avi snaps.

The three of us fall silent as we contemplate our next move.

After a moment, Lore sighs. "I have an idea how we can do it."

"Great," Avi groans.

"All that's left is getting him into the chamber," I point out.

"The pantheon will assist with that part," Lore interjects.

"We're putting a lot of faith in your deities, Lore," I whisper.

Her shoulders straighten. "Do you not trust the Aztec gods?"

Avi and I glance sideways at each other. "Um . . ."

"Have they not agreed to and produced everything we've asked of them?" Lore asks.

"Convincing the deities to allow Hope to exist as a dark soul after they cursed you and Vassago to drain her divinity isn't necessarily the best argument," Avi argues. "And while you were able to persuade Vassago to wield the weapon, Stolas will not be as easily distracted by your pretty goo-goo eyes as Vas was."

Lore makes a disgusted face at Avi. "My father was also able to steer the pantheon's decision, ending in the result we had agreed on, Vassago claiming the throne so that Stolas doesn't have to suffer with a calling he wants no part of," she adds.

"That is true," I interject. "They have assisted quite a bit. And to be honest, I'm not sure the three of us are going to be able to entrap Lucifer in a spelled chamber alone."

"What if Hendrix helped?" Avi throws out.

"I think he's done enough," I reply. "At some point, we are going to have to share what we've done with Stolas, Vassago, and Leviathan. And when we do, it's best if Hendrix's part is small." I close my eyes for a moment. Then I open them and catch Lore's gaze. "Are you sure that Lucifer will treat me like a dark soul? Like a weapon to leverage against the divine to create war? Instead of a punching bag?"

"I'm certain," she says, unwavering.

"What about Vassago and Stolas?" Avi points out. "Won't they be punished for Hope's existence and their disobedience?"

I meet her gaze before looking back at Lore. "She has a point. I think it's time for us to execute the second part of our plan."

"Agreed."

"Second part?" Avi asks with a whine.

"Are you sure you're ready to face this?" Lore confirms.

"There is nothing that Lucifer could throw at me that I haven't already seen, thanks to your transference, or suffered from over the past two years in the mortal world. My mind has been battered enough. When it comes to Stolas, I will face anything," I state.

"I wish you'd stop being noble," Avi sighs.

"It's not nobility," Lore's voice is low.

"No one can save him but me," I state.

"She's right. When you love someone, you do what's best for them, not yourself," Lore points out.

Avi gives us a slight nod, reluctantly agreeing. "Alright, ladies. Let's execute phase two then and save their sorry asses."

When my eyes meet Lore's, relief fills her gaze.

Vassago and Stolas need to be free of all of this.

And we are going to free them.

29

WAR WITH THE DIVINE

VASSAGO

S tolas lifts his eyes for a second time to meet mine. I don't look away. Instead, I study his reactions as he contemplates what we're seeing in front of us. When he finally breaks away from my gaze, it's to meet Lev's. The prince is furious, but even worse, he is suspicious. Not just of the scene in front of us, but probably of everything now.

"Well, this is an interesting turn of events," Stolas clips.

"Actually," Lev smirks around his unlit cigarette, "it's fucking brilliant."

"No one asked you," I scold.

On alert, I look around the room. Two pestilence demons stand guard at the door behind us. Six more of the faceless creatures are in the office, three on either side of the room. And three of the female-bodied demons stand behind the desk, holding weapons.

Their wings are out, ready to attack. The stringy black-and-red feathers all along their slim bodies have gone rigid as they watch us. All talking ceases as we approach.

Leviathan and I bow our heads slightly to Lucifer out of respect, trying not to flinch as we all catch our breath, trying to figure out what the actual fuck is going on.

"My Lord," Stone greets first, as is protocol. His voice drips with rage as he pins our father with a hard glare. "You demanded our presence?"

Lore's face pales when our eyes lock.

Lucifer doesn't rise from his seat behind the desk. Instead he tilts his head at us, assessing. Studying our reaction to the fact that he is casually seated, flanked by Lore, Hope, and Avi. None of them look like they're being coerced or forced.

"I believe I have something that belongs to you, Stolas," he taunts.

Stolas takes in a sharp breath, like he's been sucker punched, as the three of us shift our focus to Hope, standing to Lucifer's right. She swallows but doesn't speak, respecting the protocol of the Circles. Oddly, she isn't fidgeting either, as someone would if they're uncomfortable. Instead, she watches us with her head held high. Cool and calm. Just like Lore always is. Avi stands on Hope's other side, with the same controlled expression.

It's as if they've been trained.

When Stolas's gaze meets Hope's, his stance becomes rigid.

Lucifer gives a knowing smirk at the shift in the prince.

A tense silence fills the room before Stolas manages to speak.

"I—"

Lucifer holds up his hand. "Save it."

"I think if I explained—" he tries again.

Our father lets out a bark of laughter. "Explained what, exactly? Hmm, Stolas?"

"I'd actually like to speak, if I may," Hope interjects.

My lips part at her brazenness. I chance a sideways glance at Stolas, who is looking at Hope as if he's never seen her before. Lore and Avi remain stoic, their expressions unreadable.

"This should be fun," Lucifer growls. "By all means, tell him."

"I told your father what you did, Stolas." Her voice is cold. Detached. "I also expressed that I'm pissed as hell that you put me in this position. I've always wondered what kind of bastard doesn't take responsibility for his actions. Now I know. The prince of the Nine Circles of Hell. I've been on my knees—and on my back—with your seduction. I've bled out. I've fallen all over myself, willing to go to the depths of Hell and back for you. And this is how you repaid me. Without my permission, you had your brother coerce me into removing my divinity, then you marked me and turned my soul dark. I was the oracle of lost souls. I was created and protected by the divine. I was supposed to protect you. I had no idea what loving you would cost me." Her voice quivers. "My soul."

Stolas shakes his head, gearing up to lay into her, but stops when Hope's eyes narrow dangerously, preventing him from speaking, before she looks away, as if too disgusted to even make eye contact with him.

"Hope seems very upset with you, Stolas. You too, Vassago." Lucifer gifts us his calculating smile. "Not so much with you, Leviathan. Apparently, she just thinks you're a fucking moron."

"Thank you, my Lord," Lev replies. "And how nice of you, to hold me in such high regard in my Lord's presence." His voice drips with annoyance.

"My pleasure," Hope retorts snottily.

"I have to say, when Lore and Avi first walked Hope into this office, I almost ended them all. My rage was . . . well, let's just say pushed to its limits, given that you yourself told me she was no longer in existence," he says, the loss of control teetering at the edge of his voice.

Lucifer stands, walks around the desk, and steps toward us. Once he is in front of Stolas, he stands taller and his expression hardens. "Then I remembered that scorned women tend to betray."

"Scorned women?" Lev repeats, confused.

"Are you outraged that Hope is still alive?" Lucifer asks. "Hope tells me you left her for dead. Cruelly restraining her to a bed at the mental health facility she was hiding in, in Switzerland. Leaving her to bleed out, to make it look like she committed suicide."

Stolas shakes his head, confused. "What I am, my Lord, is fucking outraged to see her standing in this room. By your side. With my guards acting as if they are protecting her."

He barely manages to keep his demon in check. Stolas takes a menacing step in Hope's direction before Lev and I step in front of him. Each of us take a side, placing our hands on his chest to prevent him from attacking.

"Easy, my Lord," I whisper. "Let this play out."

"Someone explain what the fuck is going on here," Stolas rumbles.

"When you left me at the facility and restrained me to the bed, Gabriel appeared," Hope explains in a firm voice. "Sensing my distress, he healed me. He had no idea I was marked by the Circles. Or that you and I shared a blood bond. Therefore, he required I shed my divinity and he left me there, while my soul turned dark."

My brows pinch because it sounds like they're twisting truths. Then it hits me. My eyes snap to Lore's. She refuses to look at me, but the pulse at the base of her neck jumps.

When I trained her on how to deal with Lucifer, I used to tell her to keep her stories as close to the truth as possible. It's the only way he won't sense deceit. You can lie to the Devil if your story is full of truths.

"What the fuck," Stolas exhales.

Completely lost, he ends his fight to get to her.

"Lore told me you sent her to confirm that the oracle was dead," Lucifer adds. "Is this true? Did you send Lore to Shadowbrook to check in on Hope?" he challenges.

Stolas's gaze darts around the room before he spits out, "Yes. I did." It's the truth.

"At your request, I found her. Alive. Her soul was dark, and she was marked. My apologies, but I had no choice but to return with her, my Lord. And alert your father that she is no longer mortal, or divine." Lore states. "She belongs to the Circles."

"How convenient," I counter.

Lore's eyes snap to mine, narrowing.

"This is un-fucking-believable," Stolas scoffs.

"Oh, I agree." Lucifer smirks with a wicked edge to his smile.

"She doesn't belong here," Stolas states with fury lining his tone.

"On that, I disagree," our father says. "Dark souls belong in the Circles. Not only is Hope a dark soul, Stolas, but she is marked as yours. It would appear that her love for you, combined with your blood link, has set off a mate bond between the two of you."

"Imagine that." Lev mutters. "Looks like you've got yourself a girlfriend, Stolas."

Stolas takes in the room as his nostrils flare. The vein on his forehead is pulsing with each breath he tries to pull in.

"Love has no place in the Circles," he says.

"It is clear to me that you do not feel love toward her, Stolas."

"I thought you wanted her dead?" I point out.

"A knee-jerk, misguided reaction to her existence."

Stolas looks like he's about to blow the fuck up.

I step in front of him. "Are you saying that you want her to remain in the Circles? As Stolas's chosen?" I ask our father.

Lucifer's gaze slides back to Stolas. "You have claimed your birthright to the throne and proven yourself worthy. It's clear you despise her. So she won't be a distraction to you. Of course, you can have as many consorts as you like if she displeases you that much."

Stolas's jaw clenches.

"Her soul is dark," Lucifer points out. "And Lore has convinced me that Hope will be an asset to my end goal."

"Which is?" I inquire.

"War with the divine."

30

ONLY A MOMENT

LORE

My gaze slides to the wall of windows. It's the middle of the night and Vassago hasn't returned to the Seventh Circle. I roll onto my back and stare up at the ceiling, trying to push away the emptiness I feel from our connection. I shake my head at my own pathetic state. Am I really worried about a demon who tortures dark souls on daily basis?

I knew the second Vassago figured out what we were doing. I felt his gaze on me as it darkened with realization. And I know his wrath is coming. Stolas is pissed too. Actually, I'm pretty sure everyone in the room except Lucifer and Hope is upset with me.

Hope's and my deceits run deep on this one.

Avi's too.

But it's only for a moment, I remind myself.

My chest aches and suddenly I feel it. Rolling over,

my hand slides under the pillow and I grip my dagger, yanking it out quickly. With a snap of my arm, I point it at the shadowed form in the corner of my dark room, ready to attack. It doesn't flinch.

"Goddess." Vassago says it like a curse.

"How——" I look around, confused.

"I blocked you from sensing me," he says. "Cute trick, right?"

Swallowing, I sit up and push back against the headboard. On a good day, Vassago is scary as fuck. But when you've pissed him off, frightening doesn't even begin to describe what he is. I grind my teeth together, holding my breath, watching him.

"But then again"—his voice is low and cold—"I guess it's not a cute trick when you already know how to do it. Hendrix showed you. It's how you prevented me from knowing about the little stunt you all pulled today. Am I right?"

I don't reply. What's the point? He already knows.

He takes a step toward the bed and when he does, the amber lights from the fire raining down on the plain light his features through my windows. Vassago angles his head, his eyes digging into mine as if trying to look into my soul. My heart drops to my stomach as he stares at me like I'm nothing and everything at the same time.

"You're awfully quiet," he points out.

"What is there to say?"

"You don't want to know what I'm thinking?"

"It's not like I don't know," I whisper.

"And what am I thinking?" Vassago's jaw cracks.

"That you can't trust me. Not anymore."

"What you and Hope did was fucking stupid." His voice is quiet, but it has the same effect on me as if he shouted. "You've put yourself, her, Stolas, and me at risk."

"And I'd do it again," I darken my tone. "Over and over again. I would sacrifice everything I am and every soul in this realm or the next to ensure you exist freely."

Vassago stands taller, rolling his shoulders back.

Pissed, I drop the knife on the bed.

Sliding out, I walk over to him in the darkness, standing in front of him with my chin held high. Every so often, amber fire falls from the sky outside, lighting the room.

"You want to pretend you don't feel what is between us. Fine. You want to make us only about sex. Fine. But your actions contradict everything you say. You've been watching me for years, keeping me safe. Protecting me. I'm done standing by and allowing you to dictate what we are. I am a goddess. A warrior. And I will fight for you. I will save you from this shithole existence we live in. I will free you from Lucifer. And you will not get in my way, because if you do, Vassago, so help me, I will destroy your ability to stop me. In the end, I will choose you. Over bloodlines. Over duties. Over family. My only vow is to you. Eventually, it will be time to take your place. And when you do, I will be there to protect you. Have I made myself clear? My position on us clear?"

Silence.

"I know somewhere deep inside of you lies a being who had a good heart once. Or I wouldn't be mated to you. You've lost your way, become compliant. It ends, today."

Vassago doesn't move.

He doesn't make one sound.

Each second of stillness that passes between us makes me realize I'm right and he knows it. I peer up, taking in the faint shadow of his beautiful face and sinful gaze.

Something about the way he is looking at me reveals a deep pain. I've never seen him appear so internally conflicted before. I stand tall, allowing him to fight whatever internal battle he is waging with himself as he watches me with no expression.

With his eyes holding mine, wordlessly he takes a menacing step closer to me. I become rigid, sliding into my warrior stance in the event I need to defend myself.

Catching me off guard, he grabs my waist roughly, pulling me closer as his fingers grip me tightly, before he drops to his knees and places his forehead against my stomach.

The entire time, I hold my breath, confused at his reaction. He shudders against me and instantly, I wrap my arms around his neck, holding him to me. I lean forward and drop my lips to the top of his head, his vulnerability becoming too much for me to bear.

We stay like this for a while before I slide to my own knees and take his face between my hands, so I can look into his eyes. That's when I feel it—the wetness on his cheeks.

My gaze searches his as a few tears escape his eyes.

Frowning, I wipe them away.

"No one has ever loved me in this way," he says roughly.

Exhaling, he holds me tighter. His touch burns me, creating a need so possessive within me that my entire body begins to shake with want. One minute I'm furious with him, the next terrified. But through it all, I love him. So fucking much it actually hurts.

His eyes flick to my lips and before I can stop myself, I kiss him. Our mouths collide with an intense desire. Vassago stands, lifting me, growling as one of his hands slides into my hair, giving it a rough tug so that he can kiss down my neck.

My eyelids flutter with need as the bloodthirst presents itself in the back of my throat again. He tosses me onto the bed roughly and covers my body, his chest heaving as his arms cage me in while he looks down into my gaze.

"I'm sorry," I whisper. "I know you hate me."

His eyes harden. "I don't hate you. I crave you. I worship you. I fucking love you."

"And what I've done?"

He levels me with his glare. "My father's day of reckoning will come. And when it does, there is no one else I want by my side. Fighting for me. For us."

I suck in my bottom lip and search his gaze.

"We're in deep." His voice is hoarse.

"I know."

"There will be death, goddess."

"Just not yours."

"In the end, I need to know that you'll do as I ask."

"I won't."

"I know," he sighs. "And that's the fucking problem."

Vassago leans toward me with a feral glaze in his eyes and our mouths collide in a slow, torturous kiss. With languid movements, his lips dance across mine. The feather touch of his finger's trails along the skin on my neck, leaving scorching imprints.

My body comes alive, feeling everything as I get lost in him. The world is an ugly place. It doesn't matter where you live, or who you are.

All that matters is that you have someone who will love and protect you, no matter the cost.

And in turn, you let their love guide you through the darkness. Even if it's just for one moment.

31

BROKEN STRINGS

STOLAS

The door to my penthouse slams shut before Hope can even look up. I stand in front of it for a few seconds, flexing my fists at my sides, fuming. She crosses her arms and presses her lips together, watching me from a healthy distance in the sunken living room.

Avi and Leviathan stand near the wall of windows.

After the shitshow in my father's office, I ordered that Hope be brought here while Vassago and I dealt with the fallout from their fucking idiotic plan.

"Leave us," I bark out.

Avi and Hope share a look and I lose my shit.

"She is not in charge here!" I roar, causing them both to startle. "I FUCKING AM!"

"Of course, my Lord," Avi whispers. "I just—"

My lethal gaze snaps to hers. "Get. Out."

Lev takes her hand in his. "Come on, pretty girl."

Avi hesitates. "I'm not sure it's safe."

"Get her out of here, Lev. Or I will kill her." I order, unraveling.

"Well, it's definitely not safe for us," Lev counters.

Within seconds, their forms dissolve, leaving Hope and me.

"That's a cool gift." Her voice is small. "Teleporting."

When my hard gaze meets hers, she swallows the words. Trying to calm myself down, I stand here with my hands in the front pockets of my jeans, just looking at her with no emotion.

When Hope's eyes soften, I want to stay lost in them in this moment, savoring the way she's looking at me. Even now, when all I see is red, I'm ill prepared for the churning emotions of having her in my home again.

It's as if we are the only two people who exist.

"Stolas," she whispers.

"Don't," I stop her. "I realize you come from a different world, Hope. But in the Circles, you will treat me with some fucking respect. I AM THE PRINCE HERE!"

I know throwing my weight around isn't going to end well. But I don't give a shit.

What she's done is unforgiveable.

With a menacing glare, I step down into the living room, pushing the imaginary line of her boundaries. Not caring that she looks taken aback. Not for one fucking second.

"What is your fucking problem?" she hisses.

"Don't," I growl in a cold and detached tone.

"Don't what? Talk to you? Look at you? Touch you?"

"I'm warning you."

"Warning me?" Her eyes narrow.

"Yes."

"I am not a dog you can bark orders at."

"I am not in the mood for your bullshit!"

Hope jerks back. "You're a fucking asshole."

"I'm an—" I stop my demon from killing her.

She folds her arms over her chest, standing taller. Letting me know she isn't going anywhere. I roughly run my hands through my hair, trying to compose myself, but it's no use. I'm too pissed, too hurt, too over all the bullshit we keep putting each other through.

"I am here, Stolas. Trusting you. Wanting you. Loving you. You can be pissed all you want, but what I did for you today is because I love you."

"What you did." I laugh without humor. I fervently shake my head, my emotions releasing the demon inside of me. I can feel him taking over. "Thank you," I say, my voice dripping with sarcasm. "No one has ever done anything quite like that for me before. No one has ever cared to! You're the best."

"Why are you so angry?" she challenges.

"Because it was fucking stupid," I yell through my emotions.

"Fucking stupid was restraining me to a bed in a mental facility."

"No. Fucking stupid was walking into Lucifer's office of your own free will. Letting him know that you were alive. And that his two sons fucked him over," I shout.

"Well, at least Lore and I did something."

"What the hell is that supposed to mean?"

"You and Vassago act like the big bad demon princes, but really . . . you're pussies."

I don't move.

I don't speak.

I'm pretty sure I'm not even blinking.

"Something has to be done to protect you both."

Her words were all I needed to lose my shit completely.

Hope's angry glare doesn't waver as I stand in front her.

"Did you call me a pussy?"

"Yes," she confirms.

My eyes widen, stunned by the way she is standing in front of me in a dominant, demanding, arrogant stance. Her presence looms over me like I'm a bunny and not a demon.

"I told you not to push me," I seethe. "Didn't I warn you that I am not in the mood for fucking bullshit tonight? I told you not to provoke me. And now, you've messed with the Devil's son, sweetheart." I use the nick-name she hates. I stretch my neck from side to side. "You want to meet my pussy of a demon?" I mock in a threatening tone.

"What are you—"

Not allowing her to finish her question, I lift my hands and produce two fireballs, throwing them to either side of her. They hit the walls behind her, leaving large black sooty holes as they burn and climb up the wall. She immediately growls as she stares at the walls before she snaps her focus back to me, narrowing her eyes.

"Did you just fucking throw fire at me, demon?"

"Gonna do something about it, mortal?"

Tilting her head, she produces her own balls of fire in her hands, only these are larger. Each is whipped at me with incredible speed, requiring me to dodge them before they knock into my artwork on the opposite wall. Everything goes up in flames behind me. I don't falter. Creating two more, I throw them on the ground in front of her. Angrily, she waves her hand at her feet, putting them out, before pointing to the Oriental rug.

"I loved this rug."

"You created my artwork." I motion behind me.

At the same time we both start flinging fireballs at each other. Each of us is careful not to actually hit the other. They fly back and forth, landing all over my penthouse. By the time we're out of demonic magic, fire surrounds us, burning everything I own.

With a final growl, I close the distance between us. She doesn't say anything more; her breathing is erratic and her face flushed with anger mixed with something else. Her eyes hold mine, pleading for me to kiss her. To touch her. To tell her I'm sorry and thank her for loving me enough to save me. I don't. I can't. My lips hover over hers, on the verge of connecting, as she pants. I want to give in to her, because I do love her.

But I let her go, causing her to hiss at the sudden loss of contact.

I can't do it.

Everything about us is wrong in this moment.

"Speak freely!" I yell, sensing their presence.

"Holy shit!" Lev's voice breaks Hope's and my angry standoff.

I turn as he creates streams of water, dousing the flames.

"What is wrong with you two?" Avi shrieks.

"Nothing!" Hope and I yell at the same time.

"I knew we should have stayed," Avi sighs.

A grin appears on Lev's face.

Vassago, Lore, and Avi all just stare at us in shock, like they've never seen us before.

"Why are you here?" I manage.

Clearing his throat, Vassago says, "We've been summoned. We have to meet with Lucifer and the war council now. Lore and Avi will stay with Hope until we return."

I nod, knowing this was going to happen.

After a moment, my eyes lift and lock onto Hope's. "I want you to stay in this penthouse with Avi and Lore. Do not leave it. Do you understand me?

"Do you not trust me? Afraid I'll do something unexpected?"

"Don't push me," I warn.

"Or what?"

"I mean it, Hope," I breathe out.

Seeing the seriousness on my face she dips her chin, agreeing.

"Just this once," she gives in.

Some of the worry rushes out of my expression.

"Wait." Her hands snap out, grabbing my elbow.

I try not to push her away.

"What are you going to do?" she asks.

"I have no idea what we are going to do. But I promise you this: it will be quick and I will come back to you," I vow.

She steps closer, lowering her voice as she holds my eyes.

"I'm sorry."

"Me too."

"What I did, I did for you because I love you."

"What you did was break any strings of trust connecting us."

32

NEVER LET YOUR GUARD DOWN

HOPE

When I walk into the kitchen to grab some coffee, I stop dead in my tracks. Stolas is already awake, leaning against the kitchen counter, shirtless, sipping on his coffee. He's silent, deep in thought. His eyes slide over to mine and he half smiles. For a second, I contemplate turning back around and walking out, but I really need coffee.

"Hey," I whisper.

"Hey," he replies, his eyes never leaving mine.

When I finally manage to look away from his intense gaze, I notice a plate of bagels on the counter, already coated in cream cheese. My heart squeezes that he has my favorite breakfast waiting.

With a small smile, I grab the extra coffee mug sitting next to the plate and twist to grab the coffee pot, but he's already is holding it out for me.

Without a word, I move my mug toward him. When he's done pouring, he turns his back to me, placing the pot back on the coffee maker. Staring at his back muscles, I sip my coffee in silence, wishing things weren't quite so weird between us this morning.

I woke up feeling guilty for everything I'd done and said yesterday. And, honestly, I'd be lying if I said I wasn't torn about seeing him this morning. When he turns back to me, his eyes are serene, full of stillness again, but something still feels off.

After noticing I'm staring, Stolas clears his throat. The noise breaks the uncomfortable silence between us and snaps me out of my thoughts.

"Cream?" His voice has an odd tone to it.

"Um . . . sure. Thanks." I study his face, not liking the look on it.

"Just let me know when you've had enough." His voice is low and smooth.

While he pours, his eyes hold mine.

"That's good," I whisper.

Stolas leans in very close to me and whispers. "Are you sure?"

I nod, unable to respond verbally.

My silence makes him grin. "I'd hate for you to go behind my back and add more."

I look away from him. Passive aggressive much?

"So how was the meeting last night?" I ask, trying to change the subject.

Stolas cocks his head to the side as he studies me. It's usually endearing, but this morning, it looks almost threatening. "It was . . . eye-opening." His voice is like ice.

My irritation at this odd conversation flares. "What is wrong with you?"

"Nothing." He throws me an easy smile at me and leans back against the counter.

"Look. I am sorry for last night. And for the things I did and said—"

"It doesn't matter." He laughs once, quietly. "None of it matters this morning."

"Really?" I challenge.

My breathing stops for the tiniest moment and I briefly close my eyes to block out his perfect face. Composing myself, I reopen my eyes just as Stolas leans toward me. Reaching out, he touches my cheek. His fingertips trace a line from my jaw to my lips. At his touch, an all-consuming fire ignites within me. My lips part when his fingers run over them.

"I had a lot of time to think last tonight." He eyes me up and down in a way that makes me blush. "You're a dark soul now, Hope. I need to remember that."

"I'm still in control of my decisions and actions," I reply, and give him a stubborn glare.

"I know," he whispers. "I did what I thought was best when I left you at Shadowbrook. You did what you thought was best by revealing yourself to my father. In the end, perhaps the way you ladies handled it was the better way. We're all still breathing this morning."

I stare at him, not sure how to respond. That wasn't an epic apology on his part, nor was it forgiveness. Whatever it is, I'll take it as a form of truce, for now anyway.

"My father and the war council are throwing a celebration this evening to announce that their future heir has a chosen. Your attendant will be here later to help you get ready and prepare. Everything you'll need is in our bedroom, upstairs."

"Malia is coming back?" I ask, excited to see her.

"Yes. And this time, where she is concerned," his voice deepens, "you'd do well to remember that you live in the Circles now. I expect you to act accordingly when others are in our presence," he states. "That is nonnegotiable."

I narrow my eyes. "Of course, my Lord." I don't hide my annoyance.

Like an asshat, Stolas grabs his coffee mug and grins wickedly while he watches me. His eyes bore into mine as he takes a long sip without answering. Done with his attitude, I grab my own cup and a bagel and stroll out of the kitchen without a glance back.

Even so, I can feel Lucifer Jr.'s eyes following me as I leave.

———

I STARE at the Viking helmet adorned with two delicate red horns and intricate silver wings on both sides. The beautiful young woman wearing it tilts her head and waits patiently, holding up two pairs of shoes. Annoyed, she shifts her stance and her platinum-blond hair slides over her slender shoulders.

When I first came to the Circles, Malia was my attendant, a Huldra demon assigned to me by Stolas. She helped prepare me for a dinner with the Circle leaders and Lucifer. Thanks to Malia, I've learned proper dress and protocol for His Highness's functions. And, like Beatrice, Malia prefers proper protocol even though I hate it.

I wave my hand at her, realizing she is bursting at the seams waiting to speak to me.

"Speak freely. Always. In my presence you never have to be prompted."

"Forgive me, my Lady, but they are only shoes. Choosing is not a form of favoritism."

My gaze lifts, meeting her scarlet eyes as they twinkle at me.

"I can't."

"Choose?"

"They're so high. Like, not-able-to-walk-in-them high."

She frowns at me. The last time we saw each other, I touched her and had a vision of her death—a cruel death, where she is chained to a wall, burning. Flames surround her, and her eyes are completely black and hollow, her mouth frozen open in a soundless scream. Swallowing, I shake off the image. Since I've returned the Circles, I haven't had a new or clear vision. I'm starting to wonder if I lost my oracular gifts when I transitioned, since they were given to me by the divine. I have yet to tell Stolas.

"If I may," she replies, dropping the shoes.

I watch as she heads over to the closet, getting lost in the enormity of it before reemerging with a pair of kickass black knee-high boots with a tiny heel. She holds them up, nonverbally asking for my approval, and I smile at her.

"The black dress you've chosen is floor-length, so no one will know. Also, there is a pocket inside each boot for your weaponry," she announces, approaching me.

"Weaponry?" I pinch my brows.

Out of the bottom of her red dress, she produces two daggers, sliding one in each boot.

"One can never be too prepared, my Lady, at a celebration in honor of His Highness."

I gape at her. "All right, then."

After helping me into the boots, she stands abruptly, pulling me up with her.

"Would you care to join us this evening?" I ask.

Malia bows her head slightly. "That is a kind invitation; however, attendants are not permitted. Only His Highness, Circle leaders and revered guests."

I sigh. "It would be nice to have a friend, other than Avi and Lore."

A small smile creeps onto her deep-red lips. "It is an honor that you think of me in that way. Thank you, my Lady."

A knock at the door pulls our attention to the handsome demon prince who steps into the room, wearing a tailored tuxedo. It's always so odd to see Stolas dressed formally since most days, he lives in cotton thermals and jeans.

With a swift nod to him, Malia takes her leave.

Slowly my eyes lift and meet his seductive green eyes. When his gaze meets mine, I have to hold my breath at the intensity in them. My knees become slightly weak.

Stolas swallows. "Wow. You look . . ."

Sweat starts to pour out of me as I fill with tension and anxiety. The silk collar around my neck, holding my dress together, starts to feel too tight as Stolas takes me in, inch by inch.

"Beautiful," he finishes with a smile.

"Really?" I blink quickly, not wanting to ruin my smoky eyes.

"Really."

"You clean up pretty nicely yourself, my Lord," I tease.

With a few steps, he closes the space between us. Both his hands come up and run over my hair, which is down in loose waves, before taking my face between his palms. As soon as I feel his touch against my cheeks, I relax, until he speaks.

"Whatever happens tonight, do not let your guard down."

———

THE DRIVER PULLS into the turnabout at the front of Lucifer's estate and waits patiently for some of the other cars to drop off the distinguished guests invited this evening. Stolas shifts uncomfortably next to me. My gaze slides out the window, which I have opened a bit, hoping the fresh air would help calm my nervous energy. Stolas's warning about letting my guard down didn't help.

Relief hits me when I see Leviathan get out of his parked car and run, in his tuxedo, to the passenger side. My smile falters when I hear him growl at the being sitting in it.

He plucks the cigarette of his mouth and sighs, leaning his arm on the hood of his car, while peering into the open passenger window. "Get your ass out of the fucking car, Avi."

I frown when I see Avi cross her arms, remaining in Lev's Mercedes Benz SLR McLaren 999. It's his baby. I only know what kind of car it is because he talked my ear off about it one night. According to Avi, it's the one thing he loves more than anything in this realm or others.

"No," she huffs.

Groaning, Lev closes his eyes. I'm guessing from the look on his face, he is imagining himself getting shot between the eyes.

"Avi, we need to get inside. Lucifer will be displeased if we miss dinner."

"You left." Her voice wavers a bit.

Lev's stance becomes rigid. I watch as his eyes meet Avi's. "I had to. Stolas needed me. Apparently, I have a hero complex now," he mumbles around his cigarette.

Our car moves up a bit as we sit idle. I should roll up my window—their conversation is none of my business —but I can't help but be fascinated with how they're acting together.

Avi snorts and shakes her head at him.

Lev leans in the open window. "I'm sorry I left. I'm here now. I won't ever leave your side again."

I watch as Avi pins him with a hard look. "You promise?"

"I swear it," he vows, opening the door and holding out his hand.

After a moment, she slides her palm into his before he slams the door behind her.

Standing to her full height, Avi releases his hand and with a deep breath straightens her cocktail dress. I smile as Lev stares at her with hunger in his eyes. He's taking in all her curves.

"Lev." She snaps her fingers in front of his face,

causing him to shake off whatever naughty thoughts I am sure were taking over the sane part of his brain.

When we finally pull up to the front of the doors, Lev has extended his arm to her and Avi curls her fingers around his elbow, allowing him to guide her to the front door, where we meet up with them.

"Lev. Avi," Stolas greets them. "Lev keeping his hands to himself?" Stolas asks, leveling Leviathan with a warning glare. I know that Stolas loves and protects Avi like a sister.

Avi's eyes gleam. "He's felt me up like a hundred times already."

Lev quickly places his hands up. "She likes to exaggerate."

For a moment, I just take them in and smile.

It's been so long since I've felt normal.

And as fucked up as it is, it feels . . . normal.

33

LOYALTIES

VASSAGO

I watch Lore's figure as she mingles in the crowd. Her straight hair is really smooth tonight. It catches the lights that glimmer off the crystal chandeliers. The elegant gold dress she's wearing hugs her tanned body in all the right places. Two long slits climb up her legs on either side of the gown, giving the tiniest peek of the brown leather from her sheaths, where I know the goddess is hiding her daggers--one on each thigh.

Hundreds of sets of male eyes focus on her, eye-fucking her. My jaw clenches as they gawk. Angrily sliding past the guards my father assigned to me this evening, I make my way to the goddess. Her eyes meet mine as I push through the crowd to get to her, because nobody eye-fucks what belongs to me. After tonight, the demons staring at her will have to deal with my wrath for disrespecting my chosen.

Some jerk has the balls to reach for her. Without blinking, she pulls a dagger out, and the blade meets his throat.

"Touch me again and I'll make you bleed," she spits out.

He jerks his head and slinks away like a wounded animal.

I step up to her and watch as she returns the weapon.

"You okay?" I reach out and caressing the side of her face.

She relaxes under my touch and nods. On pure impulse, I grab her hands, placing them around the back of my neck, bringing her as close to my body as possible. I wrap my arms around the small of her back, savoring the feel of exposed skin from the low-cut dress and slowly move with her in my arms.

It takes a while, but eventually, Lore relaxes.

When she does, I rest my forehead on hers, staring deep into her eyes as we sway together, as one. Lore's eyes dart around, worried, but I ignore her fear and instead focus on the feel of her in my arms. The smell of her against me. The look in her eyes as she stares into mine, as we lose ourselves in the undeniable connection we always share.

I smile at her. Unable to fight my feelings for her any

longer, I simply enjoy this moment with her. For the first time in a long fucking time, I am happy.

With her.

"VASSAGO!" my father's voice booms around us.

Lore looks up at me through her lashes and my smile fades as reality kicks in. What the fuck were we allowing to happen?

Panic claws at my throat, because I let my guard down.

"Fuck," I breathe out, stepping back and away from her.

Lore shakes her head, stepping toward me. "Don't push me away."

With a hard exhale, I look around.

All of my father's guests have stepped away from us, watching the scene play out in front of them, including Stolas, Leviathan, Avi, and Hope. They're standing across the room with unreadable expressions. Stolas's jaw is clenched and Lev looks ready to battle.

With all the strength I can muster up, my gaze snaps to the king of the Nine Circles of Hell. His cold, callous glare is pinned on me, looking ready to tear me apart.

"Just what the fuck is going on here, Vassago?" Lucifer snarls.

All talking and music ceases.

All eyes are on us.

Lore stands with her back to him, watching me. The light in her eyes instantly shuts down. The hurt is plain as day on her face. She isn't even trying to hide her defeat this time. A deep heaviness sets into my chest as everything around me falls silent.

A choking sensation takes hold of me as I stare at Lore.

"I'm done," I say to her. "Done hiding in the shadows."

The light fills her eyes again as she dips her chin.

"Then let's step out."

Standing taller, I hold my hand out to her and when she takes it, the room fills with gasps. I pull her to me, turning her around, and we face my father, together.

When his eyes fall on us, rage fills them.

"Vassago," he warns.

"Lore is my chosen!" I shout.

Stolas and Leviathan walk toward us, standing behind Lucifer.

"I have watched helplessly as those I love most in my existence have been tortured by you for no other reason than wanting to exert their free will. I am done. And if that brings your wrath down on both of us, then we will take your punishments," I growl. "I have had enough. I'm ready to let my guard down, allowing my weakness to seep in through the cracks. I will let Lore in. I will love her. And by her side, I will exude nothing but control and power, because her love makes me stronger, not weaker. I thrive on it."

I chance a glance at Lore, realizing that she is the

only reason I continue to exist. She peers up at me, searching my eyes for answers that she desperately wants, but I don't have. There is no ease or reassurance I can provide to her in this moment.

This is the reality of falling in love with the Devil's son.

"I knew you couldn't be trusted. It's Lilith's fault, really. I should have let my guards end you at birth. Your actions today have proven that your humanity cannot be controlled or removed. No matter how hard I've tried to extinguish it," he snarls. "Let me put an end to this little fantasy in both your heads. There is no room for love in the Circles."

"Bring her in," Lucifer orders.

Four pestilence demons walk in carrying a stretcher. Anger begins to violently pulsate through my blood. The closer they get to us, the more the reality of what we are doing hits me. All feeling leaves my body until there are no more thoughts or emotions left as the extent of Lucifer's wrath stares back at us. Lilith's lifeless body.

"This is what happens to those who choose love in the Circles," he says. Our eyes lock. "Welcome to Hell."

Lore shudders next to me, taking in the signs of cruelty and torture my mother endured, no doubt at Lucifer's own hands.

"This is your existence, Vassago. Beings die around you daily, at my hand and yours. We've killed to prove points, as I have today. Slaughtered without thinking twice. We are ruthless demons who prefer torture as a form of vengeance. Today, my hands are covered in your mother's blood. And soon, yours . . ."

"I am here for you, no matter what," Lore says, reaching for me.

"Don't touch me," I caution. "You need to stay away from me."

"Vassago, don't—" she pleads, in a voice filled with desperation.

"Don't fucking touch me. I am warning you."

Lore doesn't listen.

She steps in front of me with a hard expression, taking my face in her palms, forcing me to look at her. Her hands burn my skin as if she is touching me with divinity. Everywhere she touches leaves deeper scars than the ones I already carry.

"I understand you don't want me to end up like Lilith, but that isn't your choice. It's mine," she stubbornly states. "I love you. Whatever fate that leads me to."

I roughly shove my hand at Lilith's lifeless body. "The fate that leads to is torture and nonexistence."

"Then so be it." Her voice is calm.

I roughly grab her wrists, holding her in place. Seething, I lean close to her face.

"I would die a thousand deaths to spend a moment bathed in your love," she whispers.

"All I wanted was to protect you from the ugliness of my world, goddess," I state.

"You have. By showing me what love is." Her eyes fill with tears as she leans forward, pressing her lips to mine one last time.

Ignoring the chaos erupting around us, I concentrate on the feel of her lips before we come full circle and I walk away from her, leaving the darkness behind. My choice is made. It's her. Always.

My father's guards grab her and me at the same time, yanking her away from me. This is normally where I would lose my shit and fight them off, but I don't.

I let them grab my upper arms, pulling me away from her.

I don't fight what's coming. I can't, anymore.

My demons had pulled me under, dragging me further and further into the darkness.

They buried me alive.

Until she revived me.

"Last chance," my father's voice booms. "Once and for all, decide where your loyalties lie, Vassago. With love, or the Circles."

With teary eyes, Lore shakes her head, her heart breaking. For us.

"Lore has my loyalty."

34

LOVE OR HONOR

LORE

I t sickens me to watch Vassago mourn Lilith's death. She was never was by his side, protecting him. Loving him as a mother should. She only loved herself and Lucifer. And look where her loyalties got her. Vassago was naïve to think that she had any humanity left in her. His father made sure to snuff that out a long time ago.

Lucifer's voice booms around the silent ballroom. "Vassago is now considered a traitor, charged as such for acts against the Circles. His punishment: execution. My bloodline, the bloodline of your king, has been cursed by my second-born son's humanity. But rest assured, on this night, it shall no longer be cursed. I will bleed out all humanity left in him before I extinguish his existence. And I shall do so with my own two hands in the Ninth Circle."

My stomach bottoms out. I knew Lucifer wouldn't punish me this time. I am pardoned because I brought Hope to him.

My existence is his repayment.

Low murmurs run through the guests.

It feels forced. The demons here don't give a shit what happens to Vassago. All they care about is that they aren't the ones on the receiving end of Lucifer's wrath.

"Do not fear, my legions," Lucifer continues. "My firstborn son, Stolas, heir to the Circles, has chosen a dark soul for his mate. This evening, despite the treachery that has occurred, we celebrate. We celebrate their unification. We celebrate the future of the Circles." Lucifer turns to face an enraged Stolas and shocked Hope. "The Oracle of Lost Souls and Prince Stolas are mated. Their union will secure the Circles' existence for the rest of eternity."

Lucifer's smile widens, and the evil, sadistic look he normally has is back with a vengeance in his eyes. My throat becomes dry as I stare at Vassago. The demons around us have been stunned into silence by the turn of events tonight.

I look around, unable to find the courage to speak or remove Lucifer's two goons from gripping my upper arms. In this moment, all I can do is try to remember how to breathe.

Stolas steps forward. His eyes are wild as he growls. "If Vassago is to be punished by death for loving his chosen, than so shall I. I stand with my brother, for he is my blood."

Hope's gaze meets mine with panic.

I shake my head once, because this isn't how our plan was supposed to fucking go.

Lucifer's face fills with rage. "What?" he snarls.

Stolas turns around and takes a knee in front of Hope.

"My loyalty is to my chosen. My loyalty is to Hope."

"Stolas," she pleads, willing him with her eyes to get up.

"I love you," he tells her.

"Get up!" Lucifer screams.

"I forsake the Circles and sacrifice my existence, for you, Hope."

Hope and I watch helplessly as legionnaires enter the room, fully armored. Their march is a precisely choreographed dance as they line up and take their places around the room. Lucifer orders his guard to magically bind Vassago and Stolas. The weight of what we've done comes crashing down on my chest as I watch the future of the Circles crumble in front of us.

With a wicked expression, Lucifer steps up to me. With a flick of his hand, one of his minions throws Beatrice's beaten body at him.

She falls to her knees, weak.

Hope and Avi are both held back when they move to get to her.

"Did you not think I knew?" he spits in my face. "How dare you think you can outsmart me, goddess. Everyone in the Circles is my subject. I RULE THIS KINGDOM!" His voice echoes, rattling the building. "I am the king."

"I'm sorry," Beatrice whispers at my feet.

"For what?" I seethe.

Wet eyes lift and meet mine. "I told him."

"Told him what?" I spit out.

"How you wanted the pantheon to trap him in the chamber, so that Stolas and Vassago could rule the Circles. That Vassago was to be the next king, not Stolas. Everything."

My eyes snap to Hope, who shakes her head, not understanding.

"Truth serum. In her water, when I changed her bandages," Beatrice whispers, answering our silent question of how the fuck she knew. "I'm sorry. I had no choice."

Lucifer bends down and strokes her hair gently. "Well done, Beatrice. You have proven your loyalty to me and the Circles on this day. Lucky for you," his voice turns seductive, "my favorite consort is no longer breathing. I look forward to us becoming friends again," he coos. "Take her to my chambers and clean her up," he orders.

The room around us is silent as his minions drag her

off. Vassago and Stolas watch the scene from shackles. Torment and pain are evident in both their expressions.

"We have done nothing wrong," Hope shouts. "Except fight for the freedom that you have stolen from all of us who reside here in the Circles."

"HOPE!" Stolas snaps.

"What is their crime? Loving someone? Asserting their free will? Isn't that what you built the Circles on?" she shouts.

"Silence!" Lucifer backhands her and Stolas fights against his restraints. "You know what's at stake if you open your mouth again? Stolas's death. Remember your place in my world. Never cross me again. I will be damned if I let you or Lore take what's mine."

Lucifer turns to his sons. "Take them away for treason against the throne."

The legionnaires drag both of them out of the room as Lev holds Avi back from getting to them. As Stolas passes Lev he meets his eyes, holding them with a hard look.

"As if she were your own," Stolas commands and Lev nods.

Once they've disappeared, Lucifer turns his attention back to Hope and me. "My sons will die at your hands. Consider that my gift to you both. Now you know who your true king is, and what happens to those who question me or my ways. Let this be a lesson to all of you.

You now know the lengths to which I will go to ensure that you are faithful to the Circles first."

His minions release us, and with great dramatics, they march out of the room. Before he leaves with them, Lucifer turns back to Hope and me throwing us a cruel look. "Looks like the queens have fallen without their kings."

I stand taller, deepening my voice. "You may have won this battle, my Lord, but the war is just starting."

While this story is a work of fiction, designed to be read for entertainment purposes only, I would like it to be clear that I am not downplaying the seriousness of mental health conditions, or making light of those who live with any form of mental illness or depression.

Mental illness, suicide, and cutting are very real and serious conditions, which require professional medical treatment. Please find strength in knowing you're worth it. Choose life. It's hard. It's painful. It's often lonely and scary. Darkness always is.

If you think you or a loved one are living with a mental health condition and you need more information about mental illness or suicide, please reach out to:

The National Alliance on Mental Illness (NAMI) hotline:
800–950-NAMI (6264)

The National Suicide Prevention Hotline:
800–273–8255

You can also text *"home, help, hand or SOS"* to **741741** to the National Suicide Crisis Hotline

Author Randi Cooley Wilson

LEVIATHAN

DARK SOUL SERIES FINALE

He's the demon prince of envy.
She's the daughter of Medusa.
When your soul is dark, matters of the heart are rarely
simple.

Hope Annandale would go through hell and back for
those she loves—and she has, literally. The love she
shares with Stone has survived shattering heartbreak,
deep treachery, and great sacrifice. Despite Stone's
betrayal, they have returned to the Circles—together.
But at what cost? Stone is far from being trustworthy and
pretending to do Lucifer's bidding will test his fate and
their love like never before.

Sometimes love can leave you more hopeless than lies,

that is what Avi realizes after she falls for Leviathan. A demon with a reputation that rivals her own and an uncanny ability to both terrify and captivate her all at once. Leviathan struggles to keep himself away from Avi knowing their love can never be. Yet, something about the way she makes him feel sparks a need deep within him—one he struggles to keep buried.

Vengeance threatens the Circles, forcing Leviathan to choose between his love for Avi and his protection and friendship with Stone—knowing that his decision has the potential to ignite an ancient war and destroy Hope and Stone's happily-ever-after.

Will Leviathan and Avi find the strength to fight their attraction to protect the Circles from the retribution that is about to be unleashed onto it? Or will their dark souls give in to passion, ending friendships and changing the course of Hope and Stone's fate, forever?

In this last installment of the Dark Souls Series, the battle for power over the Circles comes to an end and a sacrifice is made that could destroy it all. Leviathan is a magical journey of passion and sacrifice—one that tests the theory that in the end, true love prevails.

Leviathan is the final novel in the Dark Soul series and is a riveting tale of passion, danger and forbidden love.

THE DARK SOUL SERIES

AVAILABLE FOR PREORDER

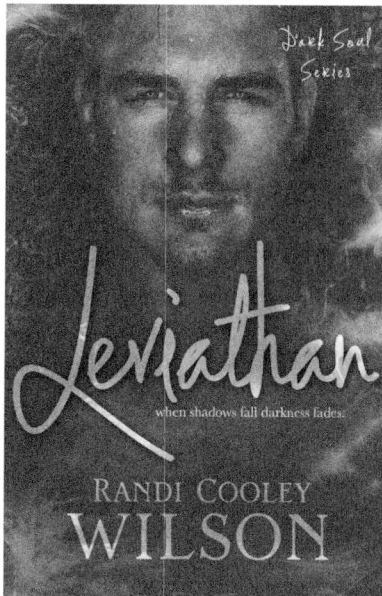

A New Adult Paranormal Romance Series

IF

A CONTEMPORARY ROMANCE NOVEL

I close my eyes and take a few deep breaths, attempting to regain my composure. The crisp evening air fills my lungs but does nothing to soothe my soul. The truth is, tonight, nothing is going to keep me calm—except maybe copious amounts of alcohol.

The brisk fall weather isn't unusual for this time of year in New England. Cooler temperatures hang in the air, chilling even with a jacket. This evening, though, there is another reason for the icy presence deep within my bones.

I shiver and stare at the closed double doors in front of me, knowing what's waiting behind them. Tears threaten to burn the back of my throat. Suddenly, I miss California.

My safe place.

Far away from the memories.

I exhale slowly, staring at the scene in front of me. The plain white church sits unassumingly on the grassy hill. Like most buildings in Massachusetts, it has a rich history and longstanding secrets. The steeple stands tall against the dusk-colored sky glowing with crimson and auburn hues.

A breeze passes over me, carrying with it the whispers of the ghosts who've passed through the sacred doors. Blue hydrangeas frame the front of the historic building, popping off the white clapboards, which look like they've just received a fresh coat of paint. It's picture perfect. On the outside. What's inside is anything but perfect.

"You ready, Emerson?" a gentle voice asks.

I unglue my gaze from the church and turn my attention to the tall, handsome man beside me, Jake Irons. When my eyes meet his, he smiles effortlessly.

How does he always appear so completely at ease all the time?

It's a gift. It must be. One that I don't possess.

My gaze roams over the tailored black suit he chose for tonight. It's flawless.

He's flawless.

"Ready," I force out, focusing on how handsome he looks.

Jake is easygoing. Calm. Steady.

Exactly what I need to keep me composed.

To keep my façade firmly in place.

He reaches for my hand with his larger one. "You okay?"

No. This is the first time my two worlds will collide, and it's impossible to be *okay.*

Lifting my gaze, I give him a watery smile and nod. "Just happy," I lie.

Jake studies me for a moment before squeezing my hand.

He's always so perceptive.

It's unnerving.

But even he has no idea what we're about to walk into. I've kept it from him, because I don't want my complicated past to tarnish my future with him. I know he senses the sadness at times, the void, but he never pushes. Never asks. He doesn't try to fix the broken pieces or make me whole. He simply accepts that this is the way I am.

With a slight tug of encouragement, he guides me toward the entrance. And with each step closer, my heart lodges itself farther in my throat. The panic crawls underneath my skin, threatening to break through the surface as I try to convince myself that my world won't fall apart the moment I step into the church.

The doors open and a friendly face greets us. "You guys made it!"

Relief crosses my friend Josh's face, and I can't help but smile at his energy.

"Sorry we're late." I step into his warm embrace.

Josh has always been my favorite boyfriend of Kennison's. The three of us went to college together—part of a larger group of friends. And while they've had their ups and downs, it really does make me happy to see the two of them getting married this weekend.

"Where is Kenz?" I ask, hoping to see my best friend.

"With the wedding coordinator, going over some last minute details. She'll be out in a minute. Come in. Everyone is already here." Josh steps to the side, letting me by so that he and Jake can shake hands and do their guy greeting thingy.

The moment I enter the church, the air around me jumps with electricity. My chest begins to cave in and my skin feels too tight all over my body. The weight of *his* stare is on me, and my skin heats under it. My head swirls and chaos grips me. I take a deep breath, trying to control what I knew was going to happen the moment I saw him again.

Lincoln Daniels is impossible to ignore.

We are impossible to ignore.

When my gaze lifts, it tangles with a set of steel-gray eyes.

And with one look, I'm gone.

Lost in the memories and heartache.

The *ifs* lingering between us.

IF | A NOVEL

AVAILABLE NOW

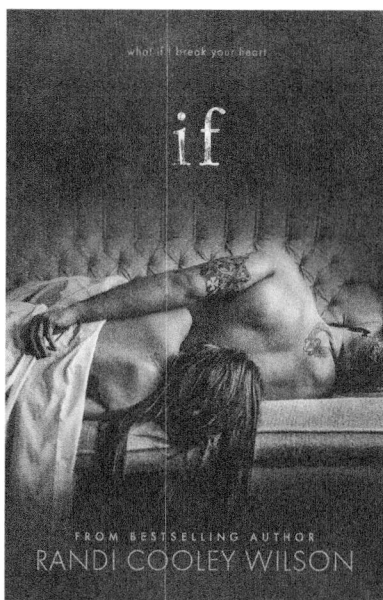

A New Adult Contemporary Romance Novel

VERNAL

THE ROYAL PROTECTOR ACADEMY
SERIES

My eyelids slide closed as the tiny drops of water cascade from the darkened sky. The warm beads hit my face, trickling effortlessly across my cool skin. The sensation of being alive wraps around me, as my spirit connects to the energy the weather bestows. Strength bleeds into my body, penetrating each layer until the energy drifts throughout my veins.

I ignore the dull ache making its way into my neck, a result of tilting of my face skyward. Instead, I lift my arms and, without thought, twirl and embrace each tiny droplet of water as the rain soaks the crenulated coastline around me in a fierce assault.

The elements heighten my supernatural powers, causing my core to hum with vitality. My lips form a small smile as I pirouette my way through the mist-shrouded, endless emerald hills. Each rise is crisscrossed by tumbledown ancient stone walls. My laughter floats in the wind. It's the only other sound encircling me, aside from the rainfall.

I loved doing this as a child. Spinning so fast I'd become dizzy and disoriented, until the earth around my feet would simply slip away, and breathlessly I would collapse onto the blades of grass. I miss the carefree days of my youth. There's something freeing—liberating—about standing in an open field, with your arms extended, allowing the rain to wash away your inhibitions. Not that I have many hang-ups, but the ones I do —they wrap around my heart like chains, squeezing until the simple act of breathing becomes almost impossible.

Another childish laugh escapes me as my body tumbles and collapses onto the soaked ground. I stretch my lean limbs and sink into the sponge-like soil, becoming one with the aged earth below my undressed body. My wet, auburn hair falls messily around my face and some of the long pieces stick to my dampened skin.

I don't care.

For the first time in days, I feel alive again.

Lying on the ground, I simply stare at the dark sky above, as the world spins around me. For a fleeting minute, the dizziness offers a brief reprieve from the musings that constantly cloud my head.

My free-spirited revel ends abruptly at the sound of a throat being cleared. I release a half moan, half sigh, knowing my moment of serenity has come to an end.

Rather than sitting up to face Rulf, the royal guard assigned to protect me, I pout like a child. My unhappiness overtakes the bliss I was feeling seconds ago.

It's not that I don't enjoy Rulf's company. It's just that his presence reminds me of my royal bloodline, my duties, and my obligations.

Knowing the gargoyle's temperament, he's probably standing with his arms crossed, aggravated by my lack of acknowledgment while he continues to get wet.

"Go away, Rulf."

"You're naked."

The statement comes from an unfamiliar, seductive, masculine voice, filled with an inherent confidence.

Definitely. Not. Rulf.

Unaware of who this stranger is, I remain still and strategize a plan of attack, should I need one. Though I'm without my weapons, I'm not concerned. Years of training with the best protectors have made me a skilled opponent. If all else fails, I always have my supernatural powers to help me kick this guy's ass.

I clear my throat and remain motionless.

"Your ability to state the obvious is mind-blowing."

The stranger releases a dark chuckle, unnerving me. I shiver in response, and my slight grin falls. My lips press together in annoyance at my reaction to something as simple as his enthralling laughter. It's like silk.

Cool.

Sensual.

Designed to pull you in and entrance you.

"I guess I missed the *clothing optional* portion of the Academy's handbook," he counters.

My stomach clenches in response as his velvety voice drifts over my exposed skin, caressing it. I swallow, in an attempt to keep myself in check and my tone even.

It is an epic failure.

"Something to work on, then." My voice is shaky.

"What's that?"

"Reading."

"Reading?"

"A prerequisite if you'll be attending the Academy."

A beat of silence passes between us before he speaks.

"Is nudity a habitual behavior of yours?" he questions, with an amused lilt to his tone.

At the sound of his deep voice, I roll onto my stomach, lift my gaze, and meet his curious expression.

He's breathtaking, in a dark and unrefined manner, if you're into that sort of thing. By the way my breathing has become erratic and my heart rate is spiraling out of control, I guess I'm into it.

"Yes," I reply.

A knowing smirk appears on his full lips. "Nice ass," he compliments, while his stare runs the length of me.

I don't shy away from his open perusal. I'm comfortable with my curves. Self-assurance comes with my title.

His eyes roam across my body, leaving imprints everywhere they go. I blush uncharacteristically at his heated intensity. My poise cracks as raw desire slithers inside me, crawling into the crevices, choking me.

Confused by the way my body is responding to him, I pinch my brows. He tilts his head to the side, watching my reaction. There's something captivating about the way he's looking at me. He's drawn to me, but can't figure out why.

I notice his self-confidence start to fade. Taking advantage of the fact that he's lost in his own thoughts, my focus shifts to his mouth, and I stare at a tiny, sexy scar on his upper lip. His breathing is smooth and soft.

Unlike me, with my unsolicited need to have him whisper dirty things to me, he seems unaffected. Cool and calm. Eerily controlled.

The stranger runs both of his large hands through his caramel hair, pushing the long pieces on top back in a sleek and sexy manner. The rain has soaked every perfect strand, and they keep attaching themselves to his sun-kissed face. It's almost as if they never want to let go.

I narrow my eyes at the wisps. They're eliciting a pang of jealousy within me. For some unexplainable reason, I feel an overwhelming sense of ownership over him. It's me who should be the one to touch his slightly scruffy, chiseled face—not those pieces of hair.

Wait, that isn't right. I don't even know him.

I scrutinize his thick eyebrows and attempt to compose myself. On most guys a brow piercing looks ridiculous. On him, it looks menacing and wild.

And hot.

So very, very hot.

I drop my gaze to the silver and hematite rings adorning his fingers. Like mine, every finger with the exception of his pinky is covered with them. I blink away the idea that our hands match, and instead concentrate on his broad chest, hidden under a white thermal.

The thin cotton is drenched, allowing me to take in his sculpted body. A pendant sits under his shirt, dangling from a black leather rope, which hangs from his neck.

Annoyingly, I can't make out what it is.

I sigh internally as my eyes trail over his rolled-up sleeves. They're pulled up to his elbows, showing off the leather-and-chain bracelets he's wearing on each wrist. At the sight of the familiar adornments, all my internal alarms go off, and something inside of me sinks. I attempt to hide the awareness that has fallen across my expression, and instead fixate on his worn jeans and heavy boots, while planning my escape.

This guy reeks of danger, and trouble. The air of cockiness he emanates is one I grew up with. It matches my father's and uncles'.

It all means this hot specimen is one hundred

percent off-limits, and being near him is like being near a bullet that you never saw coming. It wounds you so quickly and deeply that you bleed out without even knowing you've been hit.

I meet his powerful cognac glare and a shaky breath escapes me. I'm startled by the way he's staring at me.

Like I'm all he's longed for.

A light chill brushes through me. I'm not accustomed to someone looking at me and seeing just me, not my bloodline. I need to get a grip on my erratic emotions.

Standing, I put my entire unclothed body on display, hoping to throw him off balance. Pushing some of my damp hair behind my ear, I lift a challenging eyebrow at him, daring him not to look at me.

Unfazed, he holds my gaze with an unwavering stare. A silent pause beats between us.

Who is this guy?

"Are you done assessing me?" he asks.

"You're a protector?" I point to the shaded Celtic tattoo on his right forearm.

The symbol binds him to the Spiritual Assembly of Protectors, allowing him to accept divine assignments.

Of course he's a protector—he's here at the Academy.

Why can't I think clearly around him?

The stranger's expression falls, as if my accusation hurt him somehow. He doesn't say anything, but dips his chin in response, confirming my theory.

I take a step back, empathetic to the heavy burden

protectors carry. Nervously, my fingers find and play with my own piece of protector jewelry. The silver bracelet sits on my left wrist and is intricately designed with flowers and vines around the band, hiding my smaller, identical Assembly tattoo.

My aunt Eve gifted the bracelet to me for my eighteenth birthday. It was something her deceased mother Elizabeth, a jewelry designer, had made for her. Aunt Eve had the emeralds, my healing stone, added so they hang off the sides in a pretty and feminine manner. A small watch face was set on top in the hope that I would become more responsible about time management.

Not one of my strong suits.

Along with rules, motivation, education—anyway, you get the point.

It's crucial that all gargoyles wear something containing their healing stone.

The mineral rejuvenates us, increases our powers, and heightens our restorative abilities.

It's a necessary evil in my book. I despise the leather bands my family wear. They feel more like handcuffs to me than required protector accessories.

"Tristan," he says, in a way that slices through me.

Another unwelcome shiver crosses my skin at the sound of his voice.

"Serena," I reply thinly.

Tristan's pointed look drops and travels over my

body in a palpable manner, as he becomes intimately acquainted once again with my every curve.

"Are you always so . . . welcoming, Serena?"

When his eyes finally meet mine, my brow arches.

"Only to those I like."

"So you like me then?" He attempts to hide his smile.

I hold him with a glare. "Don't flatter yourself."

Tristan cocks his head and crosses his arms over his chest. My focus strays to the streams of rain dripping off his face. He steps closer to me, so close that I trap a breath he's exhaled in my lungs, when the bare portion of his arm brushes my own.

Why am I so reactive to him?

Slowly he bends down, piercing me with an amused expression. "And here I was, completely impressed with myself that I had a beautiful girl naked—and wet—within five minutes of meeting her," he seduces.

"That a record for you?" I quip.

I offer a shy grin, unable to stop myself.

"It would seem so."

"Maybe you're just having an off year," I surmise.

Tristan stares at me with an obvious sadness that stretches over us. "You have no idea just how off."

My eyes trace his lips. I start to speak, but he abruptly cuts me off when his hands lift to my face, cupping my cheeks. I stop breathing and my eyes widen at the unexpected motion.

At his touch, a warmth runs through my veins, igniting something foreign within me. His thumb lightly brushes a drop of rain off my bottom lip, and I watch with a rapidly beating heart as he brings the thumb to his mouth and sucks the bead of water off, watching me the entire time.

"It's been . . . interesting meeting you, Serena."

My name sounds like a test on his lips.

He releases my face and takes a step back, roughly sliding his hands into the front pockets of his soaked jeans.

I swallow, regarding him for a moment longer.

"You too, Tristan."

"See you around, raindrop."

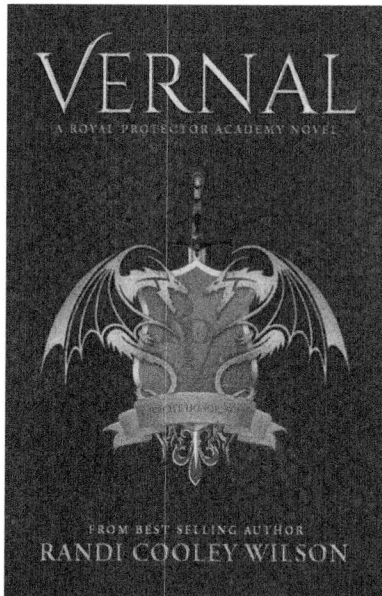

A New Adult Paranormal Romance Series

ACKNOWLEDGMENTS

There are so many people to thank for making this one possible. It truly does take an amazing team to be able to pull off publishing a novel. So, if you'll indulge me . . .

Dave and Maddison, my husband and daughter, thank you for loving me and being understanding of my deadlines. It's because of you, I get to live my dreams.

Regina Wamba at Mae I Design, thank you for the covers! And for being amazing. Love you, ninja!

Liz Ferry, thank you for making my stories shine.

Colleen Oppenheim, thank you for . . . everything!

Sarah Hershman, and the team at Hershman Rights Management, thank you for your ongoing support.

Sarai Makni, Pot&Kettle, thank you for Stone

and Hope's beautiful love song, *Stolen*. You've brought their love story to life. Listen on my website!

Chasity Michele Rece, thank you for reading this in advance, as a mental health professional, and guiding my sensitivity to mental health conditions and those who live with them daily.

Randi's Rebels, y'all are the best reader group a girl could ask for. Rebels Rock!

To My Family and Friends, I love you all.

To The Readers, thank you for reading my stories.

JOIN RANDI'S REBELS

STAY CONNECTED WITH RANDI'S
READER GROUP

ABOUT THE AUTHOR

Randi Cooley Wilson is an award-nominated, bestselling author of **The Revelation Series**, **The Royal Protector Academy Novels**, **The Dark Soul Trilogy, "if",** and the upcoming **Knightress Series**.

Randi's books have been featured on *Good Morning America, British Glamour Magazine, USA Today,* and in the Emmy's Gifting Suite. Her books range in genre, and include contemporary romance, urban/high fantasy, and paranormal romance, for both young adult and adult readers. Randi makes stuff up, devours romance books, drinks lots of wine and coffee, and has a slight addiction to bracelets. She resides in Massachusetts with her daughter and husband and their fur-baby, Coco Chanel.

Visit **randicooleywilson.com** for more information about Randi or her books and projects.

Or via **social media** outlets:

Printed in Great Britain
by Amazon